To: Des

CHARLES C. BROWN

Hope you enjoy this one!

JUSTICE
by the
Numbers

Charles C Brown

JUSTICE BY THE NUMBERS, Copyright 2018 by Charles C. Brown
Published by Trojan Horse Publishing
Cover design by Charles C. Brown
Interior layout: www.formatting4U.com

DEDICATION

This one is dedicated to my cousin,
Mary (Sis) McMullen.
Thank you for all your support.

ACKNOWLEDGEMENTS

I would like to express my appreciation to Lana Fitts and Colleen Carroll who work at City Drug, Davis, Oklahoma, for their help with pharmaceutical questions. And I definitely want to say "Thank you" to my wife Carolyn Brown who uses her computer savvy to turn my photographs into book covers for me. I would also like to thank my brother, Sgt. Dennis Brown (retired), for driving me over the route Daniel Miller took in his return from the house on Route 994 south of Huntingdon. Lastly, and possibly most important, I want to thank my readers and those who leave reviews and tell others about my books. I hope you all enjoy this one.

Until next time,
Charles Brown

CHAPTER ONE

"I asked you to come here tonight because I want them dealt with," Rosalynn Holder said matter-of-factly. "I want it done now, and I want it done with extreme prejudice."

The statement was so unexpected that Daniel Miller had no time to brace himself and keep the look of shock off his face. She had met him at the door earlier in her usual collared blouse—this one silky and pale pink—and gray dress slacks with the usual knife sharp creases, gray flats on her feet. Her hair was streaked with silver, which was a surprise. Her face was free of makeup and her nails free of polish. She had greeted him with a hug and a kiss on the cheek, and he had been surprised at how frail she felt when he put his arms around her.

"I think I like your hair that length," she had said. His straight, dark hair just brushed his shoulders. "I don't remember you earning a letter jacket."

"I didn't," he had confessed. "I bought it at a garage sale. I guess someone decided there were more important things in life than the glories earned in high school. Or maybe they just put on too much weight and outgrew it."

1

She had led him into her living room, a room that had changed little since he and her daughter had lain side by side on the carpet with coloring books and crayons. It had always been sparsely furnished and immaculately clean, free of the bric-a-brac his mother cluttered their house with.

"Is that a new recliner," he asked.

"I didn't want to spend the money," she said, "but the springs had let go in the old one."

She had waved him toward the couch and taken the seat in a recliner, but she hadn't raised the footrest. She congratulated him on passing the bar exam, and they made small talk—had he been well, had he found the bar exam difficult, did he have any promising job possibilities—for some twenty minutes before she turned the conversation to her daughter Rose and the boys who had assaulted her: Dexter Landis, Jordan Harris and Ryder Robinson.

"You do know that extreme prejudice means..." Daniel got out before she interrupted.

"I know exactly what it means, and there's no need for either of us to say it out loud."

What could a person answer to that? He sat and stared at her, his brow furrowed.

"It's been ten years," she said, still in that matter-of-fact tone. "They've had ten years more than my beautiful Rose had on this Earth, and that's ten years too many. If the system had worked the way it's supposed to, they would have spent some of those years in prison, and Rose would still be alive. You were her best friend. No, I know very well you were more than that. If things had gone differently, you and Rose would likely have been married by now and had

2

children. We owe it to her to make things right, to see that justice is done, and I need your help."

"But don't you think we should discuss…," Daniel struggled to find the right words, "…what you're suggesting? Give it some thought?"

"I have thought of little else these past ten years," Rosalynn answered. "Every second my mind wasn't occupied with lesson plans and lectures and making out worksheets and tests and grading papers."

"I heard that you resigned, that you're not teaching anymore?" he said, a little wonder in his voice. He knew beyond doubt that she wasn't old enough to draw retirement pay and wondered what she was living on.

She had turned her head and was staring at a framed photograph of Rose that hung on the wall, and her only answer was a nod. She shifted her eyes to the flat screen television which sat in an entertainment console he had never seen before.

"Since I turned that thing off, I've had lots of time to think and to plan."

"You don't watch television anymore?" Daniel asked.

Rosalynn shook her head slowly. "I did when I first retired but not for a couple of months now. I thought it would take my mind off… things," she finished after a moment's hesitation. "But the more I watched, the more angry I became. I stopped watching detective shows because every one of them ended with the criminals getting apprehended and sent to prison. Not always right away, of course. Sometimes they stretched it out over several weeks, I imagine just to keep the viewers in suspense, but eventually, the lead detective, or whatever you call him, solved the case and the guilty party was punished. I suppose it's part of the formula, good triumphs over evil—always. But we both know that's far from true in the real world.

"I thought maybe comedies would be better, but it didn't take long for me to realize I was supposed to be laughing at behavior that should be condemned and attempts made to modify it. Young men and women insulting one another over things they couldn't control, like their height, their weight, or their level of intelligence. I would have sent students to the office for behaving like that. And some of the shows have older men doing stupid things in an effort to impress someone—usually a woman who's hardly worth impressing. And all of that is supposed to be funny?

"The commercials were just as upsetting and absurd," she continued, after a thoughtful pause. "Makeup companies doing their utmost to convince women that their products are essential to their happiness and well-being. As if a person couldn't get the most out of life if her lashes were too thin or her lip gloss was the wrong color." She blew air through her lips, making a sound that expressed her disgust at the idea. "Advertisements for electronic gadgets that turn on your radio or your lights for you or order your pizza—things anybody with two hands is quite capable of doing for himself. And having been a teacher, one of the most upsetting to me was amusement parks encouraging parents to waste money on entertainment rather than save it for their children's education. It's no wonder so many people have their priorities scrambled."

For several moments, she was silent, blinking slowly, her eyes back on the photograph of her daughter.

"Maybe the most irritating of all are the pharmaceutical companies pushing drugs that have so many harmful side effects that any reasonably intelligent person would realize they might as well forego treatment and let their ailment run its course. Use whatever time they have left to get their affairs in order."

She seemed to have talked herself out, and for several moments, there was silence again. The compressor in the refrigerator kicked on in the kitchen and hummed quietly.

"I agree that something should be done," Daniel said after some thought, "but shouldn't we, maybe, go to the police and see if they might reopen the case first?"

Rosalynn shook her head and wrinkled her upper lip in a sneer. "They wouldn't pursue it back then, and I have no doubt they would refuse to even consider looking into it after so much time has passed. And if we go to them now and they turn us down, suspicion will fall on us when we get the job done."

"Still," Daniel hesitated. "Extreme prejudice? And three people?"

"Four," Rosalynn corrected.

"Four?!" he exclaimed.

"I want the person who fed her the pills to pay, too."

"But Rose committed suicide!" Daniel objected.

"Did she?" Rosalynn asked. "You know as well as I do that after her surgery, Rose had the mind of a five-year-old child at best. Where did she get the pills? How would she know what kind of pills to use? Did you get them for her?"

"No!"

5

"Well, neither did I," Rosalynn assured him, sounding angry for the first time. "Whoever it was must have worn gloves and wrapped Rose's hand around the bottle when he was finished. Hers were the only finger prints they found on it when I finally talked them into checking it. And unfortunately, that only made them more convinced than ever that her death was a suicide. Nothing I said, nothing I pointed out to them could change their minds. I was just a distraught mother, grieving the loss of her only child.

"They said she took her life because she was distraught because nobody believed her when she testified during the trial. That she was upset because it looked like the boys who raped her were not going to be punished. She wasn't even sure what they did to her was wrong and was more concerned about losing her watercolor kit! So why would she be so upset about the trial that she would take her own life? When we left the courthouse, I took her home and fed her some ice cream, and she was fine, as happy as she had ever been after her surgery. It was like the assault, the entire experience, never happened.

"They were right about one thing, though. *I* was distraught after the trial. The way Ronald Parsons went after her on the stand, demanding she name names when he knew she wasn't capable of it, harassing her until he had her in tears and the DA finally raised an objection. He secured his place in the hearts of a lot of Bearcat fans, defending those boys. How else do you think he got the backing that put him in the DA's office later? Sometimes I've thought about adding him to the list, but if we tried to deal with everyone who had a part in it, we would be busy for years."

"What?" Daniel asked. "You think others were involved?"

"I don't just think. I know."

"And who would they have been?"

"Think, Daniel," Rosalynn said, and her tone was a bit harsh. "It was the year everybody thought the football team had a chance of winning State, and everyone was rooting for them. Dexter Landis was the quarterback, Jordan Harris was a split end, and Ryder Robinson was the center. They were all seniors, and without them, the possibility of a State Championship vanished. They were essential. Parsons managed to get a couple of members of the Booster Club in the jury box, and the outcome was predictable—a hung jury. So we would have to add the holdout on the jury, wouldn't we? And if the person who supplied the pills wasn't the same person who gave them to her, that would add another one to the list. If Rose's death had been investigated as it should have been, there's no telling how many would have been implicated."

"How do you know all of this?" Daniel asked.

"It doesn't matter how I know, I just do. As I said earlier, I have thought of little else these past ten years when my mind wasn't occupied with other things. Rose was murdered, and I have always felt partially responsible. I wasn't doing very well back then, and Doctor Barnes prescribed Ambien to help me sleep. I was afraid Rose would get up and get into things, and I wouldn't hear her, maybe hurt herself, so I gave her one of my capsules the night she died. Someone *had* to have come into the house after we fell asleep, but I didn't wake up. Whoever it was didn't wake me, and Rose would have been too addled to resist."

7

"But what reason would they have for wanting to kill Rose?" Daniel asked. "What would have been their motive?"

"I kept pressing DA Snyder for a retrial." Rosalynn said. "A new trial would have interfered with the football season and put their hopes of winning the State Championship in jeopardy. The boys wouldn't have been free to practice, possibly wouldn't even have been allowed to participate until the trial was over. After Rose died, the charges were dropped, and as far as everyone else was concerned, that was the end of it. If I hadn't been so determined to see things done right back then, maybe she would still be with us. Hindsight is twenty-twenty. But I've come to believe it's never too late for justice to be done. *We* just have to be willing to *see* that it's done."

She had presented her case. Now it was up to Daniel to decide if he wanted to be involved. He slouched down far enough so that he could lay his head on the back of the sofa and stare unblinking at the ceiling. The compressor in the refrigerator kicked off, and the two of them sat in silence.

How could he refuse her, this woman who had been more of a mother to him than the woman who had brought him into the world? She was right about his relationship with her daughter. Rose Lynn Holder had been his first and only love to this point in his life. His anger at her assault and his grief at her passing were what had prompted him to study law. As a lawyer, he intended to be an advocate for victims like Rose, mentally challenged individuals whom the powers that be in society often seemed to consider expendable when they got in the way. But he had to consider what would happen to his career in law if he did what Rosalynn was asking of him. Would he ever feel right practicing law?

Daniel sat up and leaned forward, elbows on his knee. "Sexual assault is not a capital crime," he said.

"No," Rosalynn agreed, "but murder is, and as far as I'm concerned, those boys were as complicit in Rose's death as the person who put the pills down her throat. If two people are committing armed robbery and one of them kills a clerk, both of them are guilty of murder according to law. What they did to her started the process that ended her life, and the only thing they have to give that's of equal value is their own."

"Do you want them to suffer?" Daniel asked.

"No," she answered. "I just want them gone, and I want them to know why it's happening. I want them to know, 'This is for Rose'."

Daniel pursed his lips and gave the idea another minute's thought. In a very real sense, they had taken his life, too—the life that he had envisioned for himself and Rose even though, after her surgery, they could never have been man and wife. His mind made up, he nodded his head and looked Rosalynn in the eye. "Alright," he said. "I'm in. What do you need me to do?"

She gave him a smile that never quite reached her eyes. "Let's go into my office," she said, pulling herself out of the recliner. "There are some things I have to show you."

CHAPTER TWO

Like the living room, the office hadn't changed much. At a glance, Daniel saw that the bookcase still held the books he and Rose had read together. The walnut kneehole desk he had always admired was still there, and on it were an HP desktop computer, a mouse pad and a wireless mouse, a small calendar and a round, black wire container with several ink pens in it.

"Pull up a chair," Rosalynn said. "This will take a minute." She sat down in the office chair and set about booting up the computer. "Time will be of the essence once we get started. I think it needs to be done in two weeks if possible, three at the most."

"And why is that?" Daniel asked.

"If too much time elapses between the first and the last, whoever's last will get suspicious and be more cautious," she said. "Jordon Harris will be our first concern because he is the most distant. Word of his fate shouldn't get back to Huntingdon County before the others are dealt with. And he's the least intelligent of the lot, so you should have no problems with him. When the three of them were in my eighth grade English class, he had trouble maintaining a passing grade, actually wouldn't have passed if I hadn't been generous."

"And where is he now?" Daniel asked.

"In San Antonio, Texas."

"Whoa! What is he doing way down there?"

"Some kind of menial task, I imagine, like changing oil in trucks or fixing flat tires."

"But why is he down there—in Texas, I mean."

"He spent some time in the Air Force," Rosalynn said, "so that's likely where he did his basic training. Maybe he likes it down there, or maybe he's estranged from his family. There's no way to tell."

"How could he get into the Air Force with a criminal record?"

"He was never convicted of anything, so I suppose, technically, he wouldn't *have* a criminal record," she said. "Or if there is or ever was such a record, Parsons managed to get it sealed or have it expunged."

While she talked, she used the keyboard and the mouse to bring up the site she wanted. A small shack of a house appeared on the monitor.

"And this is…?" Daniel asked.

"The house where Jordan Harris lives. I have the address, and I want you to memorize it before you leave. Write nothing down."

"What color is that, and why would anybody paint their house that color?"

"I think it might have been turquoise before it got faded by the sun, and I imagine the place is a rental. The owner probably purchased the paint because it was on sale."

"And is that asbestos tile? They painted asbestos tile?!"

"Yes, I believe it is. Now watch carefully."

11

Rosalynn moved the mouse to the left, and the image on the screen shifted left. Neighboring houses and then an empty street showed on the monitor. It was like someone with a video camera was turning in a circle in the middle of the street.

"Where did you learn to do this?" Daniel asked.

"I took classes at the vo-tech in Mill Creek."

She kept moving the mouse to the left, and images on the screen swept by until a large metal building appeared with semis parked in the foreground. There she stopped.

"I have reason to believe that Jordan Harris works for this trucking company in some capacity. I don't think he's a truck driver, because I understand one has to take a rather detailed test to get the kind of license that requires, and I doubt that he could pass the test."

"Wow! You really have given this a lot of thought," Daniel said. "That looks like a major highway there in the foreground. Do you have any idea what highway it is?"

"I believe that's Interstate 10. I looked it up on Yahoo Maps, and it looks to me like Interstate 10 bisects the city."

Daniel studied the screen, his brow drawn.

"Do you think you will be able to find this place once you get down there?" she asked.

Daniel nodded. "It looks to me like the house is close enough to the Interstate that it would be hard to miss. How did you know where Harris was?" he asked. "I mean who did you ask?"

"I didn't ask anybody," she said. "I found him online, using this computer. I know where all of them are, so you don't need to get online and look for them.

I already have all the information you need, and if forensics shows are to be believed, every site you access goes into your computer's history and remains on your hard drive, even after you have erased it. I've already done the research, so don't do anything that would leave evidence some tech could find. I imagine there will be some kind of investigation eventually."

"What about *your* computer?" Daniel asked. "There will be evidence on it."

"When it's all done, I'll wipe the hard drive or destroy it. You don't use yours for any part of this. Agreed?"

"Agreed," Daniel said.

"Okay then." Rosalynn pulled a briefcase he hadn't noticed out from under the desk. "Next, I need to show you this."

She opened the briefcase on her knees and turned it so he could see what was in it.

"I thought a stun gun might come in handy," she said, picking the item up. It was black and looked to be about six inches long, two and a half inches wide and maybe an inch thick. "It's rechargeable, and the charger is right here with it. The instruction booklet that came with it is here, too. You will need to try it out before you use it. There's a button on it that lets you check its charge."

She put the stun gun back in its place and picked up another item. "This is what they call a burner phone on television. I have one just like it. I bought them at the dollar store a week ago. The number of mine is programmed into this one, and this one's number is programmed into mine. Do not take *your* phone with you. It probably has a GPS feature built into it, and we don't want anyone to be able to trace your movements.

13

We will use these phones—and only these phones—until the job is done, and then I'll get rid of them."

She returned the phone to its place and picked up something wrapped in a cloth. "This is what you will use," she said, and pulled back the cloth to reveal a small, chrome-plated revolver with a black grip and no hammer. Part of it was pink.

The sight of it seemed to make what they were planning more real, and Daniel got a nervous feeling in the pit of his stomach.

"It's a thirty-eight caliber, and it's already loaded, so handle it with care. I didn't know how to get one with a silencer, so you will have to improvise." She folded the cloth back over the gun and put it back.

"Why pink?" Daniel asked.

"It is what I could get, and since I've thought about it, I believe the color will work to our advantage," she said, and before he could ask how, she went on with her inventory.

"This is a box of surgical gloves." She put an index finger on it. He could see from the lettering on the outside of it that the gloves were black, size large, and powder-free. "Use them if you need them, but don't leave them behind if you do. Forensic people can supposedly turn them inside-out and get fingerprints off used ones. I don't know if that is really true, but there is no need to take a chance."

She waited until Daniel nodded and then went on.

"These four envelopes contain items you will leave at each scene."

"Why? What's in them?" he asked.

"You don't need to be concerned with why," Rosalynn told him. "And you'll know what's in them

14

when you use them. Just dump the contents of one of them out each time before you leave, once the job is done. Do not touch the items unless you are wearing gloves, and bring the envelope away with you. Do not leave it behind."

"But why?"

She looked up and shook her head. "You don't need to be concerned about why," she repeated. "Just promise me you will do what I tell you. You have already conceded that I have given this a lot of thought, and there is a very good reason for everything I'm asking you to do."

"Okay," Daniel said, raising his hands in a gesture of surrender.

She turned her attention back to the items in the briefcase. "This larger envelope contains the money you will need—three thousand dollars in ones, fives, tens and twenties. You might want to purchase a prepaid Visa card with some of it. You don't need to be sparing with it. There's plenty more where this came from. You will need gas and food, and you will want to get hotel rooms. Don't drive until you are exhausted. If you get overly tired, you might make mistakes. There's enough time, so you don't have to be in a hurry. Oh, and here's a drivers license you should use if anyone asks you to see one, other that a policeman, of course. In the unlikely event that you should get stopped, use your official license and then return home. We will try again another time."

She handed him the license and he studied the photograph on it. It was his image, and apparently, he would be William D. Perkins during this trip. He put it in his wallet and thought about asking where she got the license and how she had accumulated that much cash. But answers she had given to previous questions made it clear that there were some things he would just have to accept without knowing.

Rosalynn closed the briefcase and snapped the catches shut. "Now, let's go back into the living room. This chair is nowhere near as comfortable as my recliner. Get the light, please. No point in running up the electric bill."

Settling back into her recliner, she sighed audibly. Daniel took a seat on the sofa again, and it seemed like they were right back where the evening had started. But so much had changed.

"You will take my Honda Accord," she began after taking a moment to catch her breath. "It's an inconspicuous gray, and it gets good gas mileage. I've had it checked over, and there's nothing wrong with it. No lights out that would get you pulled over and no dents or scrapes that would make it easily identifiable. If you stay within the posted speed limit, you shouldn't have any problems. I've been driving for more than thirty years and have yet to be pulled over once.

"Use some of the money to buy some baseball caps, half a dozen at least. Get them with a variety of colors and logos and change them often. Buy yourself some clothes that you wouldn't ordinarily wear, worn jeans and faded shirts. They don't have to be new, maybe even shouldn't be. Just find a Goodwill along the way and see what they have. And you shouldn't wear that letter jacket. In fact, you probably shouldn't even take it with you."

"Do you really think all of that is necessary?" Daniel asked.

"Yes, I do—all of that and more. Go by a Walmart or a dollar store and get yourself some reading glasses. Get several pair and let one pair of them have extra thick lenses. You won't have to wear them all the time, just long enough for someone to see you in them—like when you go into a store to pay for gas."

"I have a pair of aviator sunglasses with mirror lenses I can wear when the sun's bright."

"Good," she said, "but don't wear them when it's not. And be aware of security cameras. Most service stations and truck stops have them now—and Walmarts. If you stop at a Walmart, be sure to wear a cap and keep your head down. Walmart parking lots and Walmart stores are covered with security cameras, and you don't want to look directly at them. Just know where they are."

He thought she had run out of dos and don'ts when she spoke again.

"Don't bring back any souvenirs, nothing that would show that you have been anywhere but right here in Pennsylvania. Don't keep receipts either. These days, most of them have an address, a date and a time printed on them. Toss them as soon as you are out of the store with your purchases."

"Anything else?" he asked when she seemed to have worn down.

"Just be yourself," she said, "just a young man on a road trip. Don't do anything that would draw attention to yourself. Act casual, not furtive. If you *act* suspicious, people will *get* suspicious. Wherever you find yourself, just blend in. Do you think you can do it?"

"Do what? Blend in?"

"No, can you do what I'm asking you to do?"

Daniel gave it some thought before he answered.

"I can't give you a positive answer to that right now. I can tell you that I have thought lots of times since Rose's death, especially right after, about doing exactly what you have in mind. When I come face-to-face with them, will I be able to do it? I don't know. I suppose it will depend on their attitude, on whether they show any signs of remorse or not. The way they acted in high school, I don't imagine there will be any. Pushing and punching whoever got in their way. Didn't matter what gender or size their victim was. They were the stars of the football team and acted like they owned the hallways, like they were entitled to do whatever they wanted to do, especially after the way the trial ended the summer before. I always did my best to avoid being in the restroom with the three of them. And because they were expected to win State, the teachers and the administration turned their heads for the most part. Now and then a teacher would say something, and they would give them a smirk and turn their backs and just walk away. I don't think I have ever been so glad to see anything in my life as I was to see the end of our senior year, because after they lost in the semifinals, it got even worse."

"It might help if you remember those times," Rosalynn suggested and then asked, "Do you have any questions for me?"

"When do you want me to leave for Texas?"

"Do you have any commitments you have to honor in the next two to three weeks?"

"I had some things in mind, but nothing that can't be postponed."

"No girlfriend or anyone who will wonder why you aren't around?"

"Nobody," Daniel said, shaking his head.

"What about you father? Is he likely to call?"

"What time his new wife isn't keeping him busy, he's out on the lake in his boat. He calls about once every six months, and I heard from him last week. So, no, we don't need to worry about him."

"Okay. This is Friday. Let's schedule your departure for five A.M. on Monday morning. That will get you out of here before my neighbors are up and leaving for work, and it will give me time to go over what we've talked about this evening. I might have overlooked something."

The two of them stood, and she walked with him to the door. There she turned and enveloped him in another hug. They parted without either of them saying a word.

CHAPTER THREE

At eight o'clock Monday morning, Daniel Miller found himself on Interstate 81 somewhere in northern Virginia, approaching the exit to a place called New Market. At the appointed time, Rosalynn had been waiting for him just inside the front door of her home in Huntingdon, and the gray Honda Accord she wanted him to take was sitting in her driveway. She opened the door, he stepped inside, and she closed it behind him. She had turned no lights on, and the entryway was darker than the front porch.

"I'll put your car in the garage when you're gone," she had said, handing him a ring with two keys. "No smart phone, right?"

"No smart phone," he had answered. "It's at home in my sock drawer. Only the burner you gave me. I just need to get the briefcase and my suitcase out of my car and put them in yours. Then I'll be on my way."

She might have smiled in the dark, but he couldn't tell. He slipped out the door again, made the switch and was back in a matter of minutes. He handed her his keys, finding her hand by feel in the dark.

"There's an atlas on the front seat," she said, "so you can find your way, old school. If I were you, I wouldn't take the same route going down and coming back. If you do, when you come back, avoid stopping at places where you stopped on the way down." She had put an arm around his neck and kissed him on the cheek. "Call if I can be of help. Be careful."

She opened the door—his signal to leave. He slid behind the wheel of the Honda, started the engine, backed out of the drive and was off. Now, three hours into his trip, he was wondering how a person was supposed to occupy his mind when he was on his way to do what was supposed to be done when he got to San Antonio.

"There's no need for either of us to say it out loud," he muttered to himself.

The clothes he was wearing were like none he had ever worn before. The kaki dress trousers and the pale pastel, button-down shirts were gone. *Buy yourself some clothes that you wouldn't ordinarily wear, worn jeans and faded shirts*, Rosalynn had suggested. *Find a Goodwill along the way.* But the thought of wearing someone else's castoffs didn't appeal to him, so he had gone to Walmart and bought several tee-shirts and three pairs of the cheapest jeans he could find. He spent most of Saturday morning making the lot of it look worn and dingy. He cut slits in the knees of the jeans and washed and dried them, together with the tee-shirts, several times using bleach until the knees were frayed. When he was done, the jeans had shrunk so much that he couldn't get them buttoned.

So, lesson learned, he had gone back to Walmart for three more pairs of jeans—these two sizes too big— and repeated the process, shirts and all. The results surprised him. The jeans, the first he had ever worn, were more comfortable than dress pants, and there was

21

something about the tee-shirts that he liked but couldn't exactly put his finger on. He smiled now at the thought that anybody describing his clothing would be describing an altogether different person than he normally was. The smile faded when he realized he might want to keep wearing jeans and tee-shirts when all of this was over. The athletic shoes on his feet—another Walmart purchase—were definitely more comfortable than the wingtips he usually favored.

He had made a quick stop at Hibbett Sports in Hagerstown, Maryland, and picked up half a dozen billed caps as Rosalynn had suggested. The one on his head at the moment was dark blue and had a white Y with an N superimposed over it on the front. So he was a New York Yankees fan—at least until the first time he stopped for gas or to use a restroom. Then he was thinking he might lean more toward the Baltimore Orioles. With its orange bill, the Orioles cap was more colorful and maybe more memorable. More than a hundred dollars worth of caps in the backseat, the price of camouflage, he thought and smiled. The eyeglasses she wanted him to get would have to wait until he found a Walmart or a Dollar General store. He had forgotten about them when he was buying the jeans and tee-shirts.

Stay within the posted speed, she had said. Blend in, she had said. Already he had discovered that, on the Interstate, everybody exceeded the posted speed limit by at least five miles per hour, some by ten. So, poke along at the posted speed and appear to be trying to avoid getting pulled over? Or go with the flow and keep pace with everybody else? He decided to do the latter. Apparently the thinking was that if everybody was speeding, the highway patrol couldn't stop them all.

To keep his mind off the near future, he turned it back to the past; all the way back to the day he found the opening in the hedge that separated his backyard from Rose's. A shy little boy of four-years-old had come face-to-face with a shy little girl six months his senior and found his soul mate. He smiled at the memory. After that, it was always out the back door and through the hedge. If she wasn't outside, he knocked at her back door, and either she came out or he went in, and they played inside. He was always welcome at Rose's house, but Rose at his house, not so much. His mother did not like children "under foot" when she was working on her quilts—which was probably why he could be gone all day, and she never called out or came to check on him, not even at lunch time. If he was "over there at Rose's," they would feed him. His dad had been gone all day, every workday, through the summer months, and sometimes for several days at a time. A construction worker had to go wherever the job was, and sometimes the job was hundreds of miles away, too far to drive home every evening.

Rosalynn had been at home all day every day for most of their preschool years, taking online class and working toward her teaching degree, but she had always doted on her daughter. And she had always sympathized with his plight, both of them having been "change of life" babies.

"Your parents love you, and my parents loved me," she told him. "It's just that we came along after they had given up having children, and they were involved in other interests."

Maybe so, Daniel thought now and not for the first time, *but it wasn't our fault we came into the world late.*

23

Rosalynn seldom talked about her past, but eventually, he came to know that Rose had been born when her mother was only sixteen. She had given herself to an eighteen-year-old man whose National Guard unit was deployed to Iraq the next day, and she never saw him again. He had been in-country only a short time when he and a couple of his buddies were killed by an IED. Daniel knew the soldier's last name had been Jaymes, but when he asked why Rose's name wasn't Jaymes, she said it was to avoid confusion. When he pressed her for details, she said she didn't want to talk about it.

Her parents had not been happy about their teenage daughter being pregnant, he knew, and weren't willing to help much when Rose was born. Rosalynn had just about all she could do, trying to keep up with her school work and take care of a baby at the same time. The elder Holders didn't warm to the idea of having an illegitimate granddaughter until Rose was almost two years old. And just days before her second birthday, they were both killed in an auto accident, neither of them yet sixty years old. Rosalynn used the money from their life insurance policies to live on and to pay for her online college classes.

For a few minutes, he was able to put everything from his mind and just enjoy cruising along. The country he was passing through was beautiful, and the weather was nice, the sun bright and so warm he turned the Honda's air conditioner on. *Not bad for mid-October*, he thought. W*onder what the temperature will be like in Texas?* And there it was again, the very thing he was trying to avoid. *Think about Rose. Think about Rose.*

They had walked into the school on their first day of kindergarten holding hands. Rosalynn had driven them there, and somewhere in her possession, he was certain, she still had the photograph she had taken of them, looking back over their shoulders and smiling. He had a copy of the photo somewhere, too, and wished he had brought it with him. His own mother had likely already been busy in her craft room at the moment the picture was taken. She had paid little attention to the grade cards he brought home, and she never attended any of his school programs. Rosalynn was his surrogate mother, driving him to the school whenever he needed to be there and home again, him and Rose always together in the backseat. It was her encouragement that helped him to keep his grades up and graduate with honors, and she was the one who took the picture of him at graduation. By then, his mother was gone, having succumbed to dementia and died when he was in the fifth grade. She had spent her last couple of years in a nursing home. And Rose was gone then, too. He had gone to her funeral a week before the start of his senior year.

He had to slow down and get his mind more focused on his driving because a semi truck had decided to pass another semi on a hill. The one doing the passing couldn't go any faster than the one being passed, so everybody got bogged down to between sixty and sixty-five miles per hour. Eventually, the left lane became clear again, everybody got back up to speed, and his mind went back to where he had left off.

Middle school had been fairly pleasant. He and Rose were in many of the same classes, and the two of

25

them became increasingly inseparable. He smiled now, thinking about their first kiss when they were thirteen. Neither of them really knew what they were doing, never having kissed anyone on the lips before. But it was a milestone, so to speak, and he remembered being amazed at the softness of her lips. They got better at it over the next year, and her mother, aware of their budding romance, was careful not to leave the two of them alone too much or too often.

His home life was different then but not much better. With his mother gone and his father still working on construction, he was left in the care of a succession of housekeeper/babysitters. Dear old dad even managed to find jobs so far south during the winter that he got home only once a month. Harold Miller did manage to be at his only son's eighth-grade graduation, a man who was more like a stranger than family. That had been the night Daniel first met the woman his father would later marry.

They were looking forward to high school, he and Rose, never dreaming of what would happen that fateful summer between their eighth and ninth grade years. One morning, she got out of bed and her left leg gave way. She hit the floor with a thud, and her mother came running even before Rose called out to her. Together, they got her up and onto the side of the bed, and then they discovered that her left arm wasn't working very well either. A tumor in her brain was pressing against the nerves that controll motor function. It had to be removed or it would continue to grow, the doctor told them, and that would undoubtedly lead to complete paralysis and end in death. Surgery was the only option. Rosalynn signed the papers.

The memory of sitting in the waiting room, wondering if Rose was going to make it, brought a frown to Daniel's face now. In a lot of ways, he realized, she hadn't. The Rose that went into the operating room that morning was not the same Rose that came out that afternoon. She had always been shy and a bit introverted, and she had been of above average intelligence. The girl who came out of the operating room was little more than an infant—a toddler at best. When the surgery was over and she was back in a private room, he and Rosalynn had gone in to see her. Rose looked at her mother for the longest time, confusion on her face. "Momma?" she finally said and began to cry. Then she pointed a finger his way and asked, "Who him?" Something like a weight settled in his chest at her question, and the feeling had never quite gone away. When the pain of surgery subsided and she was back at home and in a familiar environment, she began to remember bits and pieces of what Daniel thought of as their previous life. But even at fourteen, he realized the life he had envisioned for their future could never be. His dream was gone forever.

Rosalynn was ecstatic that her daughter had survived, but for him the next six months were the saddest of his life. Rose had to learn to walk and to be potty trained all over again. The shy, introverted, above average teenager was gone, and an outgoing and perpetually happy five-year-old who didn't know a stranger had taken her place. The doctor's best prognosis was that she would forever be a child in a woman's body.

Daniel's stomach told him it had been too long since breakfast, and he swung off the Interstate at an exit that advertised a Hardees. A burger and fries, maybe a milkshake, and he would be good for another five hundred miles, he thought. But his first stop turned out to be a Walmart he discovered on the way. He didn't tarry long in the store, just long enough to collect the eyeglasses—four pair, he figured was enough—as per Rosalynn's suggestion.

His visit to the Hardees was almost as brief because he was tempted to get his order to go and eat it in the car. But the place wasn't crowded, and he needed a break from driving. He had been on the road for nearly six hours. In that time, he had stopped once for a fuel and restroom break, and he walked into Hardees wearing the orange and black Baltimore Orioles cap with a bird on the front.

* * *

The moment her gray Honda Accord disappeared into the morning with Daniel at the wheel, Rosalynn went through the kitchen and hit the switch to raise the overhead garage door. She got behind the wheel of the gray Honda Accord that was sitting there and backed it out into the street. It wasn't an exact match for the one Daniel was driving, but a person would have to look very closely to tell that it was a different vehicle. In the next few minutes, she drove Daniel's red Chevy Impala inside and lowered the overhead door again. Then she went back outside and pulled the gray Honda onto the driveway. When her neighbors woke up, everything would look just like it had the evening before.

She ate a breakfast of granola and milk and washed it down with a cup of strong, black coffee. Her bowl rinsed and in the sink, she took a second cup into the living room and sat in her recliner. Getting the footrest up required two hands and about as much effort as she could muster. The job done, she picked up her cup from the little table beside the chair and sighed. It would be a couple of hours before businesses opened, and there was nothing she had to do but wait and sip her coffee. For a few minutes, she wondered idly how far Daniel had gotten and what route he had decided to take. *No matter*, she told *herself. The less either of us knows about what the other is doing, the better for both of us.*

The sun brightening the room woke her, and she was surprised at herself for falling asleep. Her coffee cup had fallen from her hand onto the cushion of the chair. Fortunately, it had been empty. She decided to leave the footrest up and managed to pull herself to a standing position. It was time to go to town and make her presence in Huntingdon County known.

* * *

His hunger satisfied with a burger, fries and a shake, Daniel pulled back onto Interstate 81 and headed south. Sipping a cup of carry-out coffee, he tried to keep his mind solely on his driving, but found it impossible. The old idea of telling someone to go stand on a corner and not think of pink elephants came to mind, and he smiled. A person's mind is on something all the time, he realized, and if he or she is doing something that does not require extreme concentration, it wanders where it will. Better to keep it on something of your choice. Once again, he chose to think about Rose.

29

She had been embarrassed and frustrated those first few weeks after she came home from the hospital. Somewhere there in what was left of her brain, she seemed to know she had been able to do things before that she couldn't do anymore. Wearing adult diapers mortified her, and she hated the crutches Rosalynn insisted she use long after they were no longer necessary.

She missed a year of school while she recuperated—not that she would have been capable of learning much had she been able to attend. And when it was finally decided that she was physically able to go back to school, she went to a different one than he did. They never had classes together again. He missed her, missed sitting beside her in the classrooms and the cafeteria, missed seeing her in the halls. Missed riding to school with her. Rosalynn had gotten a job teaching eighth grade English that year and had to leave home early to drop Rose off at what amounted to adult daycare. He started walking to school and found that he enjoyed it—another of life's unexpected discoveries.

For a number of minutes, he had to forget about the past and pay attention to the present while he threaded his way through Bristol, Virginia/Tennessee. The highway was four lanes wide, and some drivers seemed to be in too much of a hurry to even signal lane changes. Then the speed limit lowered to sixty-five because he was in the tri-cities area, and he spent a few minutes wondering what cities were involved. Eventually, the Interstate narrowed to two south bound lanes again, traffic thinned out a bit and some of the tension went out of his neck and shoulders.

* * *

Rosalynn spent much of the day away from home. She parked her Honda in a lot on Penn Street and walked. There was nothing in particular she wanted or needed, but for more than an hour, she went in and out of stores, browsing and being seen. At ten o'clock, she went to the appointment she had made at Stylin Hair & Nail Salon on Mifflin Street and had her hair washed and set, and for the first time ever, had her nails done professionally. She thought about having some of those fake nails glued on but decided that would be too much.

For lunch, she went across the river to Wendy's and had an Apple Pecan Chicken Salad and a diet Pepsi. She made it back home a little after one o'clock, exhausted, snuggled into her recliner under a quilted throw she had made for Rose and slept until after three. She woke up with a start when a vehicle with a loud muffler passed on the street in front of the house. It took her a few moments to remember what day it was and to remember handing Daniel the keys to her Honda. It seemed to her like that had been days ago, and she sat for a moment, wondering how far he had gotten on his way to San Antonio. She looked at the framed photo of Rose on the opposite wall and nodded. "It's in the works now, Sweetheart. It will all be made right soon."

With some difficulty, she pulled herself out of the recliner, again leaving the footrest up, and went into the bathroom. She was washing her hands, when she looked up at her image in the mirror, and it seemed to say: *Are you sure you're doing the right thing?*

"What *is* the right thing?" she asked her reflection. "And why didn't someone do it earlier?"

She shook her head, upset about second-guessing herself and went to the kitchen for something to drink. Tea this time, she decided. She put water into her hotpot and turned it on high. While it came to a boil, she got out a mug and a tea bag. Minutes later, the water poured and the teabag properly dunked and tossed in the trash, she set her mug on the little table and eased back into her recliner.

An hour later, she struggled out of the chair once again and made her way to the Honda in the driveway. Her route took her across the river again, this time to Hoss's Steakhouse where she ordered a six ounce sirloin with buttered mushrooms and a loaded baked potato. Most of it she took home in a box, her appetite not being what it once was. She left a ten dollar tip on the table.

* * *

Intestate 81 seemed to merge with Interstate 40, which was a surprise. Daniel had not expected such a smooth transition. The terrain was still hilly but nothing like the steep ridges of Virginia. He had in mind to spend the night in Nashville, but going through Knoxville with its five lanes brought the tension back to his neck and shoulders. It eased up some when the city was finally behind him, but by the time he reached Cookville, he had been on the road for twelve hours, give or take, and he was exhausted.

He checked into a Days Inn using the William D. Perkins driver's license and wearing the pair of glasses that had the lowest prescription. Then he headed for the Cracker Barrel that road signs had advertised at the next exit west. He had a ten ounce rib eye, a baked potato and a house salad and returned to the hotel. Once in his room, he took a shower and put on a pair of plaid pajama bottoms and a tee-shirt, kicked back on the bed and watched reruns of *Law and Order*. It was some time after nine when he finally turned the television off and crawled under the covers. Tomorrow would be a repeat of today, and he was not looking forward to it.

CHAPTER FOUR

Even without an alarm clock, Daniel woke up at five-thirty, a habit he had acquired from getting up at that time all through his years at college and law school. Also by habit, his first stop was the bathroom, where he took care of what polite folks might call his toilet. Then he washed his neck and lower jaw with the hottest water he could stand and applied shaving cream. He looked at his reflection in the mirror, razor in hand, and hesitated. Maybe a bit of scruff would add to the confusion if someone was asked to identify him? He bent down and washed away the shaving cream, looked at his reflection again and smiled. The smile slowly vanished when he began to wonder if maybe he wasn't getting too good at this subterfuge thing.

After a satisfying breakfast, provided by the hotel, he studied the atlas Rosalynn had sent with him. In hindsight he wished he had taken I-75 just west of Knoxville down to Chattanooga, then I-59 down to catch I-10 north of New Orleans. Rather than backtrack, he decided to take I-55 south at Memphis and cut I-10 just a little farther west.

By eight forty-five, he had already traveled a hundred and fifty miles. Driving through Nashville during the morning rush hour taught him a lesson. Always be on the other side of a large city—whichever direction you were heading—before you stopped for the night. Traffic had moved steadily, and there had been no accidents to avoid, but moving along with so many other vehicles to keep track of and making the lane changes required created tension all the same. Now, west of the city, he could relax and let his mind wander. And it wandered into the past again rather than the future, all the way back to the months after Rose's surgery and the new personality that had emerged—Rose, fifteen going on five.

He smiled at the memory of lying on the floor with her, the two of them on their bellies, coloring with crayons; both of them seventeen and nearly five feet-eight inches tall, coloring like preschool children. Rose bright-eyed and giggling because she had accidentally bumped his arm and made him color outside the line, then her face going serious and her offering an apology. For some unknown reason, colors seemed to fascinate her more after her surgery, and she showed quite a talent for painting, trees and landscapes mostly. Rosalynn's comment about her being upset over losing her watercolor kit came back to mind. It had confused him at the time, but now he remembered she had talked Mr. Griffin, the high school art instructor, into teaching Rose how to use watercolors one evening a week, and she had been on her way home from one of their sessions when the attack happened. How could he have forgotten so many details? he wondered.

Daniel pulled his mind away from that night with some effort and tried to get a mental picture of the post-surgery Rose. The doctor insisted on chemotherapy, and she had gone completely bald. That brought tears and confusion. She could not understand, though he and her mother tried to explain it time and again, why her hair was falling out. Then it had come back in thicker and curlier than it was before, and even when her mother kept it cut short, she couldn't take care of it herself. Like any five-year-old, Rosalynn had to brush it for her. She had to be reminded to keep her skirt tail down so her panties wouldn't show, to brush her teeth after meals, and if he was visiting, she whined when she was told it was time to go to bed. *Something in her mind must have given her a premonition that she wasn't long for this world,* Daniel thought, *and she didn't want to waste time sleeping.*

As if it had a will of its own, his mind went to the ones who had orchestrated her departure: Dexter Landis, Jordan Harris and Ryder Robinson. He frowned and shook his head. No, that wasn't right. Landis, Robinson and then Harris was the rank of importance with the three of them. Dexter's father was a moderately successful realtor, and his mother came from money. Ryder Robinson's father was dead, and his mother did seamstress work from their home. Jordan Harris's father worked on construction like Daniel's own father had, except Mr. Harris sat at home during the winter and drew unemployment every year. Dexter and Jordan both had cars, but Ryder didn't. For some reason, anytime Daniel had seen the three of them together outside of school, they were in Jordan's '78 Chevy Impala, a pale green thing with lots of rust spots, and Dexter was driving. Dexter had a two-year-old Camaro he had gotten new on his sixteenth birthday. But you never saw the three of them in it.

36

Likely, Dexter didn't want to give his friends a chance to mess it up, Daniel thought now.

He had figured out just how important Jordan Harris was early in their junior year of high school. At that point, Dexter was already first string quarterback. Harris was a split end and Dexter's favorite target when it came to passing. Like he had told Rosalynn, they thought they owned the halls. Harris got into the habit of slipping up behind him and slapping him on the side of the head anytime he got the chance. That ended the day he turned around suddenly, grabbed Harris's shirt and gave him a good, solid knee in the crotch. Harris hit the hallway floor in agony, and his two buddies stood with their backs against the far wall and laughed while their supposed friend threw up his lunch. So much for: All for one and one for all. He wasn't proud of what he had done, but it had stopped the bullying—at least where he was concerned.

What kind of greeting will I get from Harris when I reach San Antonio? Daniel wondered. For a while as he drove, he tried to come up with a plan that would throw Jordan Harris off guard. Several scenarios came to mind, but he discarded them all. There were too many unknown factors; he would figure out what to do when he got there.

To take his mind off where he was going and what he was supposed to do when he got there, he turned it back to where he had been. Already on this trip, he had gone through all of his hats and all of his eyeglasses and was starting over again. Wearing the strongest pair of glasses long enough to pay for gas at a Pilot Travel Center had given him such a headache that he didn't think he would use them again. Besides, he was beginning to wonder about the need for all the drama Rosalynn had created where his appearance was concerned. It didn't seem like anybody was giving him a second glance, and he had only seen a few highway patrolmen so far. But he heard her voice in his head saying, *Don't get careless,* and he pulled the bill of his Yankees cap down over his eyes a little farther and slouched to a more comfortable position, low in his seat.

* * *

Tuesday was another day of roaming around Huntingdon for Rosalynn. Monday had been exhausting, and she didn't get out of bed on Tuesday until almost ten, nearly three hours past the time when she usually got up. She ate a light breakfast since it was so late, and she planned to have lunch somewhere at noon when restaurants would likely be the most crowded. She spent the morning sitting in her recliner and drinking coffee. Caffeine, she thought, gave her strength. She wondered how far Daniel had gotten and worried a little over the thought that she might have missed something, forgot to tell him something. The corners of her mouth turned up slightly in a smile that never reached her eyes. *You've thought of little else for the last ten years*, her own voice inside her head told her. *If there was anything more that needed to be done, don't you think you would have thought of it years ago?*

"I think I gave him everything he needs," she said aloud, looking at the photograph of Rose on the opposite wall. "He will get the job done, Sweetheart. We can count on Daniel."

At a few minutes before noon, she got dressed and headed for Wendy's. As she had expected, the place was busy when she arrived. She smiled when she saw that the person taking her order was a former student of hers, a young woman who was now a student at Juniata College.

"Hi, Mrs. Holder!" she greeted. "It's nice to see you! What can we get you?"

"Just a hamburger and a chocolate Frostie," Rosalynn said and then asked, "Why aren't you in class today?"

"I only have classes Monday, Wednesday and Friday this semester."

"How are you doing?" she asked when the girl had taken her money and handed back her change.

"I'm not making straight A's, if that's what you mean, but I'm doing okay. Nothing lower than B."

"Keep up the good work," Rosalynn said and then stood aside to wait for her name to be called. She smiled to herself and decided that leaving the house again for supper wouldn't be necessary. A trip to Walmart for something that wouldn't take too much energy to prepare—maybe a Marie Calendar chicken potpie—and she could go home and stay in for the afternoon.

A young man who reminded her of Daniel came in with his wife or girlfriend, and she wondered again how far he was from San Antonio and when he would get there. *I suppose it will depend on their attitude, on whether they show any signs of remorse or not,* he had said when she asked him if he could do it. And if they showed signs of remorse and he came away without getting the job done? Or if taking care of the first one bothered him to the point that he wouldn't finish the job? But it had to be done, and it had to be Daniel. There was no one else she could ask.

Her name being called brought her back to the present. She picked up her order and found a small table near a window. *Take it one day at a time*, she told herself. *That's what you have been doing ever since the day Rose was taken away. It will be what it will be, and then...* She left the thought unfinished, and went to work on her sandwich.

Some twenty minutes later, she dumped half the burger and almost all of the Frostie into the trash and headed for her car. Walmart wasn't far, and she had wasted enough energy eating.

* * *

He had been on the road nearly twelve hours by the time he reached Baton Rouge Tuesday evening. He had made good time, stopping only for fuel, restroom breaks and fast food, which he ate on the road. A lot of truck stops, he had discovered, had restaurants attached now—a Hardees, a McDonalds or a Subway. Food and restroom stops he limited to fifteen minutes. Fuel stops took a little longer. It was after eight o'clock, and he was concerned about finding a room for the night, but he managed to snag the last single at a Holiday Inn Express just off I-10. After a nice, hot shower, he stretched out on the bed in pajama bottoms and a tee-shirt and fell asleep almost immediately. No *Law and Order* reruns tonight. An early start in the morning would put him into San Antonio by late afternoon on Wednesday, he thought. With any luck, he would get the job done and be on his way back home tomorrow night.

* * *

Daniel got a late start the next morning. He thought of eight o'clock as late anyway. Still, he passed the San Antonio city limit sign a few minutes after four. The terrain was fairly level compared to some of the states he had passed through. He was on just a slight downhill grade, and the weather was warm and sunny. The highway was lined on either side with businesses of all descriptions, randomly spaced and backed by grassy fields. This particular area of San Antonio didn't look much like a city at all, he thought. For another mile or so, there were no houses. Then there it was—on the north side of the Interstate, and not fifty yards off the roadway, the blue shack-looking place from Rosalynn's computer. The one-story structure faced west, and passing it from behind as he was, Daniel could see that it was not set on a foundation but about eighteen inches off the ground on square wooden pilings. Immediately, his mind began to work on possibilities.

He took the next exit and turned right at the bottom of the ramp, took two more rights and found himself in front of the house. The street had once been paved but now was mostly gravel, and it ended right there, seemingly cut off by the Interstate. *Simple enough to get to* went through his mind. *Now think of an excuse for being here.* He sat there thinking, and then noticed the time on the instrument panel. Harris should be getting off work soon if he was on the day shift, and he would likely be hungry. A smile spread across his face and he turned around and went back the way he had come. He took a left and then a right and kept going until he found a convenience store. Stepping inside, he overheard a conversation between a customer and the clerk.

"Two six packs of Corona, is that it?"

"That's it,"

"You drinking heavy tonight or is this supper?" the clerk joked, smiling.

"The wife will have supper ready when I get home. This is for later. Got friends coming over."

"Good stuff. I sell more of it than any other brand."

Daniel got a six pack of Corona from the cooler and set it on the counter.

"What else?" the clerk asked.

"How long will it take to make one of those Hunt Brother's pizzas advertised in the window?"

"About twenty minutes, give or take?"

"I'd like a large pepperoni then."

When the pizza was done, he took his purchases and drove back to the blue house. He turned the car around, tail end toward the Interstate, so the Pennsylvania license plate wouldn't be showing and prepared for Harris's arrival. He got the stun gun and the pistol out of the briefcase and put them in the pockets of a light, tan jacket he took from his suitcase—stun gun in the left pocket, revolver in the right. One of Rosalynn's 6 X 9 envelopes he put inside the jacket and zipped it up. That done, he slid behind the wheel and settled down to wait.

Harris pulled up a little after six-thirty in an old white Chevy pickup. Night had fallen by that time, it being late-October. Even so, in the light coming from the truck yard across the Interstate, Daniel could tell the pickup was in bad need of a trip to the carwash. Harris got out and stood for several moments, staring at the strange gray car. Then he headed for the house, his gray work uniform as much in need of washing as his truck. Daniel waited until he had gone inside and a light came on in the back of the house. Then he got out of the Honda and followed. On the porch, he managed to balance the pizza box on the arm holding the six pack and knock on the door. He heard footsteps, then the door was jerked open, and Jordan Harris stood there frowning.

"Who the hell are you, and what do you want?" His tone made it a demand.

"I got beer and pizza," Daniel said, holding both items out.

Harris's expression didn't change. He stood there, one hand on the door, the other on the door frame, and glared.

"Mind if I come in?" Daniel asked. "We could eat and talk."

Harris looked at the beer and then the pizza. Without saying a word or losing the frown, he stepped back and allowed his uninvited guest to enter. Daniel smelled beer on the man's breath and smiled.

The place didn't look any better from the inside than it had from the outside, he noticed immediately. The living room carpet had probably once been a cream color but was now a medium brown and looked like it had never been cleaned or vacuumed. An ancient sofa sat against the wall to his left, its arms thread-bare and some of the wood framework underneath the upholstery showing. The scarred and battered coffee table in front of it looked like something Goodwill or a Salvation Army store would have tossed in the trash. Its round legs were scarred, and one of them had lost its metal end cap and was sitting on some folded newspaper. Part of its laminate veneer was missing. The only thing that was obviously new in the room was a flat screen television that sat against the wall to his right. The thing was on a length of unpainted two by twelve that rested on two stacks of cement blocks, each four blocks high.

The kitchen was straight ahead and separated from the living room only by a recliner that was in worse shape than the sofa. It sat at an angle just beyond a door that likely led to a bathroom and bedroom, Daniel thought. The floor covering in the kitchen had once been off-white but was now cracked and yellowed with age. He took a step to his right and could see a stove against the left wall just beyond the recliner. A Single-tub sink, probably cast iron, took up part of the back wall to the left of a back door. A refrigerator of some kind of green color and a small table and two chairs took up most of the remaining space.

Daniel looked at his host and noticed how little Harris had changed. He was still the same tall, lanky red-head with the face full of freckles he had been in high school.

"Welcome to my humble abode," Harris said. "Now who the hell are you?"

"You don't recognize me?" Daniel asked, stepping around him and bending to set the pizza and beer on the coffee table. Straightening up, he removed the Yankees baseball cap and the horn-rimmed glasses he didn't need. "How about now?"

Harris squinted at him for more than a minute,

saying nothing. Then his eyes got big and his frown got deeper.

"Miller?" His tone made it a question. "What the hell are you doing here?"

"Had some business to attend to here in San Antonio and heard you were in the area. Just thought I'd stop by and we could catch up. I haven't heard much about you since we graduated."

"What kind of business?" Harris asked, sounding a bit suspicious.

"I just graduated from law school and passed the bar exam in Pennsylvania. I had a job interview. Pennsylvania winters are miserable, and I'm thinking about moving south." No need for the man to know the interview had been in Pennsylvania and was already over.

"How'd you find me?"

"Oh, you know. A friend talks to a friend who talks to a friend. Word gets around. I believe they call it the grapevine, don't they? Let's eat before this pizza gets cold and the beer gets warm." Daniel suggested. He stepped around the end of the coffee table, took a seat on the edge of the sofa and flipped the box open.

Harris took a slice of pizza, shoved more than half of it into his mouth and went into the kitchen for a bottle opener. When he sat back down on the sofa, the other half of the slice was in his mouth, and his cheeks were bulging. He popped the caps off two of the bottles of Corona and handed one to Daniel.

"You bring any limes?" he asked when he finally managed to swallow.

"Limes?"

"People around here squeeze lime juice in this

kind of beer." He chugged half the contents of his bottle and reached for another slice of pizza.

"So how are things going for you?" Daniel asked. "How have you been? I heard you spent some time in the Air Force. How many years were you in?"

Harris finished his beer and reached for another one. Daniel started to set his down on the table most people have at the ends of their sofas, remembered there was no table there and rested it on the arm of the sofa itself.

"Year and a half," he said.

"A year and a half?" Daniel tried to keep the surprise out of his voice. "I thought enlistments were for four years or six years? How did you manage to get out after a year and a half?"

Harris's face and neck turned red. "None a yer damn business."

Daniel nodded and took a small sip of his beer. It was as good as any he had ever tasted, but he had never been a beer man. And he needed to keep his head clear. He had no intention of drinking the whole bottle.

"Have you been home lately?" he asked.

"This *is* home."

"I mean back to Pennsylvania."

Harris finished his second beer and reached for a third. "Why the hell would I go back there?"

"You have family back there, don't you?" Daniel asked. "Your mom and dad are still alive, aren't they? And don't you have a couple sisters?"

"And none of them give a shit if I'm alive or dead. Let's talk about something else."

"What about your friends, Landis and Robinson? You don't want to see them?"

The redness that had faded from Harris's face and neck came back. "Friends," he said, and his tone made the word derogatory. "We didn't have nothin' in common except football. When the season ended our senior year, they didn't want nothin' to do with me anymore."

Especially after you dropped that pass in the end zone in the last few seconds of the semi-finals, Daniel thought. But he kept the thought to himself. He tilted his head to the side, nodded in a kind of silent okay and changed the subject. "So what do you do for a living? Work for the trucking company across the Interstate?"

Harris finished another bottle and nodded. "Yeah."

"Have you been there long?"

The question—and likely the beers he had already consumed—got him started. Harris ran through his work history from the time he got discharged from the Air Force until the present. Daniel got the impression that, early on, Harris had not had much choice about whether he would stay with a job or not. Possibly fired for unreliability or insubordination? His tone when he talked about some of his former employers suggested he hadn't left them on good terms. He had been with the trucking company longer than he had been anywhere else and thought he would stay with them awhile. Daniel didn't ask what kind of work he did now. The state of his clothing said it all.

"You gonna finish that?" Harris asked, nodding toward the beer Daniel still had in his hand.

Without a word, Daniel handed it over. A corner of the envelope inside his jacket poked him in the armpit and reminded him why he was there. He took a deep breath and thought, *it's now or never.* "So tell me about the night you and Landis and Robinson assaulted Rose Holder."

Harris had his head tipped back, the last bottle of beer at his lips, and his eyes wandered over the ceiling for a second or two. Then he lowered the bottle, set it down on the coffee table and looked Daniel in the eye.

"And we finally get around to the real reason yer here," he said. "You come all this way just to ask me that? Well, we had a trial, and they found us innocent, so I don't have to tell you shit."

"Technically, you weren't found innocent," Daniel said with a calmness that surprised even himself. "The trial ended in a hung jury, which means the three of you weren't found either innocent or guilty. But the statute of limitations has run out, so nobody could try you again, even if they wanted to."

Harris stared at him through and alcohol-induced haze.

"So why not tell me about it?"

"You can't do nothin' about it?" he asked. "Nobody can?"

Daniel shook his head. "Nobody," he said, and he could almost see the wheels turning in Harris's head.

This guy was Rose Holder's best friend. This was the guy that kneed him in the crotch and had everybody laughing at him. Why not tell him what he wanted to hear? Why not rub it in his face?

"Okay. You really wanna know. I'll tell ya."

CHAPTER FIVE

"We were just out, cruisin' around," Harris said. "Dex and Ryder and me, lookin' for some tush, like the song says."

"In your car?" Daniel asked.

"Yeah, in my car."

"And Dexter Landis was driving." He made it a statement.

"Yeah, Dex was drivin'. What of it?"

"I was just wondering why you weren't driving since it was your car, that's all. If Dexter wanted to drive, why weren't you in his car?"

Harris's face and neck got red again, and it would have been obvious to anyone that he realized his attempt to rub things in Daniel's face was getting turned back on him.

"You want me to tell ya about that night or not?"

Daniel held up his hands and nodded a concession.

"Anyway," Harris began again, and this time Daniel let him talk. "We was just cruisin' around in *my* car with *Dex* drivin' when we see this person walkin' down the street. We didn't know who it was at first, and Ryder says something like, 'That girl's walkin' funny.' Then she walks under a street light and I saw

49

who it was, and I said, 'That's old lady Holder's *re*-tard.' And I told 'em, 'People like her like to get it on.' And Dex says, 'Bullshit.' And I said, 'No, really! It's like when they get that way, not able to learn anything anymore, sex is like a instinct with them.' And Ryder says, 'Yer full a shit, Harris. Ya know that?' And I tell 'em, 'No, man, it's for real. I have a cousin down in Maryland. He's a *re*-tard, and my uncle had to have him cut, he was so horny. They was afraid he'd turn into a rapist.'

"And Ryder said, 'That's bullshit! They don't cut people.' And I said that maybe they didn't actually cut him, like with a knife, but they did something, and he settled down. Then I told 'em, 'Yer missin' the point. Them kinda people like it. Maybe she does too.' And Dex thought about if for couple of minutes, and then he says, 'Let's find out.' So he pulled up beside her in the middle of the next block, and I opened the door and drug her into the back seat. We took her out on that back road by the Hockenberry place, and you know the rest."

"Actually, I don't," Daniel said. "I wasn't there. What happened next? Did she try to resist? Did she tell you no?"

"She kept sayin' she needed to go home, and when we got her out of the car, she looked around and said, 'This not home.' It was kinda funny really. Then Dex took her down in the grass and started pullin' up her dress. She fought him at first, but then he got a hand inside her panties and a finger on her clit, and that was it, man. Once he got it in her, she hunched up to meet him like he couldn't give her enough. There wasn't no more fight until Dex got done and Ryder started to mount her. Once he got it in her, though, she was all into it again, buckin' like a bronc at a rodeo. Same thing happened when it came to be my turn."

"So you all had her?" Daniel asked.

"Hell, yeah! Dex and Ryder and then me."

"And nothing about it bothered you?"

"It pissed me off that they went first. It was kinda my idea anyway."

"And that's it? That's the only thing that upsets you about the whole incident?"

Harris shook his head and made a face. "What else is there to be upset about?"

"How about the fact that you took advantage of a young woman with special needs?" Daniel asked. "How about the way the three of you brought her home with her clothes torn and bloody and threw her out on the sidewalk like trash? You don't regret any of that? Which one of you killed her?"

"What?! None of us killed her! She killed herself!"

"Did she?" he asked. "She had the mind of a five-year-old. How would she know what kind of pills to use? Where would she get them?"

"How the hell should I know, and who the hell cares? She was just a retarded piece of ass!" Harris said, standing up, "and it's time for you to git the hell out a my house."

"You're making this easy for me," Daniel said. In one smooth motion, he stood, took the stun gun out of his jacket pocket, shoved it against Harris's chest and pressed the button. When the voltage hit him, Harris jerked erect as if he were coming to attention. Then he toppled to the right, landing on the coffee table and

51

sending splintered pieces of wood and empty beer bottles flying across the room.

Daniel turned him onto his back with a foot and leaned over him.

"What the fu…" Harris got out before a second jolt from the stun gun hit him.

"This is for Rose?" Daniel said, looking into the man's eyes. He pressed the barrel of the thirty-eight tight against the left side of his chest and pulled the trigger. Harris's body jerked like a flat-lining patient getting hit with the paddles in a Code Blue. The air left his lungs in one final slow exhalation, and he was still.

Improvise, Rosalynn had said, and in the absence of throw billows, he had. When he thought about it later, he would realize there was no *Bang!*, only a *Whomp!*, like the sound it made once when he had dropped a large plastic jar full of peanut butter on the floor of his apartment. Even Harris's closest neighbors wouldn't have heard it.

CHAPTER FIVE

Daniel stood erect, a foot still on either side of Harris's body, and looked down at the weapons in his hands—the stun gun in his left and the revolver in his right. He put both of them back in the pockets of his jacket. For a minute or two, he thought about what he had just done and how he felt about it. There was no feeling of guilt, he decided, but then he wasn't proud of himself either. He had done what needed to be done, he told himself—what should have been done ten years ago. Now there was more to do before he could take his leave, and it had to be done quickly.

He got into a position where he could grasp the back of his victim's shirt collar and began dragging him toward the door in the kitchen. Once he got past the carpet, the job was easier. Harris's belt snagged on the doorsill, but a jerk brought him out and down over the steps. Daniel dragged him to the left, away from the light coming from the truck yard across the Interstate, and pushed him under the house, using a foot to get him in far enough to be out of sight. Then he went back inside for a broom to sweep away the drag marks. That job done and back in the house, he checked the floor for blood stains. There were none. There had been no exit wound.

53

"What does she have this thing loaded with?" he whispered aloud, his hand on the pocket of his jacket.

Thinking of Rosalynn reminded him of the envelope inside his jacket. He took it out, undid the metal clasp and looked inside. The only item in it was a tube of lipstick.

"What in the world?" he asked himself and wondered what to do with it, where to put it. Finally, he shrugged and dumped it out on the floor. Maybe whoever found it would think it had been on the coffee table when it got smashed.

Moving quickly, he collected the beer bottles, the cardboard carrier they came in, the pizza box and the slice or two of pizza that was left, and everything, including the envelope, went into a plastic trash can he found under the sink. He carried it to the front door, then turned and looked around. He had touched nothing but the knob on the backdoor, the collar of Harris's shirt, and the broom handle. He set the trash can down and went into the kitchen, found a ragged dishtowel and used it to wipe his prints off the broom and backdoor knob. There was nothing he could do about Harris's collar. Taking the towel with him, he used it to turn off the lights and to wipe off the inside and outside frontdoor knobs as he left. Then it went in with the rest of the trash.

He wedged the trash can between the front and back seats in the Honda and made one last mental check of what he had done. The stun gun and revolver still in his pockets, he got behind the wheel, started the engine and drove slowly away. He would stop somewhere up the road and put things where they belonged. No spinning wheels and slinging gravel as he left, nothing but the sound of a visitor leaving the house next door. He left the headlights off until he got past neighboring houses and came to the first left turn. No porch lights came on, and nobody stood on porches watching. No one pulled back window curtains.

Two left turns and a right, and he was back on Interstate 10, heading west toward the city and the state route he had chosen for his return trip. He refused to think of it as his getaway.

* * *

Just before he got into what he thought of as San Antonio proper, he took the 410 bypass north. He could have caught Interstate 35, which would have taken him north through Austin, Waco and Fort Worth and possibly gotten him into Oklahoma more quickly. But he was tired of Interstates, for one thing, and thought that, if on the unlikely chance Harris's body was found too quickly, there would be fewer cops patrolling state highways.

Daniel's route of choice was State Highway 281, which ran almost directly north to Wichita Falls, Texas, and went through no large cities. Speed limits would be lower, and passing through small towns would slow him down, but if he pushed himself, he thought he could make it into Oklahoma by sunrise Thursday morning.

By the time he reached Lampasas at ten P.M., he was beginning to regret his choice of routes. He had yet to see a policeman since leaving San Antonio, as he had expected, but he hadn't given a thought to the near absence of the all-night truck stops and the fast food restaurants that he would have found frequently along an Interstate. He dropped the trash can in a dumpster behind a Stripes Convenience Store in Johnson City and transferred the stun gun and the thirty-eight to the suitcase in the trunk while the Honda's tank was filling at the pumps, so running out of gas wasn't going to be a problem.

Traffic was almost none-existent, and stretches of road between the towns were pitch black beyond the reach of his headlights. When his eyes began to burn, he realized that he had been up and going for more than sixteen hours.

Getting a hotel room and stopping for the night was out of the question because there were no hotels, only one-story motels that looked like they had been built in the nineteen-fifties, and even they were few and far between. Anyone of them would have likely had a vacancy, but a patron driving a vehicle with a Pennsylvania license plate would be remembered. At one point, he passed an abandoned service station and thought about pulling in behind the pumps and catching a few winks. But then he thought about the possibility of waking up to a cop or a sheriff's deputy knocking on his window and asking if everything was okay, and he kept going.

Between Adamsville and Evant, he passed a red Ford pickup abandoned on the west side of the road. Even before a plan was fully developed in his mind, he hit the brakes to slow down and make a U-turn. He pulled in behind the truck and smiled. There was a silver toolbox just behind the cab. He reached into the back seat and pulled the briefcase into his lap. A pair of Rosalynn's latex gloves were about to come in handy.

It took him less than fifteen minutes to pull the gloves on, find a Phillips screwdriver in the toolbox and remove the license plates from the front and back of the truck. Then with the plates and the screwdriver on the floor of the backseat, he made another U-turn and was on his way north again. No vehicles had passed, and he smiled to himself. Luck—or something like it—seemed to be on his side. Just a mile or two north of the little town of Evant, he pulled nose-first into a side road and swapped his Pennsylvania plate and the vanity Rosalynn had on the front of the Honda with the Texas plates from the pickup. Looking at the vanity plate in the headlights—a single red rose on a field of black—he wondered if it wouldn't have been a good idea to have taken it off before he left Huntingdon. Too late to think about it now, but when he put the Pennsylvania plates back on, he would leave it in the trunk.

A few miles up the road in the small town of Hamilton, he was able to get a room at the Hamilton Inn. As a precaution, he put the Pennsylvania and vanity plates in his suitcase and took both it and the briefcase to his room for the night. He was almost asleep before he hit the bed. His last thought before sleep actually took him was that he should have called Rosalynn, but it has been a long and tiring day. He would call her in the morning.

* * *

At a few minutes before noon on Wednesday, Rosalynn Holder backed out of her driveway in her gray Honda and headed for town. Two doors down from her house, Jason Bookheimer was raking leaves into a pile in his front yard. She pulled to the curb and rolled her window down.

"When you get finished here, you can do my yard," she said, smiling.

"I don't imagine I'll have the energy," he said, returning her smile. "I still have my backyard to do, and these cottonwoods seem to produce more leaves every year."

"Do they really produce more leaves every year, or do we just have less energy?"

Jason's front door opened and his wife Sara stood behind the storm door, glaring. Rosalynn smiled and gave her a finger wave.

"Seriously, if you have the time, I would appreciate you getting the leaves out of my yard for me. I just don't have the energy this year, and I would gladly pay you to do it. Give it some thought," she suggested. "And if you don't have the energy, maybe you could help me find someone who does." She gave Sara another smile and finger wave and drove off.

Mission accomplished, she thought. *Sara is the jealous type and that little exchange with her husband will be burned into her gray matter permanently. I can stay home and take a nap this afternoon.*

CHAPTER SIX

Daniel Miller woke with a start and sat up in bed, staring at the light coming through the opening in the window curtains. It took a minute or two for him to remember where he was and why he was there. His stomach growled, and he wondered when he had eaten last? Oh, yeah, the pizza in San Antonio, he thought, and pulled his mind back to the present. No point in dwelling on the past; what was done was done.

He threw back the covers, got his Dopp kit from his suitcase and headed for the shower. He was working the shampoo provided by the hotel into his hair when the events of the previous day and night came flooding unbidden into his mind. He stopped what he was doing and stared at the tile in front of him. Had he really done what he was thinking he had done in San Antonio? In retrospect, it all seemed like a bad dream. Had he actually done it? *There's no need for either of us to say it out loud.* If so, why was he not feeling bad about it? Why was getting out of Texas and back home his main concern?

Finding no answers on the tile of the shower, he rinsed the shampoo from his hair and decided to forgo the conditioner provided. Then he used a washcloth to soap himself, rinsed off and stepped out onto the mat.

59

With a bath towel wrapped around his waist, he stood in front of the vanity and used the hair dryer to take the fog off the mirror. As his reflection emerged in the clear spot, he looked for changes in his image. Other than the two-day scruff of beard, there were none, nothing that would attract anyone's attention. Regardless, he felt an urgency to get his things together and move on. The sooner he got into Oklahoma and tossed the Texas license plates, the sooner he could relax.

At a little after ten o'clock, he walked through the lobby with his suitcase and the briefcase, careful not to seem to be in too much of a hurry and not to be too rude or too friendly with the young woman on duty. He handed her his room key and smiled.

"Come back and stay with us again," she said and returned his smile.

Daniel nodded. "Maybe I will do that someday," he answered, conscious that saying too much might give away his Pennsylvania accent. He left the hotel wondering again if he wasn't beginning to get too good at this.

With the two cases stowed in the trunk, he headed north. In the little town of Hico—the supposed home of Billy the Kid—he found a Sonic and ordered a Breakfast Burrito and a cup of coffee. A young lady brought him his food; he backed out and drove away. A mile or so out of town, he found a spot where a tinhorn gave access to a gate that opened into a pasture. He backed in toward the gate and ate his breakfast. Then he got the burner phone out of the glove compartment and called Rosalynn. She answered on the first ring.

"Hello, Daniel. Are you okay?"

"Yes."

"Where are you now?"

"Just north of the little town of Hico, Texas, on Highway 281, on my way back."

"You've already been to San Antonio? How did you manage that in just three days?" she asked.

"I pushed it a little on Tuesday so I could get there by what I figured would be quitting time on Wednesday."

"You be careful doing things like that. You don't want to get too tired and make a mistake. You got the job done then?"

"I did."

There was a brief pause. Then she said, "Tell me about it."

He told her in detail, sparing her only the language Harris had used to describe her daughter.

"Did you wear gloves?" Rosalynn asked.

"I didn't see how I could," he said. "I figured showing up out of the blue with a pizza and a six pack of beer would make him suspicious enough. Doing so with latex gloves on would have been too much. But no problem, I wiped everything I touched with a towel and put the towel in with the rest of the trash."

"Nobody saw you?" she asked.

"Only a clerk in a convenience store and a couple of customers—and Jordan Harris, of course."

"Putting him under the house was ingenious. I can't imagine anybody will go looking for him until he has missed work for a couple of days, maybe not until after the weekend on Monday. You bought us more time."

Daniel made no comment.

"Are you okay?" she asked again.

"I guess that, considering the fact that according to the law, I am now a felon and I'm still free to come and go as I please, I'm doing fine."

"Don't think about it like that," Rosalynn said. "Just think of it as evening out the numbers. That's not a felony."

"What does that mean—evening out the numbers?"

"I keep forgetting you weren't in the courtroom when Parsons and the ADA made their closing statements. Summations, I think they're called, aren't they?"

"Yes, what about them?"

"When Parsons ended his, he gestured toward those three boys he was defending, looked at them and said something like 'three fine young men whose lives will be ruined by a guilty verdict.' Then he swept a hand toward where Rose and I were sitting, and without even looking our way, he said, 'One alleged victim who can't even tell us the young men's names. Do not ruin their lives with a guilty verdict. You must find them innocent.'

"When the ADA made his rebuttal, he told the jury we don't do justice by the numbers here in this country. Three against one did not mean the three accused were innocent because there was only one accuser. He reminded them that DNA from all three of the defendants was recovered from inside my Rose; and that, given the fact that she had the mind of a five-year-old, she could not have legally given consent.

"So what we are doing is evening the numbers. Rose has been gone a long time now. Someone eliminated the victim and took the prosecution's side down to zero. It's time for the defense to be brought down to that same number. I, for one, will not be happy until it's done. So as far as I'm concerned, it's one down and three to go."

When Daniel didn't respond, she asked again. "Are you okay? How are you feeling? *What* are you feeling?"

"I'm not really feeling much of anything," Daniel said. "I haven't *let* myself feel much of anything since the day of Rose's funeral, and now I'm into this and I don't know how I feel about it. All my life, I've been told it's wrong to kill, but now I've done it, and there doesn't seem to be that much to it if there's a good reason for it and it's done quickly."

"So you're okay to continue? Do you think you will be able to finish what we've started?"

He thought about the question for a moment. *In for a penny, in for a pound,* came to mind, followed closely by: *You might as well be hanged for a sheep as for a lamb.* Somehow, both idioms seemed to fit the situation. If he was caught, tried and convicted, the sentence would likely be the same; it wouldn't matter if he stopped now or kept on.

"Yes," Daniel said. "Who's next and where do I find him?"

"That would be the Robinson boy, Ryder. He lives somewhere near Chambersburg and works at the Walmart there."

"Works at Walmart? There's a Walmart right there in Huntingdon. Why doesn't he work at that one where he could be near his family?"

"He did when it first opened for business, but

everybody in this area knows what he and his cohorts did. I imagine the looks he got from the customers made him uncomfortable and he asked for a transfer. That's what I hear on the grapevine anyway."

"Chambersburg is right on Interstate 81," Daniel said. "I can do the job on the way back and save a few miles. You said he lives somewhere near Chambersburg? He doesn't live in town?"

"No, he lives south of the city, just off Route 11. I have his address on my computer. You should come back and let me show you his house like I did with the last one."

"Just describe it to me," Daniel said. "I was planning to take Interstate 81 all the way to Greencastle, and Chambersburg is only a few miles farther on. I imagine I'll be following him home from work anyway."

"All right," Rosalynn conceded after a brief hesitation. "It's a two-story, frame house with a porch across the front of it, probably built sometime in the first part of the twentieth century, maybe earlier. The door and window trim is white, and the roof is a rusty corrugated metal. It looks like brick at a glance, but it's covered with that asphalt siding that was made to resemble brick. It's a kind of bluish-gray. I don't think they make it anymore. I believe the place might be or might have been a farmhouse at one time, but I have no idea what kind of acreage it sits on or how close the nearest neighbors will be. You'll just have to…"

"Improvise," Daniel finished for her.

"I'm sorry," she said.

"Don't be. It would be impossible to come up with a plan for what we are doing that accounted for every little detail in advance. There are too many variables. You have done a remarkable job considering possibilities and probabilities. I'll just have to be on the lookout for possible problems and surprises." And after a pause, "I do have one question, though. There was no exit wound with Harris. What do you have that thing loaded with?"

"I *knew* I had forgotten to tell you something, but for the life of me I couldn't remember what it was. They're called frangible bullets. I thought it would be wise to use them because they disintegrate on impact and leave no bullet to be matched with bullets from other crimes."

Daniel gave it some thought. "What if they hit bone? Like a rib maybe?"

"I suppose they might come apart prematurely. You'll just have to be careful, and you might have to use more than one round. Or you could buy a different kind of ammunition. I'll leave that up to you."

When Daniel remained silent, she asked, "When do you think you'll be home?"

"I don't really know," he said. "It's right about eleven o'clock here, and I've got maybe two hundred miles to go before I get out of Texas. I want to be somewhere east of Oklahoma City come nightfall. I'm thinking I'll be in Chambersburg sometime Sunday. Then, depending on whether or not I run into problems with Robinson, I could be back in Huntingdon Monday or Tuesday."

"Well, don't push yourself. You bought us time with the way you did things in San Antonio, so there's no need to be in a rush. You want to be rested and ready when the time comes."

"Okay. Take care." He ended the call, put the phone back in the glove compartment and pulled back onto the highway.

* * *

It was nearly six o'clock when he got to Wichita Falls. Traffic was light for the most part, and he had enjoyed seeing a part of Texas that wasn't flashing by on an Interstate. At the same time, he was looking within himself and wondering what kind of changes this thing he was doing would bring in *him*. Confessing to Rosalynn that he hadn't allowed himself to feel much since the day of Rose's funeral, something he hadn't even realized he had done until he said it out loud, woke memories he had apparently suppressed. That day itself had been agony, and the first several weeks after, he had gone through a period of depression that almost ended in his own death by his own hand. But Rosalynn needed him, and that thought had kept him sane enough to live.

Then his senior year had started, and passing Rose's attackers in the hallway, enduring their smirks, and knowing they were sitting behind him in some of his classes—they always chose seats in the back of the room—made it difficult for him to concentrate. And knowing that if he wanted to go to college, he had to earn a scholarship, he had made himself block everything out. He heard nothing but the teachers' voices, saw nothing but the notes they wrote on the whiteboard or the power point presentations flashed on the screens, read only the pages of whatever textbooks had been assigned to him. He realized now that the habits he had developed then had to be given the credit for his success in college and law school. He had been the top of his class but had no friends at all. And he had come to like it that way.

Now, in the back of his mind, he remembered hearing Rosalynn talking on the telephone back then. *She did not commit suicide; she was murdered. And you are doing nothing to find the person who killed her.* She had been adamant that something should be done, and he had shared her anger. But that, too, was interfering with his ability to concentrate, and he had suppressed it—distanced himself from it. Much to his regret, for several months, he had stopped going over to visit her when she needed him most.

Snatches of conversations he heard in the hallways at school came back to mind as he drove. *That bitch is gonna be a distraction and cause the guys to lose State.* And: *I heard someone say she probably did it herself.* They were speaking of Rosalynn, no doubt, and he had not defended her. She had given her daughter one of her Ambien capsules, Rosalynn had told him, because she was taking them herself and didn't want Rose to wakeup and maybe hurt herself. He remembered now that, when she kept insisting on a retrial, the authorities made accusations and investigated Rosalynn herself. They confiscated her medications, had them tested and compared them to what had been found in Rose's stomach during autopsy. What they discovered was that Rose had been given a massive dose of Restorial, not Ambien, and they backed off. But after that, Rosalynn had given up, too—until now.

Just south of Wichita Falls, Daniel pulled to the

shoulder of the road and looked at his atlas. If he took Highway 79 up through the little towns of Petrolia and Byers, he could be in Oklahoma in an hour or less. Not too far north of the Red River, he could catch Highway 70 at a place called Waurika, then take Route 81 north to Interstate 40. If he took that route, he would have to go through Oklahoma City. Highway 70 ran almost due east to Ardmore, Oklahoma, which was right on Interstate 35, and he could go north from there and catch Interstate 40. East was where he was going, so he chose the latter, tossed the atlas on the passenger seat and pulled back onto the highway.

He smiled a few miles farther on when he realized the route he had chosen pretty much skirted the city of Wichita Falls, and he wouldn't have to be fighting city traffic. Soon, he found himself driving through open country again, his mind free to take up where his thoughts had left off. For a minute or two, he couldn't remember exactly where that was. Then it came back to him. *Oh, yes. Rosalynn's medications.* Not the kind of sleeping pills that Rose had been given. And there was something else—alcohol in her system, quite a lot of it. The Chief of Police himself had delivered the warrant and stood by while his minions took her place apart, looking for the source of it. They found nothing—not even an empty bottle. Rosalynn had never been a drinker and kept no alcohol in her house, and whoever had given it to Rose had taken the bottle away with them.

Daniel smiled as he drove. She had been a thorn in their side for months, but they had won in the end. His smile faded when he remembered something else that he had pushed to the back of his mind:

peppermint. One of the things that had made Rosalynn so sure that her daughter had been murdered was the smell of peppermint on the morning she found Rose's body. There hadn't been peppermint of any kind in the house, no candy and no oil. Whoever fed her the pills and helped her wash them down with booze—vodka, Daniel suspected—had given her a piece of peppermint candy to mask the smell.

Approaching the bridge over the Red River now, he felt ashamed of himself when he remembered there had been a time back then when he had wished that Rosalynn would just stop, just accept the fact that Rose was gone and learn to live with it. *Like you did?* He asked himself. *And how does that make you feel now?*

He didn't answer himself because at that moment, he came to the Texas end of the bridge across the Red River and discovered there was a pull off where fishermen likely left their vehicles. He slowed crossing the bridge and found a similar pull off on the Oklahoma end, swung into it and stopped. There wasn't much traffic on the road this time of night, and this would be as good a place as any to swap the license plates out.

He turned off the headlights and, leaving the motor running, got the Pennsylvania plate and the screwdriver out of the trunk. Wearing a pair of Rosalynn's latex gloves and working mostly by feel in the dark, he made the exchange, and then sailed the Texas plates out into the river. The screwdriver and gloves back in the trunk, he slid behind the wheel and pulled back onto the highway. No vehicle had passed. He had not been seen.

69

Some five or ten minutes later, he cut Highway 70, and not more than fifteen minutes after that was passing through the south end of Waurika, Oklahoma. At the junction of 70 and 81, he swung into a truck stop to fuel up and discovered it also had a restaurant. It was almost seven o'clock and he hadn't eaten anything since the Breakfast Burrito. He was tempted to go in for a good meal, but the place looked crowded. Best not to show his face to so many people. He paid for his gas and pulled back onto the highway. He would pick something up at a convenience store and eat it in the hotel room he was planning to get in Ardmore.

By then, Daniel had been on the road for nine hours with only a few stops to get a cup of coffee and to use the men's room. Night had fallen with a vengeance, pitch black with no moon or stars. Staring into the darkness beyond his headlights made his eyes burn. He knuckled them and was tempted to let them close for just a second, give them a little rest. When he gave into the temptation, his right tires dropped off the pavement and he woke up with a jerk. *Just what I need*, he thought, *to roll this thing and get picked up by the highway patrol*. He brought the Honda to a stop on the shoulder of the road, got out and walked around in the cool night air to wake himself up. *Should have gotten a cup of coffee to go back at the truck stop* went through his mind. *Too late to think of it now.*

Feeling better, he got back behind the wheel and pulled back onto the roadway again. *Don't push yourself*, Rosalynn had said. *Be rested and ready when the time comes.* Maybe it was time he started taking her advice; get a room at the first hotel he came to. But the road went on and on, almost as straight as a plumb line. There was very little traffic at this hour, a few pickups and a couple semis. Then he had to negotiate a slight curve going into the little town of Ringling. The only motel there was a one-story, mid- to early-twentieth century model that looked like it had been turned into apartments for migrant workers. He kept going. Another stretch of open road and then he passed through the somewhat larger town of Lone Grove— still no hotels. Another fifteen minutes and he passed under Interstate 35, and there was a Quality Inn on the north side of the highway with a Denny's attached. Some forty-five minutes later, he had a room, and had taken a shower, which revived him somewhat, and was kicked back on the bed in his pajamas, watching a rerun of *Law and Order* and eating takeout from Denny's.

CHAPTER SEVEN

After a good nights sleep, which still surprised him given what he had done on Wednesday evening, Daniel used the voucher provided by the hotel and enjoyed a leisurely breakfast of eggs over easy, bacon, toast and coffee at Denny's. Then he had studied the atlas long enough to determine that if he took Highway 70 a little farther east, he could catch Route 177, which ran straight north to Shawnee and Interstate 40. By doing so, he avoided Oklahoma City, and at ten-thirty, he found himself passing the second exit to Henryetta, Oklahoma.

His appearance this morning was altered somewhat. The scruff on his neck was gone, and his beard was neatly trimmed. He was wearing his Oakland A's baseball cap—green with yellow trim—to begin the day, and the sun was bright enough that he felt it safe to wear his mirrored sunglasses. A pair of wire-rimmed glasses lay in the seat beside him, the pair he thought made him look more scholarly and less geeky, to be worn the next time he stopped. He had on his last clean pair of jeans, the pair he had not cut slits in, and figured he would still be wearing them when he got back to Huntingdon. Just sitting and riding in a car all day would not get them dirty. But, he smiled at the thought—a smile that didn't quite reach his eyes—that there was a possibility they might get blood on them in Chambersburg. Maybe he would have to stop by a laundromat before he got home.

Traffic was fairly heavy on the Interstate, but his mind still tended to wander from one thing to another. An episode of *Law and Order* he had watched the previous night kept coming to the fore. It involved a young girl who had a tumor similar to and located in the same area of her brain as the one the doctor removed from Rose's brain. The girl did not want to have surgery, but because she was a minor, her parents had the final say, and they signed the papers giving the doctor permission to operate. To avoid the procedure, she swiped a hypodermic needle full of some unidentified medication and ended her life. Detectives got involved because her boyfriend was arrested for helping her push the plunger down.

Henryetta, Oklahoma, in the rearview, Daniel could not remember how the trial had turned out. What he remembered most was the reason the girl did not want to have the operation. A friend with similar issues who had been communicating with her online had suddenly stopped, and apparently the girl had gone to see her. Some of the episode's details had slipped his mind, but he didn't think he would ever forget what Olivia Benson and her partner found when they went looking for the second girl. Her mother greeted them effusively. Oh, yes! Her daughter was doing fine. She was in her room, and no, she didn't mind if they spoke with her. Nothing could have prepared them—or him—for what they saw when the woman opened her daughter's bedroom door. The girl was sitting in a wheelchair with some kind of helmet on her head and staring unblinking at the wall. Her eyes were open, but there was no indication that she was aware of her surroundings or that anyone else was there.

Until that moment, Daniel had not realized just how blessed he and Rosalynn had been to have had the Rose she was post-surgery and post-recovery. *The happiest, kindest, least-selfish, most sweet-natured person I will likely ever know,* he thought now, *and the most vulnerable. Whoever ended that beautiful life and the guys who caused the end of it deserve everything I'm bringing them.*

To quell the anger his thoughts engendered, he made himself think of the time he had gotten to spend with the post-surgery Rose and the things they had done together. She had loved going to the movies, especially cartoons and comedies, and always seemed to know the right moments to laugh. And he had loved sitting beside her, holding her hand and smiling at her profile. He tried to remember the sound of her laughter and was saddened to realize that it was fading from his mind. Her smile was still there, though, the way it made her dark brown eyes almost disappear and her upper lip seem to fold up against her nose and reveal small, even, white teeth not much bigger than the baby teeth both of them had lost in first and second grade. He had teased her about them once until he made her cry, and then he had apologized and held her in his arms and promised to never to do it again.

He missed so much about his Rose, like the feel of her arms clutching his when they went for walks. Post-op, she had been capable of walking on her own, but her left leg had never regained all of its feeling and

74

strength. Unless she had someone to hold on to, she had to swing her leg in an arc, and the action caused her to stagger a little. *Ryder Robinson spotted her because she was "walking funny,"* Daniel remembered Jordan Harris saying. *So she walked funny. That didn't give anybody license to assault her.*

Not that pre-op Rose was dull and boring. A little introverted maybe, but when we were together, Daniel thought, *she came out of her shell and we enjoyed each other's company and had fun.*

That had been especially true of the last several months before the surgery. Their kisses had become—what was the word people used?—steamier, and they had learned how it felt to have their bodies pressed together—fully clothed, of course. He had seen Rosalynn smiling at them a time or two, so he knew she approved of their relationship. But she didn't want her daughter suffering from the same stigma she had endured, and she had taken pains to keep them from going too far. For the most part, they had stolen kisses while they were looking at the *National Geographic* magazines Rosalynn kept stacked on the lower shelf of an end table.

Thinking about those magazines now brought back memories of the places they thought they would like to see and things they wanted to do together when they were older. The Eiffel Tower in Paris, the Parthenon and the Coliseum in Greece, castles in the Scotland, Ireland and Wales, Mardi Gras in New Orleans and a dozen or more other places and events were on a list Rose kept in a notebook—places they wanted to go and things they wanted to see someday. Daniel smiled at the enthusiasm she had for travel, though she hadn't ever been out of the state of Pennsylvania. His smile faded when his mind added: *And never will be.*

The operation left her unable to read and with little memory of the plans they had made together. When she found her list post-op, she brought it to him and asked him to read it for her and tell her what it meant. He told her it was a list she had made of places they wanted to go and he read it to her. When he read 'the Parthenon and Coliseum in Greece,' she looked confused.

"Grease?" she said. "We want to go in a skillet?"

He had assured her that, no, they didn't want to go in a skillet. Greece was a place, and they had talked about wanting to go there. He got the magazines out and showed her the photographs that had inspired her list. And he had sadly discovered that she was no longer interested in any of it. Places like Walmart, Wendy's and the movie theater were her only interests now. And places that sold ice cream. She would have eaten a half gallon of chocolate ice cream at one sitting if her mother had let her. But the doctor cautioned them about watching her weight. With her leg compromised as it was, she could have an accident that left her unable to walk or stand, he told them. If something like that happened, excessive weight gain would make it hard for her mother to care for her.

A sign for a McDonalds up ahead caught Daniel's attention, and he decided that since he had eaten a decent breakfast, a burger, fries and a soft drink would be okay for lunch. When the restaurant came into sight, it was just to the south of the Interstate. He took the exit to a place called Alma, made a right at the bottom of the ramp and a second one into the parking lot. He pulled into a slot just across from the entrance, traded his mirrored sunglasses for the wire-rimmed reading glasses, got out of the Honda, stretched and headed inside.

* * *

Rosalynn awoke at seven-fifteen Friday morning and immediately thought about Daniel. Where was he? Had he taken her advice and not pushed himself after they talked on the phone Thursday morning? Would he be able to finish what she was asking him to do, and what kind of a man would that leave him if he did? It had to be taking its toll, she thought, and yet he had sounded perfectly normal on the phone.

Still lying in bed she wondered, *what do I do, and where do I go today? Wendy's again? Maybe showing up there three times in one week after not eating there for more than a year would look suspicious.* After giving it some thought, she smiled to herself, that smile that never quite reached her eyes. Getting them to be suspicious of her would take suspicion away from Daniel. So Wendy's it would be.

She tossed back the covers and got out of bed, slipped on a robe, went to the kitchen and put on a pot of coffee. When it had dripped through, she poured a mug full and carried it into the living room. Still in her pajamas, she snuggled into her recliner and raised the mug to the photograph of Rose on the opposite wall.

"One down, three to go," she said. "And the next one will be taken care of soon. When they're all done, we can rest in peace, Sweetheart."

She sipped on the coffee until the mug was empty, then she set it on the little table beside her chair. On impulse, she picked up the remote and turned the TV on. She watched fifteen minutes of an inane conversation between Kelly and Ryan, and then punched in the numbers for the weather channel. A cold front was moving into the area, and that caused her some concern. Had Daniel taken a heavy jacket with him? Not to worry, she told herself. There was enough money in the envelope for him to buy a winter coat if necessary, and she had told him there was more where that came from. She flipped through channels until she found a rerun of *The Golden Girls*. After watching it for several minutes, she looked at the photograph of Rose again,

"That should have been us, Sweetheart," she said out loud. "I would have been Granny, and you would have been Doris, not the Rose that lives with them. You would have been so much smarter and sweeter. I guess it wasn't meant to be."

Tears threatened—tears that she thought had dried up years ago. She hit the button to turn the television off, struggled out of her recliner and went into the kitchen for another cup of coffee. Back in her recliner, she considered having a bowl of cereal but decided against it. More and more, even the thought of food had a tendency to make her gag. She sipped her coffee and thought about how to draw suspicion to herself and away from Daniel. Nothing significant came to mind. So, if not suspicion, then attention, she decided, and a plan began to form in her mind. When she walked out of Wendy's today, she decided, everybody in the place would know she had been there.

At a little after twelve, she dressed in a pair of her signature sharply-creased pants, silky blouse and flats—these ones gray to match the pants. It was time to put her plan into action. Wendy's was packed, as she had hoped it would be, and she placed her order and waited for her name to be called. When it was, she took the tray and headed for a table at the far end of the restaurant. Half way there, she pretended to trip and dumped the entire contents of the tray into the lap of a portly man who was dressed like a banker. She caught herself on his table and began to apologize immediately.

"Oh! I'm soooo sorry!" she said and picked up a napkin and started wiping at the chocolate Frostie that was running down his peacock blue necktie and the front of his light gray suit coat. "How clumsy of me!"

"This is a twelve hundred dollar suit and a hundred dollar tie!" Banker Man said, his tone angry. He grabbed her by the wrist and took the napkin from her hand. "How could anyone be such a klutz?"

"I'm sorry," Rosalynn said again, looking at the floor behind her. "I must have tripped on something. I'll pay to have your suit cleaned."

"Just get away from me!" the man snarled.

She turned to face him again just as he raised a handful of French fries from his lap and dropped them back onto the tray. The sight was too much. To hide the guffaw that was about to escape, she grabbed a napkin and used it to cover the lower half of her face. At a near run, she headed for the door.

Once back in her Honda, she covered her face and let the laughter take her like it hadn't since Rose's death. Anyone who saw her shoulders shaking would have thought she was crying.

"Try to un-see that, people," she muttered into the napkin. "A hundred dollars for a tie! Ridiculous!"

When she finally got control of herself, she started the engine and headed home. There was no need to spend any more time out in public today. Her presence in Huntingdon had been established beyond a doubt. And a grilled cheese sandwich and a cup of tomato soup would suffice for lunch.

* * *

Another four hours of driving and a myriad of memories of Rose got him to Lonoke, Arkansas. And although there would be another hour or hour and a half of daylight, Daniel decided not to take a chance that he would find a hotel another hour down the road. Here he had a choice of several, all on the north side of the Interstate. He stopped by another McDonalds and picked up a chicken sandwich, a bacon ranch salad and a chocolate shake. Any hotel would provide coffee, he knew. Minutes later, he was checked into a Hampton Inn.

Showered and dressed in pajama bottoms and a tee-shirt, the television on, he propped himself up against the head of the bed and ate his food. No reruns of *Law and Order* this evening. Tonight he wanted something less thought provoking and more entertaining, and he found it with Steve Harvey and *Family Feud.*

CHAPTER EIGHT

Saturday became a repeat of the last several days, minus the incident in San Antonio and what he had come to think of as the near roll-over east of Waurika, Oklahoma. Breakfast provided by the hotel at seven in the morning, suitcase and brief case loaded into the trunk of the Honda, and heading east on Interstate 40 by eight o'clock. And then what was beginning to seem like interminable driving. Traffic was fairly light in the morning, and the weather was bright and sunny. Western Arkansas was hilly and made him think of home. Then the Ozarks were behind him and the terrain became flat and the highway became crowded with what he considered to be an over-abundance of semis. Once he got through Memphis, the scenery started to look familiar, and he thought of Rosalynn's advice about not taking the same route on his way back or not stopping at the same places if he did. Since Interstate 40 was the best route home, he chose to ignore the former and observe the latter.

At two o'clock in the afternoon, he found himself once again threading his way through Nashville, Tennessee, home of the Grand Old Opry. Traffic wasn't as bad as it had been when he had navigated the city east to west, and he smiled at the lesson his last passage had taught him. Tonight he would be staying in one of the hotels he had seen around Exit 407 to Sevierville—on the other side of Knoxville. And Sunday night? Well, he would just have to study the map of Tennessee he had picked up at the welcome center in Memphis and the maps of Virginia and Maryland in the atlas. Maybe he could figure out how many hours it would take him to reach Chambersburg from there. If only he had his smart phone or his lap top, he told himself, he could use either one of them, and they would tell him in a matter of minutes— possibly seconds—what he needed to know. But both of those items could be traced somehow, if television shows were to be believed. And the idea was to be so discreet and circumspect that nobody would know he had ever left Huntingdon, Pennsylvania.

In the meantime, reminiscences of earlier times with Rose and thoughts about what might have been, could have been, should have been, would have been kept his mind occupied. Sometimes the memories caused him to smile mentally, and sometimes the corners of his mouth actually turned up slightly in what had come to be a Daniel Miller smile. Other times, his brow drew down when he thought of where he was going and what he was going to do—what he had come to believe he had to do. *There's no need for either of us to say it out loud.* Sometimes it drew down when he allowed himself to wonder what kind of life he would have when the numbers were even. Would he feel... he searched for the right word... *worthy* of practicing law? Or would all of the hard work he had done and the sacrifices he had made to graduate from law school and pass the bar exam turn out to be wasted time? Then he would realize that such dark thoughts had somehow made their way into his mind, and he would push them aside and make himself think of earlier times, happier times.

With a few stops along the way for coffee, to use a restroom or just to stretch his legs, he made it through Knoxville and reached Sevierville a few minutes before five o'clock. He checked into a Holiday Inn Express and then went looking for food. Since he hadn't eaten anything all day except a cheese Danish and a chocolate bar he bought during one of his restroom stops, what he had in mind was a good plate lunch. He found it at a Cracker Barrel on the north side of the Interstate.

Back in his room after a meal of chicken and dumplings, carrots and steak fries, he poured over his map of Tennessee and his atlas. Eventually he came to the conclusion that it was four hundred and seventy-odd miles to Chambersburg, which would likely be at least a nine-hour drive, give or take, depending on traffic and the weather. So far, he had not hit any rain. But even if he left at six in the morning, he figured he would probably not arrive at his destination earlier than three in the afternoon. That wouldn't leave enough time for him to locate his target, get the job done and get on his way back to Huntingdon. And there was no way he wanted to spend a night in a hotel in Chambersburg. He got out his burner phone and called Rosalynn while he thought about it.

"Hello, Daniel," she said and then asked, "Where are you?"

"Hello to you, too. I'm at a Holiday Inn in Sevierville."

"And where exactly is that?"

"East of Knoxville, and just south of I-40, about a nine-hour drive from Chambersburg."

"You're not going to try to make the trip all the way in one day, are you?" she asked.

"I was thinking maybe I would hang around here until noon tomorrow, maybe drive a few miles south," he said. "Pigeon Forge is down there somewhere, and Gatlinburg. Maybe do some sightseeing, a little shopping. There's a lot to see around here. Check out is at ten, I think, and I was thinking I would head north after lunch. That would get me to Roanoke, Virginia, about three or four o'clock, and I would spend the night there. That's about a three and a half hour drive from Chambersburg. If I left there at seven or eight, I would be in Chambersburg before noon. That would give me the better part of a day Monday to locate Robinson and take care of business. What do you think?"

"That sounds like a good plan to me," Rosalynn said. "Just remember not to bring anything back that would reveal you have been down there. How are you feeling?"

"Same as always—okay, I guess. How about you? Are you doing okay?"

"You don't worry about me," she said. "You just be careful and get done what needs to be done and get home safely. Get some rest, and I'll hope to see you Monday night."

The line went dead, and Daniel took the phone away from his ear and looked at it for several seconds. Was it his imagination, or did Rosalynn not seem like herself? The thought brought a mirthless chuckle.

"Where do people get that expression?" he asked himself aloud. "Who else would she be?"

He closed the phone, tossed it on the bed and headed for the shower. After driving all day—again—he was looking forward to kicking back and numbing his mind with television. Mental Pablum, he remembered someone had called it, and he thought they were probably right. But tomorrow evening, he had another unpleasant job to do, and tonight, he needed it.

* * *

On Sunday morning, Daniel woke late—six-thirty was late for him anyway—dressed and went to the dining area for breakfast. That early, there were only a few of the hotel's patrons up and around, as people back home would say. He kept to himself and avoided making eye contact with anyone. *Wherever you find yourself, just blend in.* Rosalynn's words tended to come back to mind anytime he was around people, and his decision to stay in the area until noon and sightsee would put him to the test.

After breakfast, he went back to his room and turned on the television and listened to it while he shaved his neck. His beard was beginning to thicken, and he kind of liked the look of it. Too bad he would have to shave it off when he got home—for a while, anyway. He bushed his teeth, patted on some shaving lotion and put his toilet articles back into his Dopp kit.

When the hullabaloo that would likely follow what Rosalynn had him doing blew over, he thought, maybe he would grow it again. But if he decided he could go ahead and practice law, he doubted that any law firm he might hook up with would allow an associate to have facial hair. He stared at his reflection in the mirror and wondered what the future might hold. Maybe a small office of his own?

"Time, and only time, will tell," he said out loud.

At a few minutes before ten, he check out of the hotel and stowed his suitcase and the briefcase in the trunk again. Then he drove south toward Pigeon Forge and Gatlinburg, stopping at several shops along the way. At the Smokey Mountain Knife Works, he bought himself a pocket knife. His father had always carried one, and he supposed he should carry on the tradition, although exactly what he would use it for, he didn't know.

* * *

For Rosalynn Holder, the anticipation of what would be happening when Daniel got to Chambersburg was unnerving for some reason. After she had spoken with him on the phone Saturday evening, she felt unsettled and ill at ease. Was she causing him irreparable harm, asking him to do what he was doing for her? For quite a while, she stood at the kitchen sink and stared out the window into her darkened backyard. Finding no answers, she made herself a cup of tea and carried it to her recliner. Once seated, she picked up the remote and turned on the television again. She sipped her tea and paid no attention to it, but for some strange reason, the sounds coming from it seemed to make the empty house less unnerving. When the tea was gone, she set her cup aside and dozed, coming awake now and then when the sounds from the television got louder. At a little after ten, she toddled off to bed, telling herself she didn't really need a shower since she had sat around the house and done nothing all day.

She woke Sunday morning feeling somewhat refreshed. She had slept soundly through most of the night, getting up only once to go to the bathroom. Still lying in bed, she wondered again about Daniel. Where was he and what was all of this doing to him? After several minutes of contemplation, she came to the same conclusion he had. Time, and only time, would tell. She threw back the covers and headed for the kitchen. She got a pot of coffee started and then stood staring out the window above the sink, her mind blank, much as it had been the night before. When the coffeemaker gurgling brought her out of her trance, she poured herself a mug full and carried it to her recliner. Some time later, she raised the mug to her lips and discovered that it was empty.

"Rosalynn Holder," she scolded herself, "you need to stop that. Life's too short to be losing track of time that way."

She took her mug into the kitchen and set it on the counter near the sink. The clock on the microwave read 10:03, and she thought about Daniel down there in Tennessee, checking out of the hotel. She smiled that smile that never quite reached her eyes and headed for the bathroom.

In the shower, she finally realized what had been bothering here since the middle of the week. She wrapped a bath towel around herself and went looking for her phone. Daniel didn't answer, and she let it ring five times and then hung up. More concerned than ever, she laid the phone on the table beside her recliner and went into her bedroom to get dressed. She was struggling with the last button on her blouse when her phone started ringing. She hurried into the living room, afraid that he would hang up before she could answer it.

"Daniel?" she said, sounding a bit out of breath, and her inflection made it a question.

"Yes, you called?"

"Kind of silly of me to be asking if it's you when we're the only ones who have the numbers for these phones. Why didn't you answer?"

"I was on the road," he said. "The phone was in the glove compartment, and I won't answer it when I'm driving anyway. Is everything okay?"

"Yes, everything is fine. I just thought of something, and I wanted to talk to you about it. You said you didn't know if you would be able to do... what I asked you to do until you were face to face with them, and then it would depend on their attitudes and whether or not they showed any signs of remorse."

"Yes."

"Well, you were able to do the job in San Antonio, so I'm guessing that one said or did something that maybe angered you a little?"

"Yes, a little."

"Well, I don't need to know what it was. I just wanted to call and tell you not to let this next one get to you. Don't lose your temper and give him the upper hand. From things I've heard about him, he's good at that. You need to keep a level head and remain dispassionate. Don't let him goad you into making a mistake. He's quite a bit more intelligent than the last one, his choice of employment not withstanding, so you'll have to be more careful with him."

When Daniel didn't reply, she asked her usual question. "Are you okay? Where are you now?"

"I'm fine. I pulled into a service station to return your call. I'm either in Sevierville or Pigeon Forge. I'm not sure which. This area is kind of built up, and the city limits are a little blurred for someone like me that's not from this area. Is there anything else on your mind?"

"No, that's all, and I don't mean to sound…"

"Bossy?" Daniel finished for her, but she could hear the smile in his voice. "That's okay. I appreciate your concern and your advice. We'll get this done, and I believe the world will be a better place because of it."

"Thank you," Rosalynn said. "You just be careful and call me if I can help in any way." There was a click and the call ended.

"I guess she just doesn't like goodbyes," he said, then closed the phone and put it back in the glove compartment.

Since he was at a service station, he decided to go ahead and fuel up. There wasn't enough gas in the tank to take him all the way to Roanoke anyway. That job done and payment made, he pulled back onto the highway and headed for Gatlinburg. He discovered it wasn't far and that there wasn't anything there that interested him, so he made a block and headed back north.

Nothing much else attracted his attention, but he made himself hang around until he could have lunch at

CHARLES C. BROWN

Cracker Barrel, the same one where he had eaten supper the evening before. But he thought it unlikely that he would run into the same employees—and definitely not the same customers—who had seen him then. Besides, he would be wearing a different cap and different glasses, and if anyone should ever be asked to describe the man they had seen, they would describe a man with a full beard and glasses with heavy black frames. And hopefully the beard and the glasses would both be gone not later than sometime Tuesday. And his shoulder-length hair? Maybe that should be gone, too.

By a few minutes to one, he had enjoyed a meal of meatloaf, mashed potatoes and gravy and whole-kernel corn and was heading east on Interstate 40. Once again he occupied his mind with anything that would keep him from thinking about what lay ahead. Up there somewhere near Chambersburg, Ryder Robinson was living in a house with asphalt siding that resembled gray brick. There was no point in dwelling on the fact that if things worked out the way he hoped they would, come this time Tuesday afternoon, Robinson wouldn't be living anywhere anymore.

Chapter Nine

Daniel took the Wayne Avenue exit off Interstate 81 into Chambersburg a little before noon on Monday. His stay at another Holiday Inn Express on the north edge of Roanoke had been much like the one in Sevierville, except that he had not hung around the area and gone sightseeing afterwards. He had not slept well Sunday night, and he blamed his insomnia on what he intended to do here in Chambersburg today. *There's no need for either of us to say it out loud.* Still, a morning shower, another good breakfast and several cups of strong, black coffee and he felt alert and ready.

The city turned out to be much larger than he had anticipated, and he guessed he had gone several miles, passing a number of businesses and going through a residential area before he saw a sign for Route 30. It was a narrow, one-way street, going to his right. At the next intersection, there was another sign for Route 30, one-way, going to his left. He drove a couple of blocks farther, hoping to find Route 11 or maybe Walmart, and had no luck. Businesses and homes became intermingled. On impulse, he made a left, and a block later, discovered Chambersburg's Main Street, another one-way street going to his left. He crossed it and went a few more blocks, made several more turns and was basically lost. *So what do I do now?* he wondered, beginning to feel like a rat trapped in a maze.

He made what he thought were a few random turns and found himself on Main Street again, heading south. He passed a library and several businesses, then got stopped at a red light at the square. A parking slot in front of a Presbyterian church seemed to beckon, and when the light turned green, he pulled into it and shut off the engine. For several minutes, he sat there thinking, and then he reached into the glove compartment and retrieved the phone. Rosalynn answered on the first ring.

"Were you sitting in your recliner with your phone in your hand?" he asked.

"I am sitting in my recliner, but the phone was on the table next to it. Is everything okay?"

"Yes and no," Daniel said. "I'm in Chambersburg, and the place is huge. I have no idea where Walmart might be, and for some reason, I'm turned around here. I can't tell east from west, north from south. Could you get me an address for Walmart maybe?"

"Hold on," Rosalynn said. "I'll have to go into my office and find it on the computer."

He kept the phone to his ear, heard her struggle out of the recliner and then a thump when she laid her phone on the desk. Keys rattled and a minute later she asked, "Are you still there?"

"Still here."

"Walmart is located at seventeen-thirty, Lincoln Way East. Does that help?"

"Only if you can direct me to Lincoln Way East. I have no idea where much of anything is here. Right now, I'm parked in front of a church on what I imagine would be called a square."

"Let me pull up a map," she said, and again there was a thump when she laid the phone down. More keys rattled, and she came back on the line. "It looks to me like Lincoln Way East and Route 30 are one and the same."

"I crossed Route 30 when I came in on Wayne Avenue. I think I can take it from here. Thank you."

"No problem," she said. "Keep me posted and don't hesitate to call if you need my help."

There was a click, and she was gone. Daniel smiled and put the phone back in the glove compartment. He backed out of the parking spot, made a couple of lefts and found Route 30, made a right and was on his way.

* * *

Between the square and Walmart were four miles of street/highway lined on either side with businesses of every description, and a dozen or more red lights, and it seemed to Daniel like he caught them all. The Walmart store itself was one of the largest he had ever seen, its parking lot bigger than some towns he had been to. He parked the Honda in what he hoped was a blind spot at the far edge of the lot and walked toward the store, his collar turned up against a north wind that had dropped the temperature considerably and made his light jacket inadequate. Once inside, he turned his collar back down and exchanged his mirrored sunglasses for a pair of reading glasses with black frames and weak lenses.

Ryder Robertson worked here in this store, a building that seemed to cover several city blocks, and Daniel had no idea which department he might be assigned to. Short of asking someone where Ryder might be found, which he didn't want to do, there wasn't anything he could do but take a cart and push it around until he spotted the guy. For an hour and a half, he prowled the aisles, stopping occasionally to examine items he had no intention of buying. The only thing he needed was a glimpse of his prey, and he was beginning to think Monday might be Ryder's day off. Then rounding a corner into the cereal aisle, he heard and angry female voice say:

"Goddamit, Robinson! You better learn to keep your hands to yourself if you don't want to lose your job. I'm getting's sick of your shit!"

And there was Ryder Robinson in the flesh, coming right at him, and Daniel was astounded. Robinson had been fairly large in high school, but now he seemed huge—six feet tall and likely somewhere between two-fifty and three hundred pounds. A lot of the weight was centered in a gut that hung out over the waistband of his ragged jeans and made it impossible for him to keep the tail of a faded tee-shirt shrunk by too many washings tucked in. He had gone bald on top, but the rim of reddish-brown hair he had left was in bad need of cutting and possibly washing. A quick glance at his puffy face showed a smirk that suggested he wasn't about to let some broad tell him what he could and couldn't do, and that he wasn't about to learn to keep his hands to himself either. He passed by without even giving Daniel a glance. The young woman, a well-built lady with long blonde hair pulled back into a ponytail and probably in her late twenties, glared after him until he disappeared through swinging doors, and then she turned around, bent over in her skinny jeans and went back to whatever it was she had been doing before Robinson interrupted her. Daniel turned his cart around and headed for the hardware department. Given the size of his intended target, tonight's business was going to require zip ties.

Walmart's zip ties seemed woefully inadequate, but he bought a package of the largest ones they had anyway. Then he left the store and took the Honda to the Lowe's he had passed earlier. There he was able to buy ties that were twenty inches long and looked strong enough to hogtie a bull. Back in the car, he decided to call Rosalynn again, and again she answered on the first ring.

"Yes, Daniel. What can I do for you?"

"I've located Robinson. He's working today, but I have no idea what kind of vehicle he drives. I don't want to spend the night here, and I don't want to miss him when he leaves. The parking lot here is huge, and I don't want to rely on luck. Could you get me his license plate number and a description of his vehicle? Can you do that?"

"I believe I can do that, but it might take me awhile. Let me get on it, and I'll call you back."

He had a twenty-minute wait during which he sat in the Honda in the Lowe's parking lot with the phone in his lap. When it rang, he flipped it open and held it to his ear.

"He drives a two thousand-nine Dodge Ram pickup."

"What is it with these guys and pickups?" he

asked. "I can't imagine either one of them ever hauling anything."

"I wouldn't know," Rosalynn answered. "Maybe it makes them feel more manly."

"Can you tell me what color it is?"

"No, but I can give you the VIN number and the license plate number."

"Just the license plate number should do."

She read it to him and had him repeat it back to her. She asked about the weather "down there" and told him the wind was howling around her house, and just the sound of it made her shiver. When he told her the temperature had dropped where he was too, she told him to use some of the money from the envelope to buy a heavier jacket. She had stayed in all day, she said, and had no intention of going out. Then she asked him to repeat the license plate number again, and when he was able to do it, she ended the call with: "Good. Be careful. I'll hope to see you later tonight."

So he needed to find a 2009 Dodge pickup somewhere in what seemed like umpteen acres of Walmart parking lot and to sit on it until Robinson got off work. And he needed to do it without attracting attention or being picked up on any of the dozens of security cameras aimed at said lot—an impossible task. The best he could hope for was that whatever recordings might be made of his efforts, his face would not show clearly enough to be recognizable (his mirrored sunglasses would help). Or that the tapes or disks or whatever would be erased and reused before Robinson's body was found. *There's no need for either of us to say it out loud.*

He drove back to Walmart and began his

reconnaissance, checking out the areas at either end of the place first. The best parking spaces, he figured, would be reserved for the use of customers. Employees would likely be required to use the less desirable slots. Robinson's red Dodge Ram was parked near a side door at the south end of the building. Daniel found a parking spot from which he could see the vehicle and settled back to wait. He was surprised when Robinson came out the door not more than twenty minutes later, a six pack of beer in each hand. He went directly to his pickup where he set one of the six packs on the blacktop long enough to get his keys out of his pocket and unlock and open the door. Then with everything stowed to his satisfaction, he slid behind the wheel, fired up his engine and drove past Daniel and the Honda on his way to the street. Daniel started his engine and followed.

Ryder Robinson had been living in Chambersburg long enough to learn the best route to take to avoid traffic lights and heavy traffic, and he drove through town like the proverbial bat out of hell. Daniel had all he could do to keep the red Dodge pickup in sight. Robinson never brought his vehicle to a complete stop. He approached every intersection at high speed, tapped the brakes at the last fraction of a second and hesitated just long enough to make a cursory check for cross traffic. Even with Daniel doing much the same, Robinson was blocks ahead when he made the final turn onto Route 11 and headed south toward Greencastle. By the time Daniel made the turn, the Dodge pickup was just a red dot in the distance. Apparently, the man had floored it when he passed the city limit sign. Trying to set a record time from work to home?

Route 11 was three-lane, the middle lane intended to be used for turning. Robinson used it for passing. He stopped for red lights only when there were several vehicles already stopped ahead of him. If there was only one or none at all, he tapped his breaks and made a quick check for cross traffic and barreled on through.

The traffic was heavier than Daniel would have liked. He exceeded the posted speed limit but refused to run red lights in what amounted to a vain attempt to keep Robinson in sight. When the red Dodge disappeared from view, there was nothing he could do but make an educated guess about where Robinson might have turned. The next side road he came to was Frank Road, and he made the turn without much hope of spotting Robinson and was already mentally planning what he would do if he didn't. He slowed to practically a crawl and eased along, checking both sides of the roadway. Route 11 had been lined on both sides with residences and businesses interspersed. Frank Road passed through a wooded area, but homes were clearly visible back through the leafless trees. Daniel was about to give up and turn around, and then up a narrow dirt lane that wasn't much more than two ruts, there it was—the gray-shingled house Rosalynn had described for him. And there was Ryder Robinson, carrying his two six packs of beer up the front steps, his pickup parked in the grass next to the porch.

Daniel kept going until he found an intersection where he could turn around and head back toward Route 11. This time when he drove slowly past the mouth of the lane, he noticed a barn a short distance behind the house, and he smiled to himself as a plan began to form in his mind. No knocking on the door and asking to be invited in this time. Besides, the man already had his beer. Let him have a little time to drink it.

Daniel went on by, got back to Route 11 and turned south. He hadn't eaten since breakfast, and there had to be some kind of food available in a place the size of Greencastle. What he was contemplating was best done in the dark, and a flashlight—something Rosalynn hadn't thought to include in the briefcase—just might come in handy.

* * *

It was right at six-thirty, dark-thirty in October, when Daniel made a left turn onto Frank Road, and a few minutes later, he cut his headlights and turned right into the lane. With the window down, he held the flashlight out as far as his arm could reach and used it to light the way. It wasn't as bright as headlights and was less obvious and unlikely to be noticed if Robinson or any of his neighbors looked out their windows, he thought. He approached the house at idle speed and stopped behind Robinson's pickup, then shut off the engine and listened. He could hear no sounds coming from the house, and the only indication that someone might be in there was a flickering of light at a window, probably from a television.

He got out of the Honda and closed the door quietly. Then he opened the trunk and got the items he would need out of the briefcase. Shivering in the dark, he wished he had taken Rosalynn's advice and bought a heavier jacket. He pulled on a pair of latex gloves and took inventory: the thirty-eight in the right-hand pocket, stun gun in the left, the longer zip ties stuck in his waistband, smaller ones in a hip pocket. He eased the trunk lid down until the light went out and it rested on the latch. Then he took the flashlight out of his hip pocket and, keeping it aimed at the ground, made his way to the porch. At the bottom of the steps, he could hear noise from the television. It sounded like it might be a battle scene of some kind. Then standing outside Robinson's door, he traded the flashlight for the stun gun, took a deep breath, exhaled and knocked. After a few seconds, everything went quiet inside.

Even in his stocking feet, Ryder's footsteps were audible thuds that made the window to the right of the porch rattle. The door began to open, and Daniel hit it with a shoulder and rushed in. Robinson shouted, "Hey!" and tried to turn around and back-peddle at the same time, but he wasn't fast enough. The stun gun made contact with his right side just above the belt; a muscle spasm jerked him upright and he went down. Daniel gave him another jolt for good measure and rolled him over onto his stomach. By the time one of the smaller zip ties was tightened around his wrists, he was beginning to mumble and make feeble efforts to resist. Daniel gave him another shot from the stun gun and then bound his ankles together with one of the larger ties. Another one went around his legs just above the knees, and any likelihood that he might break loose was gone. Daniel rolled him over onto his back and then sat down on the sofa.

Looking around, he realized that Robinson wasn't doing much better here in Chambersburg than Jordan Harris had been doing in San Antonio. There were no pictures on the walls or curtains at the windows, only blinds of the type that rolls up and down. The floor was covered with the same kind of stuff in a floral pattern—ancient, cracked and worn and covered in places with tracked-in dirt. The sofa he was sitting on wasn't quite as frayed, and there were two end tables and a matching coffee table, all three of which were in bad need of sanding and refinishing. The television was a lot bigger than the one he had seen in San Antonio, and it was hung on the wall, not sitting on a make-shift entertainment center of planks and cement blocks. Looking at it, Daniel thought, *Complements of his Walmart employee's discount, no doubt.* The kitchen was dark, but with the light from the living room, he could see that it had probably not been upgraded since the house was built, likely some time in the early part of twentieth century if not earlier, except for a fairly decent–looking white refrigerator. Everything else was lost in shadow.

Robinson began to moan, and Daniel pushed the coffee table aside so the man could see him. Ryder was still in his ragged jeans and faded tee-shirt. Nothing had changed apparently since he had walked into the house after work, except that now one of the six packs and several cans from the second were gone, and empty beer cans were crushed and lying on the coffee table next to his keys. He rolled his head to the right and looked at Daniel.

"Who the hell are you, and what do ya think yer doin'?" he asked, and his tone made it a demand.

Daniel smiled. "You don't recognize me?"

"Why the hell should I?"

"We graduated from high school together."

Robinson's brow drew down as if he was trying to retrieve a distant memory. Daniel removed the

101

glasses and Yankees cap he was wearing and laid them on the coffee table.

"How about now?" he asked, and his own question made him pause. This was beginning to seem like a repeat of San Antonio.

"Hell, no!" Robinson said and then practically shouted, "Who the fuck are you?!"

"You'll figure it out soon enough. For now, you can think of me as the man with the stun gun, and I don't like that kind of language. Use it again, and I'll use this." He held up the item in question.

Robinson apparently didn't believe him, and he repeated his last question word-for-word. Daniel raised himself up off the sofa, leaned forward and gave him another jolt. For a few minutes, there was silence, and he glanced at the television and realized that it was still on Mute. His host (Daniel smiled at his own mental use of the word) apparently liked TV shows that resembled war games. Violence begets violence?

"I know who you are now," Robinson said when he could talk again. "Yer the son of a bitch that's gonna be dead when I get loose from these ties."

Daniel started to rise from the sofa again.

"Okay! Okay!" Robinson shouted. "Keep that thing away from me and I'll be quiet! Just tell me what ya want!"

"Tell me about the night you and Dexter Landis and Jordan Harris raped Rose Holder."

"What?! We didn't…"

"It's not a question of whether you did or didn't, Ryder," Daniel said, cutting him off. "You *did*... all three of you did. Harris already admitted it. Now I want *you* to tell me about it."

Robinson's brow drew into a frown and it seemed like recognition was about to dawn. He rolled his head and looked at the ceiling.

"You got a tape recorder in your pocket?"

Daniel shook his head. "Nope, no tape recorder, and it wouldn't matter if I did. The statute of limitations has run out."

"The statue of what" Robinson asked and rolled his head to look at him again.

"Statute," Daniel emphasized, "the statute or the law of limitations. It means you can't be tried for your crime. Too much time has elapsed." In his mind, he was thinking, *What kind of a moron doesn't know what the statute of limitations is?*

"You already talked to Harris? Why do you wanna hear it from me?"

"I just do. I want to know if your version of what happened matches his."

Robinson swallowed, turned his eyes toward the ceiling and began. "We was out ridin' around in Harris's car…"

"Doing what?" Daniel asked.

"Ridin' around! Just ridin' around, not doin' nothing! Okay?!"

Daniel nodded.

"And we see this girl…"

"Rose Holder," Daniel offered and then asked, "Who saw her first?"

"I guess I did, but what happened after that wasn't my idea."

"Just tell me about it," Daniel prompted when he stopped. "You saw Rose, and what happened next?"

"Harris told us some shit about retarded people…"

103

"Special needs." Daniel interrupted.

"What?" Robinson asked.

"Special needs people," he said.

"Whatever. He told us that them kinda people like to fu…" he glanced at Daniel, "to get it on, and how he had a retar... a cousin like that and his uncle had ta have 'im cut because he got too horny, and they was afraid he'd become a rapist. Then someone said maybe we should see if it was true."

"Who said it?" Daniel asked.

"What difference does it make who said it? Someone just did."

"It makes a difference because I want to know who?"

Robinson rolled his head away and looked at the ceiling. He took a deep breath and exhaled through his nose. The expression on his face suggested that he wasn't saying anything more. Daniel extended his arm and started to rise.

"All right! All right!" Robinson all but shouted. "It was Landis, okay? It was Landis. He said something like, 'Let's find out,' and pulled up beside her."

"And then…" Daniel prompted.

"And then I ain't sayin' nothin' more until you tell me who you are."

When it became clear that Robinson was serious, Daniel cleared his throat and said, "Think back to our senior year. We're in the hallway at school, and Jordan Harris is on his hands and knees. It's right before fifth period, and he's tossing up whatever it was he had for lunch, and you and Dexter Landis have your backs against the wall laughing."

He could tell the exact instant that recognition came by the change in Ryder's expression.

"Miller? You're Daniel Miller?" he said and rolled his head to get a better look at the man on the sofa.

"The one and only and in the flesh," Daniel said and gave him a fake grin.

"Well, let me tell you something, Danny Boy. When I get up off this floor, yer gonna think you got hit by a train."

Daniel chuckled. "I had forgotten that was your nickname in high school. How did you come by it anyway? Was it because of your initials; RR like in railroad crossing?"

"No, it was because when I came off the line on the football field, whoever I hit was on his ass before he could blink. One of 'em said it was like gettin' hit by a train. Somehow it got printed in the paper and the name stuck."

"Oh, yes, football," Daniel said. "Almost State Champs, your crowning glory and the highlight of your life. But for the moment, you're still on the floor, and I'm sitting here on the sofa all comfy and cozy. And what you're going to do now is tell me the rest of it, so go on. Landis pulled up beside her and...?"

Again, Robinson hesitated, and Daniel started to rise.

"Harris jumped out and pulled her into the back seat."

"Did she resist?"

"I guess you could call it that. She kept sayin' she needed to go home, and she kept tellin' Harris don't."

"What was Harris doing?"

"How the hell should I know? They was behind me in the back seat. I didn't turn around and look."

"What happened next?" Daniel asked when he seemed to stall out again.

"We took her out of town, and you know the rest."

"Actually, I don't. I want to hear it from you—in detail."

"We got to this place Landis knew about, and Harris opened the backdoor and pushed her out a the car. Then he grabbed her and threw her on the ground and…"

"Who threw her on the ground, Landis or Harris?"

"Landis."

"And then…?"

"He did her and I did her and Harris did her and we took her home."

"Did she tell you no?"

Robinson was hesitant to answer, but he finally said, "Yeah."

"And you assaulted her anyway." It was a statement not a question.

"Well, what the hell was I supposed to do? I was there with the guys and there she was on the ground, mine for the takin'! You think I wanted to pass it up and look like a pussy in front a them?"

"Were you the one that killed her?" Daniel asked.

"What? Hell no! She killed herself!" Robinson said.

"She had the mind of a five-year-old," Daniel reminded him. "How would she know what kind of pills to take, and where would she get them?"

"How the hell would I know?" Robinson said.

"She didn't get 'em from me. And who gives a shit anyway? She's dead however it happened. One less retard in the world, big deal."

By then Daniel was sitting on the edge of the sofa, head bowed, his elbows on his knees, rubbing his temples with the thumb and fingers of his right hand. His left hand held the stun gun and hung toward the floor. "Do you have any regrets?" he asked quietly.

"What?"

"About that night and what you did to Rose, do you have any regrets?"

"I guess maybe I have one," Robinson said, a smirk on his face.

"And what would that be?"

"That I didn't put it up her ass when I had the chance."

Daniel's head came up and he nodded. "Thank you."

"For what?" Robinson asked and seemed genuinely confused.

"For making this easy."

Daniel leaned down and gave him another jolt from the stun gun and pulled the revolver from his pocket. Then he stood over the man on the floor, a foot on either side, and looked into his eyes.

"This is for Rose," he said. He pushed the barrel of the thirty-eight tight against the left side of Robinson's chest and pulled the trigger. As in San Antonio, the only sound was a dull *Whomp!* Robinson's body gave a jerk and then was still. The pupils of his eyes dilated, and he was gone.

CHAPTER TEN

Daniel stood erect and, for more than a minute, stared through the archway into the darkness of the kitchen. He put both guns in the pockets of his jacket, stepped away from Robinson's body and resumed his seat on the edge of the sofa. For several minutes he sat with his head bowed, forearms on knees, hands hanging, his mind a complete blank.

Without looking up, he shook his head as if to clear it and reminded himself that there was still a lot to be done. This was not a television show where someone was shot, a commercial followed immediately, and when it was over, the body was gone. This was reality, and the body wasn't going anywhere until or unless he followed through with his plan to drag it through the kitchen, out the door and to the barn out back.

He stood and grabbed hold of the zip tie around Robinson's ankles and spun him around—easy enough on the slick floor. But when he tried to move the two hundred and seventy-odd pounds of dead weight, he realized he had a problem. If it required this much effort on a slick floor, there was no way he would be able to drag it over gravel all the way to the barn. And he needed to get the job done quickly and be gone. He

108

let go of the zip tie, and Robinson's feet hit the floor with a thud. Looking around, he spotted the keys to the red Dodge Ram parked outside.

"Finally, a use for one of the trucks you and Harris seem to prefer," he said out loud, picked up the keys and headed for the door. He turned off the lights, opened the door and stood listening and looking at the lights of neighboring houses shining through the trees. A pickup went by on the road, but there were no sounds of alarm. Nobody had heard the shot.

Daniel drop the pickup's tailgate and, leaving the headlights off and using the flashlight, backed it against the foundation of the porch. Then with more effort than he ever imagined it would take, he got the body through the front door and across the porch floor and rolled it over the edge. It hit the tailgate facedown with an impact that shook the entire truck.

"So far so good," he said and took a minute to catch his breath. Maybe the worst of it was over.

He got behind the wheel again and eased the pickup forward. Then he stopped, got out and pushed Robinson into the bed of the truck and put the tailgate up. That done, he drove around the house and out to the barn. He tossed aside the length of two-by-six that propped the double doors shut and swung them open. He shined the flashlight around inside, and to his surprise, the place was practically empty. So, what to do? Dump the body in there somewhere and cover it up with whatever he could find, take the pickup down the road some place and leave it? Or just leave the body where it was, back the pickup into the barn and close the doors? Either plan seemed okay. Judging from what he had witnessed in Walmart, he didn't think Robinson had that many friends, so who would come looking for him and how soon? In either situation, he would likely not be found until after Dexter Landis had been dealt with. Putting the pickup in the barn would mean he didn't have to walk back past houses from wherever he might chose to leave it. And although Frank Road didn't seem to be that heavily traveled at this time in the evening, there was always the chance someone coming home late might spot him. That possibility won the argument in his head, and he swung the pickup around in the grass and backed it into the barn.

That done, he put the tailgate down and hopped up into the bed. Using the flashlight and the pocket knife he had bought in Tennessee, he cut away the zip ties. He had not been wearing gloves when he bought them, and his finger prints would undoubtedly be on them. *Do not touch the items unless you are wearing gloves.* Rosalynn's words came back to mind.

Back in front of the house, he returned the guns to the briefcase and got out one of Rosalynn's envelopes and took it into the house. Standing just inside the door, he made a sweep of the living room with the flashlight. Nothing seemed amiss or out of place. The coffee table was still intact this time, and he dumped the contents of the envelope onto it—a silver compact this time. Daniel recognized it as a present from Rose's seventeenth birthday. There was no blood on the floor because once again, there had been no exit wound. He used the remote to turn the television off, then turned and stepped outside, locked the door and went to the Honda. He removed the latex gloves and crammed them into the empty envelope, tossed the envelope into the trunk and pushed the lid down until the latch clicked. Nothing was ever going to wake Ryder Robinson again, but there was no need to risk waking a neighbor. Sliding behind the wheel, he discovered a dark spot on the knee of his jeans, and the sight shocked him. Robinson's blood? No doubt, but where had he picked it up? From the tailgate, he suspected, and he would be wearing them until he got back to Huntingdon. He put the car in gear and headed out, telling himself to be extra careful on the way home.

* * *

He did not take Route 11 back to Chambersburg but turned south again. In Greencastle, he caught State Route 16, a narrow two-lane that took him through Cowans Gap State Park. The night was pitch black beyond the range of his headlights, and after he crossed Route 30 and turned up the ridge, only rarely did he pass a home where there was a pole light or lighted windows. At Burnt Cabins he caught US Route 522, and from there the highway was wider and less curvy but more heavily traveled. His eyes were beginning to get heavy and burn, but he didn't want to stop and walk around where passing motorists would see him. The clock on the instrument panel read 9:03 when he pulled into a convenience store in the little town of Orbisonia. By then he had been up and going for seventeen hours and needed a cup of good, strong black coffee to keep him awake for the rest of the trip. The coffee helped marginally, and he was finished with it by the time he took the bypass around Mount

111

Union, crossed the Juniata River and caught Route 22 for the last leg home.

Rounding the corner onto Rosalynn's street, he was surprised to see his Impala sitting by the curb. He pulled the Honda into the driveway, got out and stretched his legs. There were no lights on in the house, and he was wondering if maybe she had gone to bed when he heard the front door opening quietly and she spoke.

"Bring your suitcase and the briefcase and come on in."

As quietly as it had opened, the door closed. He popped the trunk of the Honda open and got out the items requested. She was standing in the entryway when he opened the door, a feeble light from the hallway backlighting her.

"Come with me," she said and turned toward the hall. She opened the last door on the left and stood aside. "Put your things in here, and then we'll talk."

"I think there's blood on my jeans," Daniel told her. "I need to get them into the washer. Let me get out of them and put on some pajama bottoms."

Rosalynn nodded without speaking and went back up the hallway.

When his jeans were in the washer, Daniel joined her in the living room, practically falling backwards onto the sofa and sliding down until his head was resting on its back. Rosalynn was in her usual spot in her recliner.

"Poor dear," she said. "You must be exhausted."

"Driving somewhere in the neighborhood of thirty-five hundred miles and taking care of two... whatever you want to call them... in one week will do that to you I've discovered."

"You had no problems with the one in Chambersburg? I thought you would call."

"No problems I couldn't deal with and I was more concerned with getting away from there and back here than making a phone call."

"Tell me about it."

He gave her a run down of all that had happened since their last phone conversation, again leaving out the ugly language Robinson had used. When he finished, she turned her head and looked toward the photograph of her daughter. It was nothing but a dark and indistinct rectangle against the lighter background of the wall.

"And Robinson denied having anything to do with Rose's death?" Rosalynn asked when he finished.

Daniel nodded. "Just like Harris, he seemed genuinely surprised that anyone would think she had been murdered. Could we have a little more light in here please? I've been driving mostly in the dark for the last two hours."

Rosalynn reached out and turned on the lamp that was sitting on the table beside her recliner. "I think that would be okay. You're a friend making a late night visit if anybody should happen to see a light in the window."

"I was surprised to see my Impala out front when I came around the corner. Shouldn't it be in the garage?" Daniel asked.

"Again, a friend visiting," she said. "I didn't back it out until it was dark, so anyone who sees it there in the morning will think you came in it. The neighbors have all seen your vehicle here before."

There was no need to tell him she thought it best

113

not to have two gray Hondas sitting in front of her house, and there wasn't room for two of them in the garage. Daniel nodded but said nothing. He sat slumped on the sofa, his head back and eyes closed, his arms resting at his sides.

"Are you going to be okay with what we're doing?" Rosalynn asked. "Or do you think it's going to haunt you?"

"I won't know if it will or won't until it does or doesn't," he said. "Right now, it doesn't bother me one bit. Given their attitudes about what they did to Rose and what they said about it, I feel like what I've done was justified. If someone were to ask me right now if I had ever committed a felony, I believe I could tell them no, and I don't think it would even shake the needle on a polygraph machine."

Rosalynn gave his answer some thought before she spoke again. "Well, you obviously need some rest, so let's get some sleep, and we'll talk about number three in the morning."

* * *

Daniel woke to the aroma of fresh coffee the next morning and marveled at the thought that he had slept so soundly. There had been no problem falling asleep. He was out like a light almost before his head hit the pillow, and there had been no dreams of any kind. From the light coming through the mini-blinds, he knew he had slept later than usual, but there was no clock in the room, and the burner phone was still in the glove compartment of the Honda.

He tossed back the covers and sat up on the side

of the bed and pulled on the socks he had worn the day before. Rosalnn's hardwood floors were cold. He headed for the kitchen, stopping off long enough in the bathroom to splash cold water on his face and to comb the tangles out of his hair. Smiling at his reflection, he ran the comb through his beard. *Maybe later,* he thought, *when this is all over, I'll grow it again.*

Rosalynn was standing by the sink, looking out the window, a mug of coffee in her hand. There was already a mug full waiting for him on the end of the table. When he said, "Good morning," she turned and waved a hand toward it.

"I heard you getting up. Good morning to you. Did you sleep well? Are you hungry?"

Before he even answered, she was pulling a skillet out of a bottom cabinet and opening the refrigerator door.

"Hungry might not be the right word. I feel like I haven't eaten in about three days." He sat down at the table and picked up the mug of coffee.

A few minutes later, Rosalynn set a plate of bacon and eggs down in front of him and turned to butter the toast that had just popped up. She brought the two slices and laid them on the edge of his plate and then took a seat at the other end of the table.

"It's wonderful to have you here, Daniel. Just to have you sitting across the table enjoying your food again," she said.

"It's good to be here again," he said after a sip of coffee. "Sorry I missed Easter, but I was giving as much time as I could to studying for the bar exam."

"Yes, I know, and it paid off. I'm not complaining. It's just that I had forgotten how good it feels to have someone here to do for."

When he had sopped the last of the egg yolk from the plate with the last bite of toast, she stood and took it to the sink, brought back the coffeepot and refilled his mug.

"Thank you," he said, "but I've gotten used to doing for myself."

She nodded and gave him a smile that made her eyes sparkle. "Let's take our coffee into the living room. The seating is more comfortable in there."

Rosalynn took the recliner as usual, and he sat down on the sofa, at the end this time, where he could set his mug on an end table. For several moments, neither of them spoke.

"Tell me about Rose's father," Daniel said.

The request seemed to surprise her. "Why do you want to know about him?"

"You said the other night that you knew Rose and I were more than friends, and you were right. If things had turned out differently, her father would have been my father-in-law and the grandfather of our children. I've just been wondering what kind of man he was, how he would have fit into our lives."

Her stare almost made him regret he had asked, and then she turned her eyes toward the photograph of her daughter and began. "He was a good-looking young man, almost pretty," she said. "And like me, he was a little bit angry with life. I believed at the time that my parents thought I was a bother, and he was rebelling against his parents because of their ultra-conservative, fundamentalist religion. When they found out that he was seeing me, they threatened to throw him out of their house if he didn't stop. My parents didn't go to church, and to them that meant I was a pagan or a heathen or both. So, we met on the sly, and he enlisted in the National Guards. The plan was for us to use the money he would receive from his monthly meetings to rent an apartment. We would move in together, and we would both get jobs. His would be full-time, and mine would be part-time until I graduated from high school.

"When his unit was deployed, we took it as a good sign. We would be separated for awhile, but he would be receiving full-time pay, and we thought we would be able to put our plan into motion sooner. But it wasn't meant to be." She paused, obviously reliving moments from the past. "We were alone together only once, for a couple of hours the night before he left. That was when Rose was conceived. My mother had never told me much about sex, and the only female friend I had never talked about such things. I knew what we were doing was how babies got started, but I thought it took more than once for it to happen." Again, she paused. "He was killed shortly after his unit arrived in the Middle East, and he never knew he had a daughter."

"What was his name?" Daniel asked.

"His name was Calvin Jaymes. His parents always thought their son would go into the ministry, so they named him after John Calvin, a man they believed to be an important figure in their church's history."

"Does his family know they had a granddaughter?"

His question was met with a mirthless chuckle. "They do."

"But...?" he prompted.

She let the silence build for so long that he thought she wasn't going to answer.

117

"After I had Rose and learned that Calvin had been killed, I took her to see them—or for them to see her. His father opened the door and gave me a look that I felt was intended to incinerate me where I stood. I knew how they felt about me, so I waited for him to speak first. He looked me up and down and finally asked, 'What do you want?' I could tell by his tone that he was thinking he would have to scrub his porch floor with Lysol when I was gone. I said, 'I thought you might want to see your granddaughter,' and I started to lift the blanket away from Rose's face. He threw his hand up in front of his face and said, 'I don't want to see that! Don't show me that!'

"I was shocked. Rose wasn't a *that*! She was a baby, an innocent little child. I said as much, and he let me have it with both barrels, as they say. He told me Calvin's death was his punishment from God for having lain with a harlot and producing a child out of wedlock. I could hardly believe what I was hearing. I asked him what *my* punishment was, and he told me it would be 'having to raise that little bastard you've got in your arms.' Those were his exact words. Then he told me to get off his property and to never set foot on it again. He started to close the door, and I told him to wait a minute.

"As I said moments ago, my parents didn't go to any church, but I had been to Bible School with a friend several times, and a few of the stories they read to us stuck in my mind. There was a flowerbed in front of the Jaymes's porch, and it was edged with stones. I stooped and picked up one of fair size and handed it to him and said, 'You cast the first stone.' His face got red and veins stood out in his temples and he threw the

118

stone back into the flower bed and slammed the door. That was the beginning and end of whatever relationship Rose might have had with her Jaymes grandparents."

"The rest of the family never saw her?" Daniel asked.

Rosalynn shook her head. "When Rose was three, their daughter graduated from high school and fled to California. And I don't use the word *fled* sarcastically or facetiously. The girl *fled*. She had been made to dress like a figure out of a painting of the first Thanksgiving and had not been allowed to attend any kind of after-school function, and she fled to get away from that. A few months later, Mr. Jaymes packed his wife and their belongings up and followed her, from what I heard later, intending to bring their daughter back into the fold. That was the last I ever heard of any of them."

Daniel spent several minutes digesting what he had heard and then asked, "What about your parents? How did they react when they found out you were pregnant?"

"They were stunned, of course," Rosalynn began without hesitation. "They had no idea that I had been seeing anyone. We had been meeting at a friend's house while her parents were at work and for just a few minutes at a time over a period of several months. They were disappointed in me and didn't hesitate to tell me so frequently, but there was none of the moral outrage the Jaymes family would have subjected their son to if he had survived. Besides, I think my mother felt a little bit responsible. She had never told me anything about sex. When I came of age, we had the usual mother-daughter talk about what to expect each month, but that was the extent of it. She never even hinted at what a man and a woman did in a bedroom, and somehow I got the impression it was something one did not ask about. My friend's mother was much like mine, so she couldn't help me.

"Not that either of us was totally in the dark. As I said, I knew that what Calvin and I were doing was how babies got started, but I thought it took more than once. And maybe there was a part of me that actually wanted a baby. It would mean a part of Calvin was with me even when he wasn't there.

"And when Rose was born?" Daniel prompted. "What did they think then?"

"She was an inconvenience, as I had been, showing up late in their lives. My mother agreed to take care of her while I was in school, but the moment I got home, she was my responsibility. I held her and fed her while I did my homework, and I got up in the night and heated her bottle and rocked her while she took it. She became my motivation, my determination. I was going to graduate from high school, and I was going to give Rose love like I never had. She wasn't going to be the ruination of my life, as my mother kept saying. And I loved her more than life itself.

"When Rose got to be a toddler, their attitude began to change. She was such a sweet natured child, and she was cute. Gradually, they seemed to forget about her illegitimacy. My mother was elated when her first word was Gammaw. I think Rose got more attention from her at that age than I ever did."

"But they died when Rose was still pretty young, didn't they?" Daniel asked.

Rosalynn nodded. "Rose had just had her second birthday when they were killed in an auto accident. The irony of it still haunts me—two innocent victims who never touched a drop of alcohol taken out of this world at the hands of a drunk driver."

For several minutes, they were both silent. A car passed by on the street out front. The compressor in the refrigerator kicked on with a rattle and then settled into a low hum.

"But enough about that. Tell me about you and Rose," Rosalynn said.

"What about us?"

"How far did your relationship go?"

Daniel chuckled. "You kept a close enough watch on us to know it didn't go too far."

"Yes, I did," Rosalynn said and smiled, "but I didn't mean it that way. Did you ever propose to her?"

"We were only fifteen when she was diagnosed with that brain tumor!" Daniel said. "And I wasn't in any position to propose to anyone at that age."

"But you would have eventually if things had gone differently?"

"Eventually, yes, no doubt, but it would have been a mere formality. I can't tell you exactly when it started, but by the time she had her surgery, the two of us just assumed that we would get married someday."

"And her surgery ended all hope of that," Rosalynn finished for him.

Daniel nodded. "But I still intended to be a part of her life and for her to be a part of mine."

"And that seems to bring us back to the ones who took her from us. I think you should rest today and take care of number three tomorrow."

121

Again, he nodded. "But while I'm resting, you could tell me what you know about one Dexter Landis and tell me where I can find him."

"That will require a trip to my office," Rosalynn said, struggling out of her recliner without putting the footrest down. "He lives in Altoona, and I've got all you will need to know on my computer."

CHAPTER ELEVEN

Rosalynn was as good as her word. Daniel sat down in the same chair he had used before and watched while she pulled up an image of the house Dexter Landis occupied. It was a red-brick one-story with white trim and a dark shingled roof. It sat about twenty feet back from the street on a terraced and immaculately kept lawn. Two concrete steps led from a wide main sidewalk up to a narrower one that led to two more steps up to the second terrace, and the narrow sidewalk ended at three more steps in front of a roofed porch. Perfectly trimmed bushes of some kind hid the cement blocks of the building's foundation. Above the red front door was a crown of fancy molding with a finial in its center. She gave him the street address and had him repeat it back to her. Tarnished brass numbers attached to a white wooden plaque fastened to the bricks to the left of the front door would make locating the place easy enough, he thought.

As with Jordan Harris's house before, she moved the mouse to the left, and the view on the monitor swept past neighboring houses, the street itself, dwellings across the street, over the street again and back to the Landis domicile, which appeared to be on a corner lot. Houses were closer together than he would have hoped, and there were no outbuildings of any kind, not even storage sheds to be seen. Some subdivisions were like that Daniel knew from studying law. Contracts specified what homeowners could and could not do on property they had bought and paid for, right down to the last detail—no dog houses, no clotheslines, no gravel driveways, etc. All of that put together meant that what he had to do in Altoona was going to require more stealth than the last two had. Closer neighbors might hear the shot, and there would be no place to conceal the results of his efforts (*there's no need for either of us to say it out loud*). Dexter was obviously doing a lot better than his two high school cohorts had been. Rosalynn's next comment told him why.

"Next, I can give you the address of the Walgreens where he is employed as a pharmacist."

"A pharmacist!" Daniel exclaimed. "Where did he go to pharmacy school?"

"I don't really know. Some Ivy League university, I imagine. I doubt that even Penn State would have been good enough for the likes of Dexter Landis. Where he went to school has no bearing on what we're doing, so I didn't bother to research it."

There's no need for either of us to say it out loud went through Daniel's mind again. He pushed the thought aside and tried to concentrate on what Rosalynn was saying.

"I haven't been able to find a map of Altoona that is detailed enough to let us trace a route from his workplace to his house. I was able to learn that the Walgreens where he works is just north and west of

124

Interstate-99 on Plank Road. If all else fails, you might have to pick him up there when he gets off work an follow him home as you did the one in Chambersburg. As you can see, the photo of the place won't be of much help. All of their stores look pretty much alike."

She was rattling keys as she spoke, and then there was the photograph of the store. It had been taken at night, and there was nothing distinguishing about it. Just some lighted windows and the usual company logo—a red mortar and pestle with a large, white *W*—in a high front window.

The two of them sat and looked at it for a minute or more without speaking. The situation seemed to dictate much of what would happen. Daniel would have to find the house and formulate a plan that would get him inside. That much was a given. Exactly how he would be able to do that was far from clear.

"This one will have to be done with more care," Rosalynn said, essentially giving voice to the thought he had earlier. "It will be done closer to home, and it will involve an individual I imagine society deems more important than a Walmart employee and an oil changer at a trucking company more than a thousand miles from here."

Daniel nodded. "I've thought about that. The Landis family is well-heeled, and white collar trumps blue collar every time. I don't imagine there will be much time between when I leave his place and he's found, twenty-four to forty-eight hours at the outside most, I'd say. At least, the ones investigating it will be in Blair County and not Huntingdon County, so there will be some confusion about jurisdiction. And I can just imagine how the Landis family will be screaming

125

for results. Speaking of family, is Dexter Landis married? Or does he have a girlfriend I need to be looking out for?"

"A wife, no," Rosalynn said. "A girlfriend, I don't know but I don't think so. He does have a three-year-old daughter, but she doesn't live with him."

"A daughter! We can't orphan a child!"

"We won't. An orphan has no parents, and she will still have a mother. She lives with her mother and step-father, so she will have family. Dexter lived with the little girl's mother until she got pregnant, and then he tossed her out. He never married her, and from what I've heard, he has no part in the little girl's life. Given her age, I can't imagine she would ever think of anyone as her father other than her mother's husband."

"But still…"

"I'll take care of her, Daniel," Rosalynn cut him off. "Trust me. It's better for her to have a step-father who is a good man and loves her than to have a biological father who is a rapist and wants nothing to do with her. She will be better off—the *world* will be better off—when we finish what we've started. If I didn't believe that, we never would have started."

"And how do you plan to take care of her?" he asked.

"You don't need to know that," she said. "We need to keep some things compartmented. They can't make you tell what you don't know should there ever come a time when you're questioned. If things go as well with the next two as they did with the last two, when this is over, you should be free and clear to live your life in whatever manner pleases you. If our plan proceeds as I am hoping it will, you will never come under suspicion. So please trust that I will not leave the child wanting. I will take care of her, I promise."

A dozen thoughts went through Daniel's mind beginning with: how she would provide for the child when her father was gone? What about the Landis family? Did they have any kind of relationship with the little girl? Where had the money come from that was in the envelope in the briefcase? How could she be so certain that suspicion would not fall on him? All of them went unasked. Maybe she was right. The less he knew, the less he could be made to confess.

He nodded, "Okay, what else can you tell me that I might need to know?"

"I'm afraid that's all I have at the moment."

"Okay, I have a suggestion," he said after several minutes of thought. "Rather than sitting around all day wasting time, let's the two of us drive up to Altoona and do a reconnaissance. We can go in my Impala and stop by the Chamber of Commerce and pick up a map of the city. We can use it to locate his address and let me get a better look at his house. I'll be in a better position to make a plan if I can see first-hand what I will be dealing with."

"I'm not sure we should do that," Rosalynn objected. "It's not a good idea for us to be seen together."

"We won't be. I'll stay in the car while you go in and get the map. You can wear my sunglasses and one of the caps I bought, maybe a pair of my jeans and one of my tee-shirts. There's not much difference in our heights. I don't think anyone has ever seen you in a getup like that, so anyone asked to describe you would be describing an entirely different person. Then you

127

can sit in the car while I pay a visit to the Walgreens where he works and get a look at him. I don't imagine he has changed much, but I haven't seen him since we graduated from high school. He might have packed on the pounds and gone bald the way Robinson did."

"All right," Rosalynn agreed. "Let's get ready and go. I might need to be back in time for a nap this afternoon."

Daniel nodded and smiled. "Whatever you need. Let me go get you your new outfit."

* * *

Daniel smiled when she came out of her bedroom in the jeans and the tee-shirt, her hair tucked up under the Yankees cap.

"You don't need to smirk," Rosalynn said, "and you had better enjoy this while it lasts. You will never see me in an outfit like this again. Go out on the front porch and check to see that there's no one on the street. If my neighbors see me like this, our entire scheme could be compromised."

"There's nobody in sight," he told her when he came back in the front door a few minutes later. "Remember what you told me about acting suspicious now. We'll just walk to the car like we normally would, no crouching and scurrying. The door's already unlocked."

He handed her his sunglasses and she slipped them on. When they got to the car, he opened the door and waited until she was settled in the passenger seat and closed it for her. He got behind the wheel, started the engine and pulled away from the curb. Her head began to nod, and she was asleep before they were out of town.

Daniel woke her when they passed the Altoona city limit sign and asked her if she knew where to find the Chamber of Commerce. She did not, and as per her instructions, he still did not have his smart phone with him. They both knew the address of the Walgreens on Plank Road, so he decided they should head there first. It was not that difficult to find, and he cruised the parking lot, looking for a car that would likely belong to Dexter Landis. When no vehicle seemed to fit the bill, he found a way to get behind the building, and there it was—a silver, late model Corvette convertible. The personalized license plate that read *Dexter-1* left no doubt.

He found a parking spot in the lot out front of the store and went in. The young lady at the checkout welcomed him to the store and then went about stocking a shelf with over the counter items. The layout was like every Walgreens he had ever visited. He roamed the aisles, looking for nothing in particular, surreptitiously working his way into a position from which he could get a glimpse of Dexter Landis. Nobody paid him any mind.

Landis was in profile, counting out pills, when Daniel got his first look. He poured them into a vial and set it aside. A young, blonde female assistant peeled the back off a label and affixed it to the vial, bought it to a customer, and collected payment. Dexter turned away and disappeared around the end of some shelves and came back into view carrying a large white bottle. Daniel got a look at his face and realized the man had changed little since high school. There

129

were the same high cheekbones and chiseled jaw line, the same straight and narrow nose, the same dark hair without a hint of gray. He might have put on all of twenty pounds, but he still looked fit—membership in a gym maybe. Landis seemed to be so focused on the task at hand that he never looked up, never saw Daniel standing there and probably wouldn't have recognized the old victim of his high school bulling days if he had. Having seen enough, Daniel turned and left the store.

When he opened the door and slipped back behind the wheel, Rosalynn awoke with a start.

"Did you see him?" she asked.

Daniel nodded.

"And…?"

"And he's working as a pharmacist, wearing a white jacket and basically ignoring everybody."

"He didn't see you then?"

Daniel shook his head. "He was too busy pushing drugs and making money."

"Where to now?" she asked.

"We need to find somebody who can give us directions to the Chamber of Commerce. You're up next," he said and pulled out onto the street.

A little farther up Plank Road, they found a CVS Pharmacy, and he swung into the parking lot. Without a word, Rosalynn opened the door and got out. Daniel had to smile at the sight of her, sauntering toward the store in jeans and tee-shirt, a light jacket thrown over it against the chill. She wasn't inside much more than a minute and came out with a look of satisfaction on her face.

"We need to keep going up Plank Road," she said. "The nearest office is northwest of here."

She gave directions as he drove, and they found the place with little trouble. Again, she was the one to go in while he waited in the Impala. And again, it took her little more than a minute to return with the map. Using it, they found Dexter Landis's place without much trouble.

"It's not on a corner lot," Daniel said when he began to turn and realized he would be going down a blacktopped driveway. He swung around the back corner of the house and discovered an overhead door. Dexter's garage was in his basement. He turned around and drove back up to the street.

"I'm guessing contracts for this subdivision don't allow its residents to park on the street or even leave a vehicle of any kind sitting in their driveways. There isn't a car in sight."

"How does this change things?" Rosalynn asked. "His garage being in his basement?"

It took Daniel a little while to answer. "I don't know. It might work to my advantage. I could hide behind the bushes and slip under the overhead door at the last second and follow him up the stairs, I suppose. Or I could maybe jimmy that pedestrian door there to the right of it. I'll have to give it some thought. The possibility of no cars allowed in driveways concerns me more. I might have to find a place to leave the Honda and walk in. We got what we came for. Let's head back to Huntingdon."

Once again, Rosalynn was asleep before they got out of town.

* * *

131

Daniel left the house on Wednesday at 7:30 P.M., taking Route 453 to Tyrone and catching I-95 down to Altoona. From a call Rosalynn had made using her burn phone to the Walgreens where Dexter Landis worked, he knew the man got off work at nine. His idea was to get there early enough to scope out the neighborhood during nighttime hours but not to be too early and risk having a strange car raising suspicions. If his own suspicions—no cars allowed on driveways—turned out to be correct, he would have to abort for the night and come back later.

Traffic was light that late in the evening, and he made the exit from I-95 onto Plank Road at 8:27. From there to the subdivision where Dexter lived was another fifteen minutes. When he turned into the first street, he was relieved to see vehicles parked in driveways, mostly cars and SUVs but a few pickups. Lights were on in most of the houses, but he found one four doors down from the Landis residence that was dark, and he took a chance that the owners were out of town and backed into the driveway.

As quickly as possible, he prepared himself to do what he had come to do (*there's no need for either of us to say out loud*). Thirty-eight in the right pocket of his jacket, stun gun in the left, larger zip ties tucked into the waistband of his jeans, smaller ones in a front pocket. He thought about a possibly dark basement garage and tucked the flashlight he had purchased for the Robinson job into a hip pocket. Lastly, he pulled on a pair of latex gloves and then headed down the street to look for a place of concealment.

He hadn't been lying behind the bushes at the front corner of Dexter's place more than twenty minutes when he heard the overhead door begin to rise. A moment later, the Corvette came roaring down the street, braked sharply and swung down the drive. He waited until he heard the overhead door begin to descend and made his move. The door was eighteen inches off the concrete floor when he slid under it, the flashlight in his hip pocket making a scraping sound. The lights of the vehicle went out, two doors popped open and he heard a female laugh. Both doors slammed and footsteps pounded up wooden stairs, both of them laughing now and the female giving a yelp. Daniel frowned, imagining what Dexter might have done to produce such a reaction. A moment later, the overhead light went out, and he found himself in total darkness.

He waited until his heart rate was close to normal and he could breathe again. Then he sat up slowly and pulled the flashlight from his pocket. He put two fingers over its lens, turned it on and used the feeble light it provided to make his way to the pedestrian door. He unlocked it, stepped outside and closed it silently. Maybe this was a stroke of luck he couldn't have hoped for? It was doubtful Dexter Landis ever checked to see if the door was locked. Tomorrow night, he would be able to wait until his target was upstairs and settled. No last second rolling under the overhead door, just opening this one quietly and walking in. On his way back to the Honda, Daniel found himself smiling into the dark.

* * *

Rosalynn was waiting up when he got back to Huntingdon a little less than an hour later.

133

"Is it done?" she asked.

Daniel shook his head and told her what had happened.

"That doesn't surprise me, him being the lecher that he is. Do you have any idea who the woman was?"

"The young blonde from Walgreens, I think," he said. "It was right at nine o'clock when he got home, and I doubt that he had time to swing by someone else's place and pick her up. In fact, I wouldn't doubt that he left the store a little early, maybe had his work caught up."

"Well, I'm glad you weren't discovered," Rosalynn said. "So what now?"

"I go back tomorrow night and see it through. I left the door unlocked, so I shouldn't have a problem getting in. I won't even have to be there when he gets off work."

CHAPTER TWELVE

For Daniel, Thursday was an agony of inactivity. He and Rosalynn had both slept late, and their first meal of the day was more a brunch than a breakfast. Strong black coffee consumed in too great a quantity made them both jittery, and there was nothing either of them could do until nightfall. At eight o'clock P.M., he would leave for Altoona, and she would walk the floor until she exhausted herself, and then if he wasn't back yet, she would likely fall asleep in her recliner. Going out for any reason was out of the question because they didn't want to be seen together while Daniel still had his long hair and beard. Besides, they had everything they needed right there in the house—everything except a way to make the clock move faster.

To take their minds off what was intended in the evening, they watched television through what was left of the morning, the lunch hour and much of the afternoon. They turned the thing off, and Rosalynn fried smoked pork chops for their supper while Daniel tore up a head of lettuce and diced tomatoes for a tossed salad. The food consumed, they went back to their seats in front of the television and fell asleep for much of the rest of the afternoon. When Daniel woke

135

up, it was dark outside, but this was October in Pennsylvania, so there was still a nearly three-hour wait until he left for Altoona.

Rosalynn roused and made another pot of coffee. They filled their mugs and carried them to the living room, where they took their usual seats. Daniel picked up the remote and turned the television off, and Rosalynn did not object. Both of them had had their fill on metal Pablum for one day.

"Tell me about your parents," Rosalynn asked, more to pass the time than anything else. "What do you remember about them from your childhood?"

Daniel was surprised by the question and had to give it some thought. "Mom was a quilter, but I guess you knew that. In my mind, I mostly see her bending over the table where she cut out pieces or sitting at her Singer, sewing them together, or fussing with that machine she had that did the actual quilting. She spent most of her time in her 'quilt room'," he said using finger quotes.

"That's it?" Rosalynn asked. "No memories of her in the kitchen, preparing meals?"

Daniel bowed his head in thought for a moment. "Maybe a few nebulous images of her at the stove or the counter, frying something or making sandwiches. She would make me a plate and have me sit up to the table, and she would take hers into her quilt room and, I guess, eat it while she worked. I learned early on that I was not to interrupt her work, so I never went in there. Of course, you know that I snuck through the hedge and met Rose when we were all of four years old. After that, I think I ate more meals with the two of you than I did at home. Breakfast was always a bowl

136

of cereal and a glass of milk I would find on the kitchen table when I woke up. She would already be busy with her quilts. When I got tall enough to reach the top cabinets, I had to get the cereal and the milk and the bowl myself."

"What happened to all of the quilts she made?"

"She sold them. People would show up at the door, she would take them into her quilt room, and they would come out smiling with a paper sack in their arms."

"So you have none of her quilts?"

Daniel frowned. "No, not a one. She sold them all and put the money in a savings account. We discovered it when she had to go to the nursing home when I was... what... eleven? There was enough money in it to pay for a used car and a couple semesters of college."

"Well, it was nice of her to think of your education and provide for it."

"I'm not sure that was her intention or that she had any idea what the money would eventually be used for. I think maybe her dementia started long before she became incapacitated. I think her quilting started out as a hobby, something to make the time pass while my father was away, but it became an obsession, something she felt compelled to do."

"Your father was away for long periods of time." It was a statement, not a question.

Daniel nodded. "Construction jobs kept him away weeks at a time sometimes. But sometimes I've wondered if he worked on construction to keep away from me and Mom. Looking back, there didn't seem to be much... affection between them. When Dad left, she would be in her quilting room, and he would stop by the door and say, 'I'm off again,' or something like that, and without even looking up from her work, she would say something like, 'Stay safe.' I would follow him to his pickup if I wasn't over here. Sometimes he would pat me on the head and say something. Sometimes it seemed like he wasn't even aware that I was there beside him. He would get into his truck and drive away without a word or a wave."

"And now he's down in Florida with his second wife. Maybe you should pay him a visit when all of this is over."

He nodded in agreement. Maybe getting out of the area for awhile would be a good idea.

"You don't have any relatives other than your father?"

"None that I know of. Mom and Dad were both only children, and if I ever met my grandparents, I was too young at the time to remember them. I don't know what happened to them, but they must have died young. I never had aunts and uncles and cousins to visit, but life was good because I had Rose and I had you."

"And Rose and I had you," Rosalynn said, her eyes filling up with tears, "until we didn't have Rose anymore." The tears spilled over and flowed down her cheeks.

Daniel went to her, knelt beside her recliner and pulled her head onto his shoulder. She cried for a minute or more and then pushed herself back.

"I don't know what's wrong with me. I haven't cried since the day of Rose's funeral," she said. "I'm sorry I pried into your life. I shouldn't have."

He shook his head. "You answered all of my questions about Rose's father and his family yesterday, and I thank you for that. And you don't need to feel bad for me. I came to grips with my upbringing a long time ago."

Rosalynn dried her eyes with the heels of her hands. He coaxed a smile out of her, and she reached out and laid a hand on his cheek.

"Thank you for all you are doing for Rose and me," she said.

He returned her smile without saying anything and went back to the chair he had been sitting in.

"Let's see if we can find something on this thing that won't make our brains rot," he suggested, picking up the remote and turning on the television. He surfed the channels until he found a rerun of *Law and Order*.

Rosalynn nodded okay and they watched it in silence. When it was time for him to go, she was asleep in her recliner.

* * *

The night sky was pitch black when he went out to the Honda and set off for Altoona—not unusual for October in Pennsylvania. He took the route he had taken the night before, Highway 453 to Tyrone and I-95 south from there. The trip took him less than an hour. He backed into the same driveway he had used the previous night and settled down to wait. Dexter Landis shot by in his Corvette less than half an hour later, slowed down barely enough to make the turn and disappear down his driveway. Daniel gave him thirty minutes to get upstairs and take a shower or do whatever else he might want to do. Then he started the Honda and pulled out into the street with the headlights off, once again navigating with and arm out the window, flashlight in hand. In front of Dexter's house, he shut off the engine and drifted down the driveway. The Honda would be hidden behind the house while he did what he had come to do (*there's no need for either of us to say it out loud*). He thought about backing it around so it would be heading out but decided to wait until there was nobody in the house that could hear the engine start. He got out and closed the door with as little noise as possible. No need to pop the trunk this night. Both guns and the zip ties were already where he always carried them, the third yellow envelop inside his jacket. The night was cold enough that he was wearing leather gloves. A pair of latex ones was in a pocket, glasses on his nose and a baseball cap on his head, Yankees again.

The pedestrian door was unlocked as he had left it. He slipped inside and turned on the flashlight. At the top of the stairs, he turned the doorknob slowly and eased the door open. Stepping through it, he found himself in a kitchen. Light coming from the front of the house made a dining area visible to his left, and an archway between the two rooms gave access to the living room. He stepped into it quietly. Dexter was nowhere to be seen.

The room was definitely an upgrade from the ones where he had dealt with Harris and Robinson. A leather sofa sat beneath a picture window in the front wall and to the left of the front door from where he stood. A matching overstuffed chair and ottoman sat to his right and was obviously positioned for watching the television—one of the largest he had ever seen— sitting in an expensive entertainment center that took up the entire wall to his right. A red brick fireplace with shelves on either side took up the wall to his left. Window curtains and throw pillows suggested a woman's touch, likely Dexter's mother.

Daniel was smiling at the clutter of athletic trophies on the fireplace mantel and thinking how proud of them Dexter must be when the man himself spoke behind him.

"Who are you and what the hell are you doing in my house?"

Daniel turned slowly and realized for the first time that there was an archway in the corner of the room that led to a hallway. He stood smiling at Dexter Landis from ten feet away and saying nothing. The man's hair was still damp from his shower, and he was wearing an old tee-shirt and pajama bottoms much like the ones Daniel himself wore.

"I asked you a question, asshole," Dexter said and started forward, his hands knotted into fists.

Daniel stood upright and let him come. At the last moment when Landis was reaching for him, he jerked the stun gun from his pocket and jammed it into the man's chest. The voltage shook him like a rag doll. Daniel stepped back and let him fall. Dexter landed face down, so there was no need to roll him over.

He used the same configuration of zip ties he had used on Robinson—small one on the wrists, large ones around his ankles and just above the knees. When they had been pulled tight, Dexter had almost recovered from the jolt.

"To be perfectly accurate, Dex, you asked me two

141

questions. Who I am, you will figure out soon enough. What I am doing in your house at the moment is looking for information. After I get the information? Well, we'll just have to wait and see. Do you want to stay there on the floor or would you like me to pick you up and put you in your chair?"

"What I'd like you to do is take these zip ties off me so I can get up and kick your ass," Dexter said when he was able to speak. "I don't know who think you are and I'm not telling you shit. Before this is over, I'm gonna need your name so I can tell them what to carve on your tombstone."

"No can do," Daniel smiled. "Floor or chair are your only options."

When the man on the floor only glared, he started to get a chair from the kitchen and sit beside him, but halfway to the kitchen, he realized there were windows in the top of the front door. He turned and reached for the tie around Dexter's feet and almost got kicked in the face. Another jolt from the stun gun made the job easier, and soon the two of them were in the dining area—Daniel sitting in a captain's chair, Landis still on the floor.

"Okay, first you tell me about the night you and Jordan Harris and Ryder Robinson raped Rose Holder."

The answer he got was the one he had come to expect. "We didn't rape anyone, and I already told you, I'm not telling you shit."

Daniel leaned down and gave him a jolt from the stun gun, a brief one this time.

"Wrong answer," he said. "Let's try that again. Tell me about the night the three of you raped Rose Holder."

142

Dexter just lay there on the floor and glared at him. Daniel leaned forward with the stun gun. Then he spoke.

"All right! All right! Just tell me what you want to know!"

"I want you to tell me about that night. Start from the beginning and tell me everything. I'll help you get started. The three of you were out driving around and…" Daniel gestured with his free hand, a silent you take it from here.

The story he got was essentially the same as the ones he had gotten from Harris and Robinson.

When he was finished, Daniel went over the details. "So Harris saw her first and told you about his cousin, but *you* were the one who decided the three of you should find out if it was true?"

Dexter shrugged and shook his head, "Yeah, so?"

"It was *your* idea to take advantage of a special needs girl, and the three of you raped her. Why?"

"Why not? She had what we were looking for and she was there."

Daniel took off the glasses he didn't need and the hat that was making his head itch and laid them on the table. He rubbed a little of the burn out of his eyes that the glasses had caused and then looked at the man on the floor.

"Do you know me now?" he asked.

Dexter stared at him for a minute or more, and then it was like a light bulb went on in his head. "Daniel Miller, little Danny Boy Miller; it's gonna be such a pleasure kicking your ass."

"Said the man in zip ties lying on the floor. Next question: Do you have any regrets about that night?"

Dexter made a show of giving it some thought, squinching his eyes and looking to the side. "No, I don't think so? Why should I?"

"You assaulted a girl with special needs! Somone who couldn't defend herself!"

"She was a *re*-tard," Dexter said, "nothing much more than a life support system for a twat, for god sakes! And once we got started, she went at it like there was no tomorrow. You and her were close. Don't try to tell me you never tapped that!"

The look on Daniel's face told him he had hit a nerve and he laughed.

"You didn't, did you? All that snatch, right there for the taking, and you were too much of a gentleman!"

Daniel's expression did not change. "Last question: Did you kill her?"

"No! She killed herself! She swallowed a bunch of pills!"

"She had the mind of a five-year-old. Where did she get the pills and how would she know what kind to use?"

"How should I know? Maybe her mother gave them to her! It wasn't me!"

"But you know who did," Daniel pushed. "Who was it?"

Dexter broke eye contact and looked down and to the left. "I don't know."

Daniel leaned down with the stun gun.

"I don't know! I swear I don't know! I just know that that bitch Holder was raising such a fuss it was impossible for the team not to be affected. None of us could concentrate, and the coach was getting pissed. Dad went to a Booster Club meeting, and when he came home, he said he would take care of it."

"He would take care of it?" Daniel repeated.

"Yeah, that's what he said. He would take care of it, and that's all I know. Now get these damned ties off me. I've had enough of this shit."

Without a word, Daniel got up from his chair and went into the living room. When he returned, he had a throw pillow in his left hand and the thirty-eight in his right. Landis started laughing.

"What? You're gonna *shoot* me now, Danny Boy? You don't have the balls. Free my wrists and I'll hold the pillow."

To make the job quick and simple, he gave the man another jolt from the stun gun. Then he leaned over him, a foot on either side, placed the pillow on his chest, and pressed the barrel of the revolver tight against it.

Looking Dexter Landis in the eye, he said, "This is for Rose," and he pulled the trigger.

There was less of a sound than there had been with either Harris or Robinson. Dexter's body jerked once, much like when he had been hit with the stun gun, and then he was still. Daniel returned the revolver to his jacket pocket and took the leather glove off his right hand and laid it on the table. He pulled on a latex one and checked for a pulse at Dexter's neck. There was none. Number three had been dealt with, and now he knew who number four would be.

What now? Take him to the basement and shove him underneath the Corvette? What would be the point? Daniel didn't feel like dealing with getting him down the steps and/or cleaning up whatever blood might be under him. If and when someone came looking, they would find Dexter's vehicle in the garage and scour the house until they found what they were looking for anyway

145

(*there's no need for either of us to say it out loud*). He rolled Landis on his side until he could get the blade of his pocket knife under the zip tie around his wrists. The ones on his legs and ankles came off next, and he went looking through cabinet drawers until he found a plastic bag. The ties and the latex glove went into it along with the throw pillow. He would toss them somewhere on his way back to Huntingdon, wherever he could find a dumpster or maybe just over a bank along the highway. He was on his way to the basement door when he remembered the yellow envelop inside his jacket. He went back onto the dining room and dumped its contents on the table—a plastic card with a leopard print pattern that Rose intended to carry the driver's license she never got in. The sight of it brought a lump to his throat. So much of life, so many things she never got to experience.

He turned out the lights and used his flashlight to leave the house the same way he came in. The clouds had separated and the moon and stars were bright, but the Honda sat in darkness in the shadow of the house. He set the plastic bag in the passenger seat, fired up the engine and pulled up the driveway without turning the headlights on. Several blocks down the street, he turned them on and picked up speed. As far as he could tell, nobody had seen him or the Honda.

He took Highway 22 to Water Street and then down to Huntingdon. The drive home seemed to take only minutes, and he wondered why the computer had routed them all the way up to Tyrone and down I-95— better highway maybe? He made it into Huntingdon by 11:30 and to Rosalynn's house before midnight with a stop in an alley downtown to get rid of the bag. He buried it deep under the trash that was already there, smiling to himself. So many crooks on television shows got caught because they tossed their evidence right on top where it would be found by the next person who lifted the dumpster's lid. Or they tossed it into the polycart in front of their own house.

Rosalynn was waiting in the living room when he parked the Honda in the driveway, retrieved the briefcase from the trunk, and went into the house. As before, the only light in the place came from the ceiling fixture in the hallway. Daniel wondered if she hadn't been sleeping in her recliner and came awake when he closed the trunk lid.

"It's done?" she asked.

"It's done," he said and told her how it had gone.

"So, Mr. Landis was the one who gave her the pills."

Daniel shrugged. "Dexter said that you were causing a fuss, and the football team couldn't concentrate. His dad said he would take care of it. That could mean he did it himself, or it could mean he got someone else to do it."

"Either way, he's implicated," Rosalynn said. "He's our number four, but we will have to put him off for awhile."

She went back to her recliner, and he took a seat in the over-stuffed chair. For several minutes, neither of them said anything.

"They will likely find him in a day or two, maybe as early as tomorrow evening," Rosalynn said. "Someone will go looking for him when he doesn't show up for work, maybe that little chippy he brought home last evening. I imagine they'll do an autopsy, and the funeral will be sometime next week. We can put it off until after that. Let them have their time to mourn."

"I guess I could go up to my place until then, maybe shave off this beard."

"I don't think you should do either just yet. You don't want to be seen with the beard up there, and you should keep it until the job is finished."

"But I can't stay here," Daniel objected. "We shouldn't be seen together, and I don't want to stay inside for a week. Besides, my car sitting out there at the curb is going to cause suspicion."

"Maybe this would be a good time to pay your father a visit."

"In Florida? That's a long drive."

"So don't drive, fly. There's plenty of money left in the briefcase for an airline ticket. Take your Impala down to Harrisburg and leave it in long term parking. Catch a flight to Leesburg and rent a car. Maybe if you let him know you were coming, he could pick you up at the airport. How long has it been since you've seen him?"

Daniel was hesitant about answering. "I guess it's been three years."

"Then it's high time you paid him a visit," Rosalynn said. "He's getting on in years, and you never know when and if you'll get another chance."

"Okay, I'll leave in the morning, and I'll take the burner phone with me. You can keep me posted as to what is happening here, and I will be back whenever you think the time is right to finish the job."

"Good," Rosalynn said, and he could almost hear a smile in her voice. "Let's get some sleep, and I'll wake you in plenty of time to be gone before the neighbors are awake."

CHAPTER THIRTEEN

Without a reservation, it took Daniel awhile to get a flight out of Harrisburg International, but he finally landed at Leesburg International Airport late Saturday evening. By the time he rented a car, a dark-blue Hyundai Accent, and drove to his father's place, it was dark. Through the three rectangles of glass in the front door, he could see a faint bluish light coming for a room at the back of the house. He rang the doorbell and waited. Moments later, he could make out a hulking shadow coming up a hallway and heard his father speak.

"Who the hell would be ringin' our doorbell this time a night?"

A woman's voice answered faintly, but Daniel could not make out what she was saying.

"Well, they better have a damn good reason," his father said.

The porch light came on and the door was jerked open. Harold Miller stood glaring at the intruder, his light-blue eyes a little more rheumy than the last time his son had seen him. Maybe down a few pounds from his usual 225, but still as muscular as ever. Full head of hair completely white now. Face clear of whiskers except for a faint stubble.

149

CHARLES C. BROWN

"Who the hell are you and what do you want?" Not exactly the greeting Daniel had anticipated but close.

"It's me, Dad. Daniel."

His father frowned and then seemed to recognize him. "What the hell do you mean, comin' here with long hair and a beard, lookin' like a damn hippie?"

"It's nice to see you too, Dad. Mind if I come in? I've had a long day, and I'm tired."

"Who is it Harold?" this from step-mom coming up the hall.

"It's my boy, and it looks like he's gone over to the dark side."

"Well, invite him in for god's sake. Don't make him stand out there on the porch." His father stepped aside and Daniel stepped in. His step-mother wrapped him up in a hug and said, "Welcome. It's so good to see you."

Daniel held her at arms-length and looked her up and down and wondered, not for the first time, how much younger she was than his father. She still had the figure of the former Miss America contestant she had been back in Atlanta, and her hair was still the same honey blonde it had been when he first met her at his eighth-grade graduation. Her face was mostly free of lines and wrinkles—the beginnings of tiny crows feet at the corners of her eyes. The thought went through his mind: *Did Dad buy her a facelift?* But she had always been sweet to him, so the thought went unspoken.

"Thank you, Charlotte," he said. "It's great to see you, too."

"We were just about to watch the news," his

150

father said, his tone suggesting that someone ringing the doorbell was a rude interruption. "Gotta get to bed early. Got plans to go fishin' in the morning."

In the first three minutes, the tone had been set for his entire visit—his father criticizing his appearance, complaining about his chosen profession, almost everything about him; his step-mother doing her best to intervene and make peace between the two of them. The thought that kept going through Daniel's mind was: *Find him soon, people. Find him soon.*

* * *

Saturday was a "normal" day for Rosalynn—at least, as normal as any of her days were likely to get. She had risen at five-thirty to see Daniel off, then gone back to bed and slept until almost noon. After several cups of coffee, she took the gray Honda—the one Daniel had used—across the river to Pizza Hut and had a salad and a diet soft drink. Hoss's Steakhouse was practically right next door, but her appetite wasn't what it had been. Why spend money on something she couldn't finish?

Her hunger satisfied, she left the restaurant and headed for Walmart. There wasn't a thing in the world she needed, but going back to an empty house did not appeal. Once inside the store, she roamed the aisles aimlessly, stopping at several sales racks and looking at shirts and jeans in Rose's size. When she found something her daughter would have liked, she smiled a smile that made her eyes twinkle. Then reality would assert itself, the smile would disappear, and she would move on to something else.

She ran into several people whose children she had taught and stopped to speak with them. Some of them thanked her for the wonderful job she had done. Others seemed to think that anything more than a hello was too much. Rosalynn didn't care one way or the other. She was passing time and wondering what kind of day Daniel was having in Florida.

She made herself stay out until nearly four, and then went home and napped in her recliner with the television on. Her intention was to watch the news at six and ten to see if there was any word of a discovery in Altoona. There was none. Maybe he has weekends off, she thought, and then again, maybe he had no friends except the little blonde that had foiled Daniel's plans on Thursday evening. Whatever. He had been dealt with, and now he was someone else's problem. When she heard something, she would use the burner phone to call Daniel and let him know what was going on. Until then the both of them would just have to find things to do to put in their time.

* * *

Daniel was awakened on Sunday morning by a soft knock on the bedroom door. He looked at the window and saw that it was still dark and thought he must be mistaken. Then the knock came again.

"Daniel?" his step-mother said quietly. "It's time to get up, hon. Your father has breakfast almost ready."

He wiped a hand down across his face and said, "Be right there."

He slipped out of bed and went to the bathroom

in his tee-shirt and pajama bottoms. A splash of cold water on his face brought him awake a little better and he headed for the kitchen. His father was at the stove, dressed in the same kind of gray Dickie work pants and shirt he wore when he worked on construction. He was turning eggs over-easy in a cast iron skillet. A plate of crisply fried bacon was already on the table, the grease getting soaked away by a paper towel under it. A small glass of orange juice sat at each of the three plates set around a small oak table, flatware on paper napkins to the side.

His father lifted the eggs onto a platter and turned around. "You think maybe you should get dressed before you come to the table?"

"Good morning to you too, Dad."

"Now don't start, Harold," Charlotte said. "Food tastes the same whatever you're wearing. Just be glad your son has come to see you."

"Yes, it does," Daniel agreed. "I'll change into street clothes when we're finished eating. What time are we leaving on this fishing trip?"

"As soon as we finish breakfast and get the table cleared off," Harold Miller said. He set the platter of eggs on the table and went back to the counter top next to the stove and came back with a stack of buttered toast on a small plate.

Daniel waited until his father had pushed Charlotte's chair in for her and sat down himself and then took the remaining place. His father slid three eggs onto his plate, selected a slice of toast and two strips of bacon and set about eating as if it was a job he had to finish in order to get paid for it. His wife took only a couple strips of bacon and a piece of toast.

Daniel followed his father's lead. There was to be no small talk, it seemed, at Harold Miller's breakfast table. For several minutes they ate in a silence broken only by the sounds of flatware on plates.

"So, how far is it to this place where you intend to go fishing?" Daniel asked.

His father swallowed. "'Bout thirty minutes."

"Do you fish all day?"

"Depends on how long it takes to catch enough for a meal."

Harold Miller was so intent on sopping up egg yolk with a wedge of toast that he did not see the fleeting grimace his comment brought to his wife's face. Daniel saw it and wondered what it meant. He said nothing more and was finishing his eggs and toast when his father pushed back his chair and carried his plate and flatware to the sink. There he rinsed them off and put them in the dishwasher to the right of the sink.

"Gotta see a man about a horse," he said, and disappeared into the hallway."

Daniel waited until he heard the bathroom door closing and then asked, "What's going on, Charlotte?"

His step-mother shook her head and grimaced again.

"Please, tell me. What was that look you had on your face when Dad said we had to catch enough fish for a meal?"

She gave her head another quick shake. "I'm so tired of fish I could scream."

"And...?" Daniel prompted when she said no more.

"If we don't have fish, we don't have meat. Your father insists on me having a Lincoln, and he trades

154

them in every two years. It stretches our budget so thin we can't afford to buy groceries like normal people. No steaks, no roasts, not even pork chops. On a rare occasion, I find chicken on sale, and we have that. He says he wants to keep me in the style to which I am accustomed—his words, not mine—and I can't make him understand it's not what I want and not what I need. When I go shopping for clothes, I get them off the sale racks, which is fine with me. But I have to hide the receipts from him because he throws a fit if he finds out how little I paid for them.

"He thinks I came from money, and I suppose compared to the income he had when we met, you could say I did. But my father was blue collar, and my mother was a teacher. Their combined incomes kept us comfortable, but we were far from wealthy. Mama and Daddy both drive Chevys, and I was driving one too when I met your father."

Any further confessions were cut off when they heard the bathroom door opening. A few seconds later, his father walked into the kitchen.

"You still in your jammies, boy? We need to be pulling out of the drive in five minutes."

"I'll be ready." Daniel pushed back his chair and started to pick up his plate.

"Leave that," his step-mother said. "I'll take care of it when y'all are gone."

Daniel gave her a nod and a smile and headed for the bedroom. He didn't look at his father, so he missed the scowl on the man's face.

"Take an extra five minutes and shave that mess off yer face."

Daniel reappeared at the archway. "This is me,"

he said, pointing to his beard. "It goes where I go, and it stays where it is until *I* decide to take it off. If that upsets you, maybe you should go fishing by yourself. I'll stay here and keep Charlotte company. What's it gonna be?"

Harold Miller's face turned red, but he said, "Get yerself changed. We need to get goin'."

It took him less than the five minutes allotted. When he came back to the kitchen, his father looked at the holes in the knees of his jeans and frowned but said nothing. He postponed his comment until they were in his pickup, the boat hitched to the rear bumper, and they were away from the house.

"I thought you was gonna be a shyster lawyer? When did you start wearin' jeans with the knees out?"

Daniel sucked in a lungful of air and exhaled with a sigh. "I studied law. I passed the bar exam in Pennsylvania. I might find a place in a law firm already established, or I could put in an office of my own. Nothing about that makes me a shyster. I studied law so I could help people, not to get rich."

"None a that explains the ragged jeans."

Daniel shook his head. "Call it camouflage."

"Camouflage? They're blue jeans. How does that get to be camouflage?"

Daniel turned his head and looked out the window at the passing landscape and refused to answer.

"'Bout time you came down for a visit," his father said. "How long's it been, three... four years?"

"When was the last time *you* were home?" Daniel countered. "The night I graduated from high school, wasn't it?"

"This is home to me now. I didn't leave nothin' up there in Huntingdon County I need to go back for."

"Yeah, I get that, Dad. Not even a son."

They rode the rest of the way to the lake in silence. Harold Miller backed the boat trailer down the ramp until the boat floated. Then he got out of the truck and moored it to a piling while Daniel watched. The truck and trailer parked, the two of them climbed aboard, and his dad soon had them in open water. There was a chill in the air that made a light jacket necessary, and the sun was bright on the water. Daniel was glad he had thought to bring a light jacket and his mirrored sunglasses They spent the next four hours and some-odd minutes, casting and reeling, switching from spinners to cut bait, moving from one area of the lake to another. The fish apparently weren't hitting very well, but between the two of them, they managed to catch four fairly large fish—Daniel three, his father one, much to the older man's chagrin. During that time, Harold Miller didn't say more than a few words to his son. Daniel followed his father's lead and said next to nothing. He waited until his father picked up a rod, and he took the one that was left. When Harold Miller switched from artificial bait to cut bait without saying a word, his son followed suit. Anyone observing would have thought the two men were strangers who didn't like one another very well, and had somehow been forced into sharing a boat. One thought kept going through Daniels mind: *Find him soon, people. Find him soon.*

They got back to the dock, loaded the boat onto the trailer and got back to the house by 11:30. His father disappeared around the end of the garage with the fish they had caught, and Daniel went into the

157

house to wash the stink of fish off of his hands. When his father came in the backdoor a few minutes later, he was carrying eight fillets that turned out to be plenty of fish for the three of them. Charlotte blackened them in the oven and brought a tossed salad out of the refrigerator, and there were canned peaches for desert. When lunch was over, Daniel said he had some business to attend to and left in his rental. If he had his way, he would not set foot in any boat again during his sojourn in Florida, and there would be meat on the table that did not come out of the water.

* * *

Harold Miller was angry when his son left and did not tell them where he was going or when he would be back. The fact that Daniel was nearly twenty-nine years old and had been on his own since he had graduated from high school at the age of eighteen did not seem to register in the older man's mind. And that was besides the fact that he had never been a large part of his son's life anyway. But what one could have called mildly angry became full-blown irate when Daniel came into the house an hour and a half later, carrying several sacks from the grocery store. Charlotte was elated when she began taking stock of what he had brought—chuck roast, smoked pork chops, t-bone steaks, a ring of smoked sausage, bacon, hot links, skinless and boneless chicken breasts. Smiling, she began stowing it all in the refrigerator.

"What do you think yer doin', bringin' that stuff into this house?" his father demanded. "You thinkin' I can't afford groceries for me and my wife?"

"Harold," Charlotte said, and there was a hint of warning in her tone.

"I'm not *thinking*, Dad. *I know*. Charlotte and I had a little talk this morning while you were seeing a man about a horse. Maybe you should listen to her now and then, find out what *she* wants you to get for her instead of getting her what *you* want her to have. One thing I learned while I was going to college is that life is much more enjoyable when your finances aren't stretched so thin you don't know where your next meal is coming from. And I know for a *fact* that *one* thing she doesn't want is *fish* everyday. Me? I never cared that much for fish either, and while I'm here, we're going to eat meat."

"When did you get to be such a smartass?" his father asked.

"Sticks and stones, Dad, sticks and stones. Some things just don't make sense. Like buying a high-end vehicle you really can't afford and then trading it in every two years and making car payments interminably. And I'm guessing you're trading them in with what... less than ten thousand miles on the odometer? You have a beautiful, loving wife who deserves a better existence than fish everyday. Listen to what she has to say and both your lives will be the better for it. Now maybe I've said enough. I've got to make a phone call." So saying, Daniel headed to the bedroom to call Rosalynn.

Rosalynn had nothing to report. She had been watching the news faithfully, morning, noon and evening. There had been no report of a body found anywhere in Altoona, Pennsylvania.

"Do you think maybe we should call in an anonymous tip?"

"No, I think we just need to be patient and let things run their course. How are things down there in Florida?"

Daniel gave her an abbreviated version of what had taken place since his arrival and finished with, "I don't know how Charlotte puts up with the man. I may go back out there now and get told to pack my bags. If that happens, maybe I'll drive the rental back to Harrisburg, pick up my Impala and be back in Huntingdon by Wednesday."

"Well, give the man a chance. Maybe you've told him what he's needed to hear and things will get better."

"I'll give it my best shot," Daniel said. "Let me know what's going on the minute you hear anything."

"You enjoy your visit. I'll let you know what develops."

CHAPTER FOURTEEN

They did not find Dexter Landis until just after noon on Monday. When he didn't call his mother at his usual time on Sunday evening, she became concerned. It was not like her son not to check in. Calls to his cell phone went straight to voicemail. Calls to his landline got picked up by his answering machine. When she still couldn't reach him on Monday morning, she called the Walgreen Pharmacy where he worked. He had not shown up for his shift, and he was more than two hours late. In a panic, she called the Altoona Police Department. The conversation went something like this:

"Altoona Police Department, Sergeant Hagans speaking; how can I help you?"

"Hello, I'm calling from Huntingdon. I've been trying to reach my son since Sunday evening and haven't been able to get in touch with him. He's not at his place of employment, and nobody there has seen him since Thursday when he left work."

"You're saying your son is missing?"

"No, I don't know. He always gives me a call on Sunday evening, and he didn't this past Sunday. I'm just concerned. Could one of your officers go by and check his house?"

"What is your son's name and where would his house be?"

161

Marissa Landis gave him the information he required and waited while he made a note of it. His breathing was heavy in her ear, and she imagined him, an over-weight man, sitting there in a uniform with buttons stretched to the limit, the receiver wedged between his shoulder and his ear, writing on a notepad with a cheap ballpoint pen.

"And your name and number?"

She identified herself and gave him her phone number.

Alright," he said. "When we have someone in the area, we'll have them check it out." And he was gone before she could say anything more.

She tried her son's cell phone again and got no answer; tried his landline with the same result. But she kept trying. Every fifteen minutes she dialed one or the other. When she had not heard back from the Altoona Police Department at 12:15, she called them again. A female answered this time.

"Altoona Police Department, Officer Latham speaking; how can I help you?"

"I called earlier and spoke to a Sergeant Hagans about checking to see if my son is okay. He hasn't gotten back to me."

"I wouldn't know anything about that, ma'am, and Sergeant Hagans is out to lunch. Do you want me to have him call you when he gets in?"

"I want him to call me," Marissa Landis said through clenched teeth, "when he has something to tell me, and I want him to send someone out to my son's house sometime between now and midnight tomorrow night. Is that too much to ask?"

"I'll let him know you called when he gets back

from lunch," Officer Latham said, and there was a click as the connection was broken.

It would not be the police who found her son's body; it would be Cynthia Beck, the little blonde assistant who had foiled Daniel Miller's plans and bought Dexter Landis an extra day by sharing his bed the previous Wednesday night. Concerned that he was missing work and knowing where he hid a spare key, she went looking for him during her lunch break. And find him she did, but never in her most frightening nightmares had she ever dreamed about finding the body of a friend and lover dead on the floor of his dining room. She turned and ran out the front door, gagging at the odor of the beginnings of decomposition. On the front porch, she sucked in air, trying to get the stench out of her nostrils and then took out her cell phone and dialed 911. When the woman on the other end of the line got her calmed down enough to tell her what the emergency was, Cynthia was told to stay where she was until the police arrived and not to touch anything. When a patrol car showed up minutes later, she was sitting with her head in her hands on the concrete steps that led up to the front porch.

"You found a body?" the officer asked as he approached. "Where?"

"In there in the dining room," Cynthia said, looking up and indicating with a thumb over her shoulder.

The officer went into the house and was back in under a minute. Taking a small notebook from his pocket, he flipped it open, produced a ballpoint pen and began asking questions. What had she been doing there when she made the discovery? What was her relationship with the deceased? Had she touched or moved anything in the house?

While he was still asking questions, a van from the local television station pulled to the curb, WTAJ followed by the CBS symbol emblazoned on its sides, and under that YOUR NEWS LEADER. It was followed moments later by a second patrol car. The officer who got out of it immediately called a halt to the men who had gotten out of the van and were approaching the house, one with a camera on his shoulder, the other with a microphone in his hand. The second officer came on to the house, and Cameraman seemed content to shoot from his place on the main sidewalk.

Cynthia answered the officer's questions as honestly as she could, but things began to get confused in her mind. Her head was beginning to ache, and all she wanted to do was go back to Walgreen's and count pills. There was no way that was going to happen. Her workday had effectively ended when she walked into Dexter Landis's house and found him lying dead on the dining room floor.

* * *

Cynthia's discovery and the interview she made with WTAJ, practically under duress, made the six o'clock and ten o'clock news. Rosalynn watched both times and attempted to call Daniel between the two, but he didn't pick up. He had left his burner phone under the pillow in the guestroom he was using and couldn't hear it ringing in the living room. The less his father and step-mother knew about what he had been doing—and what he had yet to do—he had decided, the better it was for everybody. He had already come to regret his comment about his jeans being camouflage. Given the atmosphere in the house since he had brought the meat in, his father would likely demand to know why he had a burner phone when his iPhone 6 worked perfectly well. He would take the phone outside after supper and give Rosalynn a call, maybe make an excuse to go off somewhere in his rental.

His father dozed in front of the television until the news came on at ten. Daniel and Charlotte exchanged small talk quietly until Harold Miller was apparently wakened by his internal clock and straightened up. Then everyone was silent, listening to reports of the latest government follies, natural disasters and crimes that had been committed in the area. The news ended and his father got up from his recliner and disappeared into the hallway without saying a word. Charlotte smiled and whispered, "Good night," and followed.

Daniel waited thirty minutes, retrieved his burner phone and went outside to make his call. Rosalynn answered on the first ring.

"They found him at noon today."

"And what kind of stir is that causing?"

"None at all as near as I can tell. That little blonde girl you saw him with went out to his house when he didn't come to work. That's all I know so far."

"So I can come home soon?"

"No, I'd say you need to stay there until a week from to day at the very least, Monday of next week will be plenty early. I think the funeral will be over by then. But even if it isn't, we can start thinking about a plan for number four. You enjoy your visit as much as you can. From what you told me the last time we talked, I think your father could benefit from your company. Are things going any better?"

"Yes and no. I gave him a bit of advice and he didn't take it very well. The last time he spoke to me at any length was to bitch about my long hair and beard. Apparently, when he was supervising construction crews, he had to deal with men who were too lazy to shave or make an effort to get to a barber shop. Some of them, it seems, were even too lazy to bathe or shower and wash their hair regularly. Since then I've gotten mostly grunts, what time I haven't been getting the silent treatment. Charlotte and I are getting along well, though. I just hope I won't have driven a wedge between them by the time I leave. He is obviously crazy about her, and I think maybe she's more of a wife to him than he deserves in some ways. Then again, in some ways he makes an effort to be good to her. I'll tell you all about it when I get home. I better get back inside now before one of them discovers I'm outside and wants to know who I'm talking to."

"Well, make the best of it, and I'll be looking forward to your return."

"Good night," Daniel said, but she was already gone.

* * *

Even though the cause of death was obvious and over the vehement objections of the Landis family, an autopsy was performed on the body of Dexter Allan

Landis. The coroner's search for a bullet yielded only fragments, and notwithstanding the magic of television forensics experts who are supposedly able to piece scraps of metal together, there was little hope of identifying the weapon used with a ballistics test. The autopsy did little more than confirm the cause of death—a bullet through the heart. Death had been instantaneous.

On Wednesday, the Blair County coroner's office released the body, and it was transported to Clarkson's Funeral Home in Huntingdon where it was prepared for burial. There wasn't much that needed to be done, just embalming and a little bit of makeup to hide the discoloration caused by the first stages of decomp. That completed, the body was put into cold storage to await transportation to the First Methodist Church on Friday morning where the Landis family were members but attended only sporadically.

Eldon Landis, Dexter's father, pressed for a closed casket funeral, but his wife would have none of it. Her son had been somebody in the community (at least in her mind), and its citizens needed to be made as painfully aware as she was that his life had been cut short by the heinous act of some evil person. If the entire population of Huntingdon, Pennsylvania, was behind her, she thought, the authorities would be pressured to investigate and apprehend his killer. Truth be told, most of those who saw the front page article in *The Daily News* found themselves wondering who Dexter Landis was and why his passing was considered front-page news. After all, the murder had happened in Altoona. A few diehard Bearcat fans recalled that he had been the quarterback of the team the year they were supposed to have won State but didn't, which brought a frown to their faces, and they turned to the sports section without finishing the article.

Attendance at the funeral on Friday was disappointing and the absence of many supposed friends of her son and of the family inexcusable, Marissa Landis thought. She sat on the front pew of the church, glaring at her son's casket throughout the service, hands clutching a damp tissue in her lap, hearing not a word that was spoken from the pulpit. They could not get away with this! Ignoring her son's passing at the hands of a murderer like he wasn't important enough to mourn. Just wait until some group or other needed funding for one of their projects and called on her for a donation!

Eldon Landis sat beside his wife, a foot of space between them, dry-eyed and looking bored. From the day their son was born, he had been in second place with her, and he knew Dexter's passing wouldn't change that. Very likely the Golden Boy would be elevated to a position of sainthood, and anything he did or said in an effort to console her would be met with hostility. So get him in the ground and be done with it. Life would go on as usual.

Their daughter Dianne, on the other hand, held a dry tissue to her face throughout almost the entire affair, mostly to hide the smile she knew would have made her mother violently angry. Dexter had never been a very nice brother, always self-centered and self-important, the handsome quarterback, high achiever and pride of the family. If he wanted something, he got it, no matter who it hurt or what the cost. Maybe if she had been prettier, she sometimes thought, her parents would have treated her more fairly, been as proud of her as they were of Mr. Hotshot Dexter. But it didn't matter anymore. He was no longer among the living, and with his death, her inheritance had doubled.

* * *

About the time the funeral of Dexter Landis was concluding in Huntingdon, Pennsylvania, the neighbor just to the north of Jordan Harris's rental in San Antonio, Texas was dialing 911. The weather had been warm down south, and a strong wind had been blowing out of the southwest for several days, bringing the stench of something in the latter stages of decay with it. Somebody needed to come and check it out.

Officer Parks arrived a short time later and followed his nose to the northeast corner of the faded blue house just on the north side of Interstate 10 where Harris no longer lived. Getting down on one knee, carefully so as not to soil his uniform pants, he braced himself with one hand on the ground and the other on the side of the house and leaned down to look under it. He managed to get a quick glimpse of dirty gray work pants and a pair of worn athletic shoes before a shift in the wind brought the stench of decay full force into his face. Bile rose in his throat, and he jumped up and backed away.

"What the hell?" he muttered, frowning. He stood looking at the space under the house until he was sure he wouldn't throw up. Then he went to his vehicle and returned with a flashlight. Once again down on a knee and head close to the ground, Parks shown the light under the house from fifteen feet back and verified that, yes, there was indeed a body under there. He used his walkie to call it in and was told to wait right there. Some thirty minutes later, the backyard of the late Jordan Harris's rental was swarming with Officers, the Chief of Police himself calling the shots.

"We might have to tear up the floor in the room right above the body so the coroner can get a look at it before we move it," he suggested.

"What? Hell no! Why the hell would you have to do that?" The objection came from the man who owned the house and who lived about three doors to the north.

"He has to pronounce the body dead before we disturb it."

"And you think you have to tear up my floor to do that?" the owner said. "Hell, anybody within a quarter mile north of here could pronounce it dead just from the smell!"

Fifteen minutes later, they were still arguing about what should be done when the coroner and his assistant came around the corner of the house carrying a gurney.

"So where is the body?" one of them asked.

"Under the house," Officer Parks said pointing.

"Well, let's get it out of there," the coroner said.

"Don't you need to see it before you pronounce death?" the Chief asked.

"I'd say from the smell alone there can be no doubt. I'm just here to make it official, and I'm not about to crawl under there, so get him out."

"And how do you suggest we do that?"

The coroner looked around. "Anybody got a garden rake?"

170

"I've got one in my shed," the owner of the place said. "I'll be right back." And he disappeared around the house. He was back in less than five minutes and handed off the rake to Officer Parks who went to work, wearing a mask the coroner had provided. The rest of the crowd formed a crude semicircle about ten yards back and watched Parks work. What came out from under the house did not look human. The body had begun to disintegrate, and it took several tries to get it all. In the end, it was more a pile of work clothes and shoes mixed up with mostly bones. Wild animals of one kind or another had done their work on those parts that were not covered with cloth.

"I think that's gotta be Jordan Harris, the guy that rents the place," the owner said.

"What do you know about him?" the Chief asked.

"Not much. He comes from back east someplace and he works... worked for the trucking company across the Interstate. Somebody over there might be able to tell you more."

The coroner and his assistant loaded what was left of Jordan Harris onto their gurney and transported him back to their lab. Autopsy would reveal that death had been caused by one gunshot to the left side of the chest, no bullet recovered. DNA collected by the government during Harris's short stay in the Air Force, positively identified the remains as those of Jordan Harris as expected. Authorities were eventually able to locate his family using military records, and his remains were cremated at their request and the ashes sent back to Huntingdon, Pennsylvania, for burial.

Given the fact that Jordan was estranged from his family at the time of his death, there was no memorial service. Who would have attended? his parents asked. Whatever friends he might have had in high school had moved on—many of them out of state or gone from the area—and he had had a falling out with the two young men he had been closest to, Dexter Landis and Ryder Robinson.

* * *

Daniel Miller's call to Rosalynn Friday evening brought welcome news. The funeral of one Dexter Landis had been held that morning.

"So it's clear to come home?"

"I see no reason why you couldn't" Rosalynn said.

"Did you go?" Daniel asked. "To the funeral, I mean."

"No, I did not! Whatever made you think I would?"

"I just thought you might want to see it through to the end."

"It ended for me when you came home and told me the job was done," Rosalynn said. "When do you think you might get back?"

"I'll call the airline in the morning and schedule a flight. I imagine it will be late tomorrow evening."

"Well, enjoy the rest of the time you have with your father." Before he could respond, she was gone.

In some ways his visit to Florida had been pleasant. His father had said little to him throughout most of the week, even on the days when the two of them went fishing together. But then, what could a retired construction supervisor and a possible future lawyer have in common? Time spent with his step-mother, on the other hand, produced memories he would cherish. Maybe it was because he and Charlotte were closer in age or possibly because their minds ran in similar circles. Whatever the reason, he would leave knowing that he would miss her far more than he would miss the surliness that was his father.

He managed to book a flight that did not leave Leesburg International until nine-thirty P.M. It routed him through Atlanta—where he had an hour-plus layover—and got him into Harrisburg International sometime after midnight. The drive to Huntingdon would likely take him two hours, so he would not make it home until what folks called the wee hours. When he shared his plans with his father and step-mother, Charlotte was the one who teared up and insisted they make his final day with them special. His father just frowned and nodded.

CHAPTER FIFTEEN

Daniel pulled to the curb in front of Rosalynn's place a little after two A.M. Sunday morning. A stop at an all night café for coffee and slice of pie had extended his time line by thirty minutes. The house was dark and he was thinking about sacking out in the car and letting Rosalynn sleep when the porch light blinked on and off twice. She met him just inside the door with a hug.

"I know you must be tired, but take your suitcase to your room and we'll talk a few minutes."

The suitcase stowed, Daniel found her in her recliner and took his usual place on the sofa, the only light coming from the hallway. "So how did it go?" she asked, "Did you and your father come to an understanding?"

Daniel thought awhile before he answered. "An understanding? I don't know. I think a truce, an impasse or something like that would be a more accurate description of what there is between us. After the incident with the meat I told you about on the phone, he said little to me, and I said less to him. Mostly, Charlotte and I visited. She's quite a lady."

Rosalynn nodded but said nothing.

"Have you given any thought to what comes next?" Daniel asked.

174

"I have, but if you want to rest a bit before we take it further, that would be okay. And it would maybe give the Landis family time to get past their grief. I think there's time for that."

"How long do you think that would take, Rosalynn? How long did it take you to get past *your* grief when Rose died?"

"I never have," she said.

"And why should we give Eldon Landis even a smidgen of consideration? He's the one most likely responsible for taking Rose away from us. Dexter told me his father said he would take care of it. So either he killed Rose or he hired someone else to do it. I had a lot of time to think, coming back on the plane and sitting around the airport in Atlanta. And I came to the realization that, since the day you called me and told me that Rose was dead, my life has been one long period of mourning for what was taken away from us. I had her in my life for fourteen years, and you had her four more than that. She was part of me, and it's like Eldon Landis excised her out of me, and nobody ever sutured up the incision. So no, I don't want to give them time to get past their grief, and I don't intend to rest until the numbers are even like you suggested, and that won't happen until both sides are down to zero."

Daniel had spoken calmly but with conviction, and Rosalynn nodded agreement "Have you given any thought to how we should go about it?"

"Yes, I have. He's a realtor. He has properties for sale all over Huntingdon County, and I imagine he has a website. We just get on it and find a place for sale somewhere outside of town. I call him up and tell him I'm interested in it and want him to show it to me. He shows up and I take him down, and then I take him out. Zero for the prosecution; zero for the defense. It's over."

"That sounds like a good enough plan to me," Rosalynn agreed. "Let's get some sleep, and we will get started on it in the morning."

* * *

She was up before Daniel and had already located the Landis Realty website when he came shambling up the hall, still in his pajamas and tee-shirt.

"In here," she called when he passed the door to her office. He reversed direction and came back to stand in the doorway.

"I've found several possibilities," Rosalynn told him. "Which one we use will depend on how close the neighbors are, I suppose."

"Well, could we maybe have a little coffee and some breakfast before we get into that? The pie I ate on the way up from Harrisburg is just a distant memory now."

"Oh! Yes, I'm sorry," she said leaving the computer and following him into the kitchen. "The coffee is already made. Pour yourself some, and I'll fix you some bacon and eggs."

Daniel got a mug from the cabinet, filled it with coffee and took it to the end of the table that had become "his place."

"You don't mind me sitting at your table in pajama bottoms and tee-shirt?" he asked.

"Why no!" Rosalynn said, turning to look at him. "I'm in pajamas and a robe myself. What difference does it make what you're wearing as long as you're covered?"

Daniel shrugged. "My father was of the opinion that I shouldn't come to the table until I was fully dressed. I just wondered what you thought."

Rosalynn turned her attention back to the eggs she was frying. "What I think is life's too short and uncertain to be concerned about inconsequentialities. Do what makes you happy and wear whatever's comfortable, so long as you are not breaking the law and you're using common sense. Pajamas at the table in your own home are fine with me; wearing pajamas to Walmart, not so much."

Both of them fell silent and the only sounds were the sizzle of bacon and the scrap of her egg turner on the skillet. Daniel sipped his coffee until she set a plate down in front of him.

"Thank you," he said and picked up a fork and began to eat.

Rosalynn poured herself a mug of coffee and sat down at the other end of the table. "We will have to be more cautious with this one," she said. "We will be working close to home, and the Landis family has money."

"Always makes people think they're more important than the ones who don't have any or have little," Daniel agreed between mouthfuls.

"Sheriff Kauffman and his staff will be involved, and they are pretty good at their jobs.

Daniel nodded, his coffee mug to his lips.

"I just want you to be aware of the danger and to be more careful with this one."

"I'll do that," he said, pushing back his plate. "Let's go look at these places you've found."

They had to deal with single photographs this

time, no pushing the mouse to the side and turning in the middle of the street. Several of the possibilities she had selected looked like summer cottages and were located near Raystown Lake.

"I'm thinking that neighboring cottages might be closed up for the winter and unoccupied," she explained. "But there's no way of knowing how close the neighbors are without visiting each site. I can print out addresses and directions for you, and unless you get lucky and find what you're looking for among the first several, you might be at it a couple of days."

"Whatever it takes."

He left the house shortly after noon with six possibilities, three of them just across the river and near Raystown Lake. He found the properties being offered by Landis Realty easily enough because of the company's For Sale signs in the yards. As he and Rosalynn had expected, dwellings around the lake were small and close together. Most of them looked empty, but that could have been because their occupants were off visiting relatives or doing some shopping in Altoona or Holidaysburg or wherever. If he couldn't find a suitable place in the country, he would have to come back after dark and see if there were any lights on. Farther away from Huntingdon, he thought, would be better.

It was beginning to get dark when he found what he thought he was looking for, an old two-story house south of Huntingdon, off Highway 994 and just beyond the town of Entriken. It looked much like the house the late Ryder Robinson had occupied except the siding was shiplap that looked like it had never seen a coat of paint. It sat back from the road about a hundred yards and was accessed by a gravel lane that passed back through a gap in the trees and was nothing more than two ruts with grass growing waist-high between them. Two waist-high metal posts and a heavy chain made it impossible to get a closer look. But even from the highway he could tell the place needed a lot of work to make it livable, and the high grass in the lane suggested it had been uninhabited and on the market for quite a while. The photograph of the place on the Landis Realty website had to have been taken years ago, Daniel thought and smiled. The location was ideal for what he had in mind, no neighbors within half a mile, and he thought Landis would be eager to show it.

He described it to Rosalynn when he got back, and she readily agreed with his choice. The next step would be to call Landis Realty in the morning and make arrangements for the man to show him the house. One more, and his job would be done; the numbers would be even.

* * *

He used his burner phone at nine-fifteen the next morning. Eldon Landis himself answered on the first ring.

"Landis Realty, Eldon Landis speaking. What can I show you today?"

He sounded rather chipper for a man who recently lost his only son.

"Howdy, my name's Eugene Rawls," Daniel said, using a phony southern accent. "U'm up here from Georgia. I just took a job at R and M Distributors, drivin' a truck, and I want ta bring my wife and kids up. She says she don't wanna live in no town. Wants a place in the country. A friend tol' me about that piece a property yer handlin' down on nine, ninety-four. I went down there and looked it over, and I think that's the place I want. Any chance I cou'd git a closer look at it sometime taday. I got ta be on the job tamara."

There was no hesitation, no word of caution about how badly the place needed to be repaired. Eldon Landis's pulse rate quickened at the thought of unloading that old derelict structure before another bad winter took it completely to the ground, and he jumped at the chance.

"How's two-thirty sound?"

"Two-thirty's fine," Daniel said.

"What was that name again?" Landis asked.

"Rawls, Eugene Rawls."

"I'll meet you down there at two-thirty, Mr. Rawls. See you then."

Daniel closed his burner and shook his head.

"What is it? What's the matter?" Rosalynn asked.

"Nothing really. It's just from the excitement in his voice, I imagine him pumping a fist and hissing 'Yes!' at the possibility of selling that old relic to some poor slob that's too dumb to know what he's getting. And Dad called *me* a shyster because I want to be a lawyer."

"Well, every little bit helps," she said, smiling. "That was a nice touch with the accent. Nobody listening would ever believe you grew up right here in Huntingdon

Daniel grinned. "I'm to meet him down there at two-thirty this afternoon."

The worst of it was the waiting. Four and a half hours of waiting until it was time to meet number four and make the final deduction. They watched television until noon, turned it off while they had a sandwich, then went back to watching reruns of *Law and Order*, *NCIS*, or whatever they could find that didn't give them a headache. When one forty-five finally arrived, Daniel got into the gray Honda he had used before and headed out.

* * *

Eldon Landis was waiting at the end of the lane, the chain across it lying on the ground and his silver Cadillac Escalade parked far enough in that Daniel had no problem turning off the highway. The man had put on some pounds and his hairline had receded some since the photograph on his company's website had been taken, and he was shorter than Daniel had imagined. He was wearing charcoal gray dress pants, a gold tie over a white shirt, and a dove gray sports coat. His penny loafers matched his pants and had already collected a patina of dust. Landis waved for him to follow, then got into his vehicle and led the way. They parked side by side in the knee-high grass of the front yard and got out.

"Now, you can see it needs a little work, Mr. Rawls," Landis said, beaming, "but you look like a man that knows his way around a saw and a hammer."

Daniel stood slump-shouldered in his black and orange Baltimore Orioles cap and a red and black plaid hunter's jacket he had picked up in a second-hand store on his way out of Huntingdon and nodded. "Yep, I do. I

181

surely do." The weather had turned cold, and meteorologists were calling for snow flurries, so there was no reason for anyone to question the leather gloves he wore. A cold wind was blowing out of the north.

"Well, let's get inside and out of this wind," Landis suggested and headed for the steps that led up to the front porch. Daniel followed without saying anything. The steps were wide, four feet from end to end maybe, four of them, and the right halves of the second and third ones were gone.

"Better keep over here to this side," Landis suggested.

The two of them made it to the porch, Landis opened the door, and they stepped inside. Daniel turned and pushed the door shut.

He had prepared himself as usual—stun gun in the left pocket of his jacket, thirty-eight in the right pocket, large zip ties stuck down the waist of his jeans, smaller ones in a hip pocket. Mentally it was the same. *This is for Rose*, he kept telling himself. *This is for Rose.*

"Obviously, the kitchen needs to be redone." Landis had gone on ahead to an archway and was gesturing with the sweep of an arm, his back turned.

Daniel stepped up behind him and glanced briefly toward where the man was pointing. *The kitchen doesn't need to be* redone, he thought, *it needs to be* done. With the exception of a sink and running water, the room had not been updated since it had been built, probably sometime in the late nineteenth or early twentieth century. But that had nothing to do with why he was there. He slipped the stun gun out of his pocket, stepped up behind Landis and pressed it to the man's neck.

It was the first time he had ever used in on bare flesh, but the man's sports coat made it impossible to do otherwise. There was a sizzling sound and the smell of burning flesh. His right hand was on the man's shoulder, and he kept the stun gun pressed tight until Landis started to pitch forward. As in previous incidents, there was no effort to break the fall, and he landed hard on his face. Daniel slipped the stun gun back into his pocket and went to work with the zip ties. He was pulling the last one tight around Landis's legs just above the knees when the man's ability to speak returned.

"What the hell are you doing?"

"We need to talk," Daniel said. He rolled the man onto his back, grabbed the shoulders of his jacket and set him up against the wall. Then he sat down on the floor, cross-legged and facing him. Landis's nose looked a little crooked, and blood trickled down over his lips. Daniel pulled a handkerchief out of a hip pocket and wiped it away.

"Talk about what? Who the hell are you?"

"Who am I? I'm the one who took out your rapist son about a week ago. I'm the one who's evening out the numbers. You know, one accuser, three rapists."

"What the hell are you talking about?"

"I'm talking about Rose Holder and the guys who raped her—your son and Jordan Harris and Ryder Robinson."

"Dexter and those boys were acquitted!" Landis insisted.

"No, no, no, Eldon. You're confused. They weren't acquitted. Their trial ended in a hung jury, remember? They raped Rose Lynn Holder, a young woman who had the mind of a five-year-old, a special needs person, and they got away Scott free with it—until now. Rose's mother wanted a retrial, but you killed her before there could be one."

"What?! I didn't kill anybody!"

"Then who did you hire to do the job?" Daniel pressed.

"I didn't hire anybody!"

"So you did it yourself? Your son told me the football team was having trouble concentrating because Rosalynn Holder kept pushing for a retrial. He told me you said you would take care of it, and somebody obviously took care of it. So if you say you didn't hire anybody that means you did it yourself."

Eldon swallowed hard and said nothing.

"So tell me what you did. Tell me how you went about it?"

When Landis refused to speak, Daniel pulled the stun gun out of his pocket, leaned forward and pressed it against the man's leg. The reaction he got was unexpected, and he almost got kicked in the knee. Landis's body jerked and stiffened, his head pressed back against the wall almost hard enough to make a dent in it. When his muscles finally relaxed, he gasped for air. Daniel moved over beside him and leaned back against the wall.

"Tell me how you went about it?"

"I waited until after the girl's mother took her sleeping pill and was out of it…"

"How did you know Rose's mother took sleeping pills?" Daniel interrupted.

"I just did, okay?"

"Not okay. I want you to tell me everything,

184

answer every question I ask you. How did you know she took sleeping pills?"

"Someone told me," Landis said after a stubborn hesitation.

"Who?"

The man refused to answer, and Daniel pulled the stun gun out of his pocket.

"Okay! Okay!" Landis shouted. "It was a friend of my brother-in-law's, the pharmacist she used."

"And you got the capsules you used on Rose from your brother-in-law?"

"Yeah."

Daniel shook his head. Rosalynn was right. If they tried to deal with everybody who had been involved, it would take years.

"Go on," he said. "You waited until her mother was asleep, and then...?"

"I slipped into the house..."

"How? Did you have a key?"

"No, I had an electric thing, a lock pick I got off the internet. It looked like a little drill. All you had to do was stick the end of it in a lock and pull the trigger."

Daniel nodded. "Go on."

"I went into her bedroom and I made her swallow some capsules and some vodka and I left."

"I want details," Daniel said. "Did Rose resist? Did she fight you?"

"What's the point of all this?" Landis asked. "I fed her the stuff and she went to sleep and never woke up. Case closed."

"The point is: I want details. She was my best friend, would have been my fiancé and wife eventually

185

if things had been different, the mother of my children. I want to know what the last minutes of her life were like, and the stun gun comes out again if you don't start talking."

Landis dropped his chin to his chest for a moment, and then he raised his head and began. "She was already groggy, okay? When I tried to shake her awake, she opened her eyes and smiled at me and tried to go back to sleep. I had to throw the covers back and pull her legs over the side of the bed and set her up and hold her there. She whined a little bit and kept trying to fall over, and I had to let go of her to get the lid off the pills and the vodka. I set her up again, and I put some of the capsules in her mouth and tipped her head back and poured some of the vodka in. She coughed and choked a little bit, but I had an arm around her neck and a hand under her chin so she couldn't spit them out."

"Did she say anything or try to resist?"

"Yeah, I guess, a little. She said, 'Burns,' when I gave her the vodka, and she tried to pull my hand away."

Daniel had trouble getting words past the lump in his throat. "Go on."

"There's not much left to tell," Landis said. "I made her swallow the rest of the capsules and more vodka. I gave her a piece of peppermint candy to cover the smell, and I laid her back down like she was when I got there, and I covered her up and left."

"How did her finger prints get on the container the pills came in? Did you wrap her hand around it?"

"Yeah, I did," Landis answered after a hesitant pause.

Daniel took a moment to think about all that he had just heard and then he asked, "Do you have any regrets about it? About what you did?"

"Yeah, I regret that I didn't do it sooner. If I had, maybe the team would have won State like everybody wanted them to. Those boys really felt bad about losing. It was their senior year and their last chance. Winning a state Championship was important to them."

Daniel's head dropped. "Do you think winning State was more important to them than living was to Rose Holder?"

"Look, I get it," Landis said, anger in his tone. "She was your friend and you had the hots for her. But she was never gonna be what you wanted. She was a *re*-tard, for god sakes! She would never have been able to raise children! If that bitch of a mother of hers had just let it go, things would be different. You want to know why things turned out the way they did, go talk to her!"

Daniel got up from where he was sitting and walked to the middle of the room. He took the thirty-eight out of his pocket and turned around.

"What?" Landis said. "You're gonna *shoot* me now? Who the hell died and made you judge, jury and executioner?"

Daniel's response was a mirthless chuckle. "Do you not see the irony in the question you just asked?"

Landis looked confused.

"You took it upon yourself to decide Rose Holder had to die, and *you* carried out the sentence. And you can sit there now and ask who died and made *me* judge, jury and executioner? Well, Mr. Eldon Landis, I believe it was Rose Lynn Holder, and this is for her."

187

Dropping to one knee and extending his arm, he pulled the trigger. The thirty-eight jumped his hand, a dark hole appeared in the lapel of Eldon Landis's gray sports coat and his chin dropped to his chest. Just to be sure, Daniel fired another round, and a second hole appeared, cutting the edge of the first.

Still on one knee, Daniel dropped his head. It was over. The numbers were finally even.

CHAPTER SIXTEEN

And yet it wasn't really over, would possibly never be over. Daniel had to force himself to overcome a lethargy born of depression and move. He stood and returned the thirty-eight to his jacket pocket and took stock of the situation. He was wearing gloves, so he had left no fingerprints or touch DNA on anything except the zip ties. He took off a glove and worked the knife out of his pocket and opened it. Then putting the glove back on, he went to where what remained of Eldon Landis was sitting and cut the ties off his legs and ankles. He had to pull the man away from the wall to get to the wrists, and when he did, the body slid slowly over and the head hit the floor with a thud. As a further precaution, he went through the man's pockets until he found a cell phone and the keys to the Escalade. There were no trash bags, trash cans or pillow cases to put the zip ties in, so he carried them in his hands. He picked up the handkerchief he had used to wipe Landis's nose and carried it out with the rest of the items.

In the living room, he peeked out a window to check for cars passing on the road. There were none. He let himself out and locked the door. As quickly as possible without leaving any tell-tale spin marks in the grass, he backed Landis's Escalade onto the gravel lane and drove it around behind the house and out of sight. So far, so good; still no vehicles passing on the highway. He got into the gray Honda and headed out, stopping at the end of the lane to fasten the chain back in place. When that was done, he threw Landis's keys into the weeds. The man's cell phone he took with him and would dispose of it when he found some water.

He thought about Rosalynn's suggestion that he not return from San Antonio by the same route he had taken down there and he turned right out of the lane. Left would have taken him back past Entriken and up Highway 26 through Marklesburg, both small towns, and the quickest way home, a distance of under twenty-five miles. It was unlikely that anyone in either town had taken any notice of his passing or would think anything of it if they saw the gray Honda passing through again. But he didn't want to take the funk he was in back to Rosalynn. Maybe a long drive would get him over it. It was worth a try.

The road was narrow and his route was windy. It took him over ridges and around turns that made him concentrate on his driving. Still, his mind kept going back to what the four of them had said about Rose. In their minds, she had been a *re*-tard, someone to be used and thrown away or eliminated out of convenience. He was afraid their words were forever burned into his mind. The blacktop was lined on either side with dense forest most of the way, and traffic was practically nonexistent. He kept his speed far below the posted limit. He passed through the villages of Eagle Forge and Cooks, and after nearly an hour, he reached a town called Three Springs. A half hour after that, he was in Orbisonia and back on familiar ground.

He stopped for a restroom break and a cup of coffee at the same convenience store he had visited on his way back from San Antonio and Chambersburg. Had that been only what... less than a month ago? If the checkout girl recognized him as a previous customer, she showed no sign of it.

The wind had died down somewhat, but the sky had become overcast, and it was already getting dark when he pulled back onto Route 522. Huntingdon was less than an hour away, driving the posted speed limit, and he couldn't imagine Rosalynn not having supper ready when he got there. Time and distance had not left the funk entirely behind, but it had diminished it enough to make life bearable, and he was hungry.

He slowed down enough on the bridge over the Aughwick Creek north of Shirleysburg to sail Landis's phone over the rail. If it landed on a gravel bar instead of in the water, so be it. He had taken the SIM card out and tossed it out the window somewhere between Three Springs and Orbisonia.

Thirty minutes later, he pulled into the driveway at Rosalynn's place. His Impala was still sitting by the curb, and he wondered idly if she had used it while he was gone. He went into the house without emptying his pockets this time and without getting the briefcase from the backseat. Belatedly, he remembered the forth envelop he was supposed to have emptied earlier and wondered what was in it. No matter now. It was too late to do anything about it.

Rosalynn met him in the entryway as usual and wrapped him up in a hug that made breathing difficult.

"I expect you hours ago!" she said. "Where have you been? Did something go wrong?"

191

Her concern brought a lump to his throat, and he couldn't speak. She took her arms from around him and put a hand on either side of his face.

"Daniel?" she said, looking into his eyes.

"It's done," he was finally able to say. "Everything went the way I... we expected it to."

She studied his expression, his face still in her hands. A tear escaped and ran down his cheek, and she wiped it away with a thumb. Then she hugged him again, her arms around his neck this time, and kissed him on the cheek.

"I made a roast," she said. "You go sit in the living room and rest until I get it on the table, and then we'll talk while we eat. I want you to tell me about it. I want to know everything."

* * *

She seemed to understand what he was going through better than he would have imagined. She sat at the far end of the table and listened intently while he recounted what had happened with Landis, how he had left things, and he apologized for not remembering the last envelop. She told him not to worry about it; she would see that there was enough misdirection to mislead whoever would investigate without it. His appetite was better than he thought it would be, and he finished two helpings of the roast with mashed potatoes and gravy and had lemon pie for dessert.

She did no seem elated with the results of their endeavor, merely satisfied and maybe a little glad to have it finished. He spent the night in her guestroom again and left for his apartment in State College before first light in the morning, before any of her neighbors were up and about. She had taken possession of the thirty-eight, the stun gun, his burner phone, the briefcase and everything that remain in it, promising to dispose of everything as quickly as possible. When he asked about the viewing history on her computer, she told him not to worry. She would install a new hard drive and destroy the old one. No doubt there would be consequences, she had told him, but she would take pains to see that nothing would come back on either of them from her end.

She told him she would miss him but urged him to go. When they found Eldon Landis (she refused to use the word *body*), things would get hectic.

"What about you?" he asked. "You will be right here in the middle of it."

"Don't worry about me," she said. "Everything will work out okay for me."

Get rid of the jeans, the baseball caps, and the reading glasses, she said—anything and everything that might cause anyone to have even the slightest suspicion he might have been involved in any of it. Give it away or destroy it, he asked, and she said he could do it either way, so long as none of it could ever be traced back to him.

It had taken them a month, less one day, to "deal with" the four of them, and Thanksgiving was too close. It would be best if they skipped it this year, she said. They would find Eldon Landis soon and launch an investigation and quickly find out they had no leads. Whatever they collected would eventually be put into a folder and stuck in a filing cabinet with other cold case files, she felt certain. If everything went as she expected, it would be safe for him to visit at Christmas as usual.

"Take this," she said and pushed another large envelope into his hands. "Don't open it until you get home. You need to rest for a couple of weeks—do nothing—and this will help you."

Again, she gathered him into a hug and kissed him on the cheek. "Don't forget us," she said, "me and Rose."

Driving away from her place, he realized that he would never know what had been in the forth envelope, the one he was supposed to have emptied somewhere near Eldon Landis. The lipstick, compact and plastic case for credit cards from the first three envelopes came to mind, and he found himself wondering why there had been no word, no news reports about the other two. There was no way for him to know that Jordan Harris's ashes had already been buried in an unmarked plot in a cemetery near Alexandria, or that Ryder Robinson had yet to be found. The young man had threatened on several occasions to take off for parts unknown and start over someplace where no one knew his history. Since his pickup was gone, his family assumed that he had finally done so. The man from whom he rented the house north of Greencastle would find no reason to visit the barn behind it until some time in the spring.

"We did it for you, Rose," Daniel said aloud as he drove away. "We did it for you."

* * *

Marissa Landis was not concerned when her husband did not come home Tuesday evening. In fact, she was not aware of his absence until nearly noon on

Friday when the maid told her there had been no need to make his bed for the last three mornings. Her husband had a habit of spending nights out now and then, and she knew there had been several reasons for his absences in recent years, all of them female. She had inherited money from her parents and had loaned him enough to start his realty business. Eldon Landis was moderately successful and enjoyed wearing fine clothes and driving expensive cars, and they lived lavishly, but it was mostly on her money. The problem was the more Eldon had, the more he wanted. And when she refused to let him dip into the principle of her trust fund, he began "punishing" her by having affairs. She, in retaliation, had moved his clothes and other belongings out of their bedroom and into the guestroom and had lost track of how many years ago that had been.

Her daughter Dianne stopped by with her latest squeeze late Friday evening, just a drop-by-and-remind-them-I-exist sort of visit. If one expects to inherit the family fortune, one must be attentive and available or, at the very least, visible. Marissa was in the den, watching reruns of *Family Feud* with Steve Garvey and enjoying a third double-shot of Johnnie Walker Red.

"Get yourself a drink and join me," Marissa told them. "Liquor cabinet's open."

After a couple of minutes, the two of them settled on the sofa, highball glasses of amber liquid in hand.

"Mom, this is Bryan with a *y*," Dianne said and smiled sweetly at the man beside her. "I think his parents decided to spell it that way so he wouldn't mess up and spell brain. This is my mom."

The young man laughed and said, "Pleased to meet you."

"Likewise," Marissa said and turned her attention back to the television.

"Where's Dad," her daughter asked.

"I have no idea," Marissa said. I haven't seen him since Monday morning. Or was it Tuesday?"

"What?" Dianne asked. "He's been gone all week and you don't know where?"

"I stopped trying to keep track of him years ago. He has his life and I have mine. Sometimes they overlap. When they don't, my life tends to be good."

Bryan with a *y* laughed and Dianne frowned at him and asked, "How much have you had to drink, Mom?"

"Not nearly enough, I'm afraid. I still see your brother lying in that casket." She downed the rest of her drink and handed the glass to Bryan. "Would you get me another one, please? Johnnie Walker."

"Don't you think you've had enough?" Dianne asked, and Bryan gave her a frown and shook his head. Minutes later, he sat back down and put the glass in her hand.

They stayed until after eight, and by that time, Marissa was slurring her words. Bryan helped her up the stairs to her bedroom, and Dianne helped her get undressed and into bed. It would not be until Monday when her husband failed to show up at his office, that anybody became concerned enough to call the authorities. And then it would not be a member of his family but his secretary.

* * *

Saturday and Sunday evenings had been repeats of Friday evening without the benefit of help from Bryan and her daughter. So when Marissa got the call on

Monday morning from Janet Staubs, her husband's secretary, she was nursing a hangover and in a foul mood.

"Misses Landis, I'm concerned about your husband," the woman said. "He hasn't been in his office since Tuesday when he left a note that he was going out to show someone a property."

"He hasn't been spending his nights with you?" Marissa asked, her tone surly.

"What?! I'm his *secretary*! I answer the phone and open his mail and take deeds to the courthouse to be filed! That's where I was Tuesday when he left! I'm not his hump!"

"Well, I haven't seen him since Monday or Tuesday either, so as to where he might be, your guess is a good as mine. And my apologies for that last question. I'm not feeling very well this morning."

"Shouldn't we call someone? It's not like him to neglect his business like this."

"Whatever you think," Marissa told her. "Me? I'm going to sit here at my kitchen table and have some more coffee." Without saying anything more, she hung up.

Janet called the Huntingdon Police Department and got a Sergeant Somebody who started the old song and dance about the person must be missing for forty-eight hours before…

"I believe that from sometime Tuesday afternoon of last week until now, which is Monday of a new week, forty-eight hours and then some have passed!" she said, cutting him off. "How about you get me someone on this phone who gives a damn about doing his job?"

There was a silent pause while the sergeant handed the receiver off to someone else. "Lieutenant Monroe speaking. How can I help you?" He had asked the right question, but his tone suggested he had only accepted the receiver from his underling out of necessity. There was another hysterical woman on the line.

Janet's patience wore thin, and she unloaded. "My boss is missing, has been since last Tuesday. I am reporting him missing, and I am hoping that someone there at your office will put their donuts down long enough to see if they can find him."

"Now, Ma'am, there's no need to get testy," he said and seemed to become marginally more alert.

"Testy?! You think I'm *testy* because I'm asking you to do your job? If I don't get some cooperation and respect over this phone, I'll come down there to your office, and I'll s*how* you testy! Have you ever had footprints on your desk?"

"Watch it lady! You don't threaten a policeman."

"That wasn't a threat, numbskull," Janet assured him, "that was a promise. Now are you interested enough to take some notes, or do I hang up and call Sheriff Kauffman?"

"Just calm down and tell me the name of this missing person."

"His name is Eldon Landis, and he is the owner and proprietor of Landis Realty."

"Eldon Landis?" the Lieutenant said, and for the first time there was something like eagerness in his tone, "the husband of Marissa Landis?"

There was a jingle and squeak of equipment as he reached for a notepad, and Janet smiled. Money is a great motivator, whether you're working for it or for somebody who has it. The Lieutenant began asking questions and she began answering them. Where did she *think* he might have gone? A note left on her desk said to show one of his the properties to a prospective buyer. Was he having any health issue? Not that she was aware of. Did she have a list of the properties Mr. Landis was currently representing? No, but she could make one.

She hung up the phone and began making a list of the properties the company was handling within the borough of Huntingdon. She didn't quite have it finished when a squad car pulled up out front and two uniformed officers got out of it and came in. They waited somewhat impatiently while she finished it. When she handed it to them, they turned and left without saying a word. She sat down behind her desk and heaved a sigh of relief. She had done all that she could. Someone else had to take it from here.

The two officers took the list back to the station, and Lieutenant Monroe organized a search. The list was divided among everyone who was on duty, and their top priority was to check each and every property thoroughly—house, garage, barn and storage shed— any place and every place where a man might be when maybe he had a seizure or suffered a heart attack. Or where someone might hide a body.

The search took a major part of the day, and when if was over, the officers involved had nothing to report. Wherever Eldon Landis was, Lieutenant Monroe concluded, it was out of the Department's jurisdiction. He called the Huntingdon County Sheriff's Department and handed the case off to them. With a sigh of relief, he hung up the phone. It was Sheriff James Kauffman's problem now.

* * *

Sheriff Kauffman's first action was to have his secretary, Meagan Price, call the office of Landis Realty and request a list of properties the company was representing but that were not within the borough limits of Huntingdon. Having anticipated the request, Janet Staubs had already compiled such a list. It was on her desk and waiting to be picked up. Kauffman dispatched young Deputy William Buckley to do so. Buckley was back in just over fifteen minutes.

The list consisted of nearly two dozen properties, quite a few of them scattered around Raystown Lake. One was as far north as Warriors Mark, another one to the south on State Route 522 as far as Shade Gap. Another one was still farther south, almost to the southern county line on State Route 3021 and was likely a hunters' cabin near State Gameland 121. A couple of others were scattered in between, including one that was up Black Log Valley on State Route 2017. The search was going to take them to the far reaches of the county and into areas most of them were not familiar with. It was probably going to take most of a day and possibly longer to cover them all.

Sheriff Kauffman divvied up the list, giving Chief Deputy Emory Shields the ones around the lake and nearest to home. Deputy Debra Hicks, the newest and youngest member of his staff, would accompany Shields. To William Buckley, he assigned the ones to the south, and he took the ones to the north himself. It was late afternoon and the man had already been missing for a week, so there seemed to be little cause for urgency. In Kauffman's mind, the search would be more like a recovery than a rescue mission.

"There's no need to come into the office in the

morning," Sheriff Kauffman told them. Make sure your radios are fully charged and start your search from home. You find him, call it in and let everybody know. Stay with him until backup arrives. I suspect the county coroner will be with them."

* * *

Shields picked Hicks up the next morning at her apartment. Debora Hicks was a curvy brunette about five foot eight, and had no trouble getting into the department pickup, even though it sat rather high on nineteen inch wheels. Shields said, "Good morning," smiled and wished again that he was maybe thirty years younger. She smiled and returned the greeting, wondering again how a man could look so much like Slim Pickens and not actually *be* him. They sipped take-out cups of coffee as Shields drove them out to the lake and the first address on their list.

It turned out to be a faux log cabin, likely constructed from one of those kits that had been popular the last half of the twentieth century. It sat on a narrow lot between two small cottages about half a mile from the lake shore. If a man was ill-mannered enough, he could have leaned his back against an outside wall and spit on the neighbor's house.

"Why do people want to spend their time out here?" Debra Hicks asked. "This place is more crowded than town."

"I've always thought havin' a place out here makes them feel important," Shields said. "You know? They're at a party and someone asks 'What have you and your family been doin' this summer?' and they

201

can answer 'Oh, not much, just spending some time at our place out at the lake.'"

The front door was locked and the two front windows were covered inside with mini-blinds. They made a circuit of the place and found the backdoor also locked, as expected, and there was no way to get a look inside. Back at the front door, Shields pulled a lock pick kit out of a pocket, and Hicks went ballistic.

"What are you doing? You can't do that! That's breaking and entering!"

"I'm not breaking anything. I think of it more like *opening* and entering. We're looking for someone. More than likely, a dead body. How else are we gonna see if he's inside this cabin? You wanna drive all the way back to town and get us a key?"

"You agree with Kauffman that he's probably dead?"

Shields was down on one knee, working on the lock. "Like he said, more than likely. Nobody's seen him since a week ago as of tomorrow, so far as we know. And he hasn't been answerin' his cell phone."

Deputy Hicks looked unconvinced but said nothing.

"And what about the next place, and the next? We got what... four or five more on our list? You want to run around with a pocketful of keys and spend a lot a time trying to figure out which one fits what?"

He swung the door open, braced a hand on the doorjamb and stood up. They stepped inside. The interior consisted of one large room with the back left corner partitioned off for a minuscule bathroom with a tiny wall-hung sink, a cheap commercially made shower and a commode. The right rear corner was a kitchen, complete with a stainless steel, double-tub sink and a dishwasher.

"Wouldn't be a bad place to live for a single person," Hicks observed.

"Yeah," Shields seemed to agree. "I bet it's just like the one Abraham Lincoln was born in up in Illinois." He took a quick look in the bathroom, said, "He's not here," and headed for the door.

Their second stop was a cottage—white with a dark asphalt shingle roof in the Cape Cod style. It had no curtains or blinds on its windows, but there were closets in two of the rooms. Deputy Shields had Hicks pick the lock on the front door this time. It took her a couple minutes to do what he usually did in thirty seconds, but he thought she needed to learn and praised her a little when the door finally swung open. They each took a room and looked in a closet. No Eldon Landis. No body. They locked up and headed for the next address.

They finished their list a little past two and headed back to the office. Could have been back a little earlier, but Shield made Hicks pick all the locks from the second one on, and it took awhile. They had found nothing and heard nothing from anyone else. Sheriff Kauffman was back from his run, had been since about ten o'clock. There were only two properties on his list and Warriors Mark was only twenty-odd miles from Huntingdon. His trip had been as fruitless as theirs. Eldon Landis was still out there somewhere. It looked like, if anybody in the Department was going to locate him, it was up to Deputy William (Billy) Buckley.

* * *

Buckley left home with a clear plan of how he would go about checking the five properties on his list. The one farthest from Huntingdon was the one down by Gameland 121. Although the place was only thirty miles away, the roads were so narrow and windy that getting there took just a few minutes short of an hour. Then he had to go up three dirt side roads before he found what he was looking for.

Everybody seemed to think it would be a hunter's cabin, and it was. Not much more than a tarpaper shack with a couple of windows. A set of crude steps led up to the front door, which was handmade out of one-by-fours and looked like it belonged on someone's woodshed. The place had been set on a foundation of fieldstone, and there was no way he could see in the windows without a ladder. He didn't have one, but he had thought to bring a set of lock picks, and it took him less than a minute to open the cheap padlock that secured the front door.

He swung the door open and stepped inside. Even in the dim light he could see there was no body. There was nowhere to hide one. The place was a single large, empty room. There were no cabinets, no closets, no furniture at all. He backed out and closed the door.

He was back in his pickup and about to head out when a question came to mind. What did whoever built the place use for a restroom? He left the pickup running and headed around the shack, wading through knee-high grass and pushing head-tall reeds out of the way. From the back corner of the shack, he could see an outhouse at the back of the lot.

"I just bet the state gave them permission to have that there," he muttered aloud to himself and pushed his way toward it and swung the door open on squeaky hinges.

It was a one-holer, and it was empty except for a calendar with a photo of a naked woman and half a roll of toilet tissue.

He closed the door, made his way back to his pickup and headed north and east. His next stop would be in Shade Valley on State Route 35, somewhere north of a place called Richvale, and then there was one in Blacklog Valley and another near Orbisonia on Love's Valley Road. It was beginning to look like he was in for a long day.

* * *

He came dragging into the office at three minutes of five, looking like something someone had pulled through a knothole backwards.

Emory Shields gave him a grin and asked, "What took you so long, Billy? Me and Hicks got back in time for lunch." He knew it was a lie, but he wanted to get a rise out of the kid. He was not disappointed.

"What took me so long?! The places on my list were all scattered to hell and gone, and three of them were farms! I had to do the fugitive thing!"

"What's the fugitive thing?" Hicks asked.

"You know, from the movie. Search every gas station, residence, warehouse, farmhouse, hen house, outhouse and doghouse! There wasn't any service stations or warehouses, but there was houses, barns, hog sheds, milk houses, chicken houses, granaries, storage sheds, a silo and one plastic playhouse. And that's only after I found the properties I was lookin' for. I been to places today I never knew existed. Still not sure if some of them really do. I grew up in Tyrone and didn't have any relatives on farms! I didn't know there was so many places on a farm where someone could hide a body!"

Shields laughed out loud. "Wore ya out, did it?"

"And just like the rest of us, you had no luck?" Hicks asked.

"Only if you count it luck that I found my way back."

"So, he's still out there somewhere, and we'll just have to keep looking," Sheriff Kauffman said. "But we'll start again in the morning. Let's all take it home and get some supper. Give some thought to what we might have missed. I'll see you in the morning.

CHAPTER SEVENTEEN

Daniel Miller was unrecognizable as the man who had left Rosalynn Holder's house in Huntingdon a week ago. The beard was gone, and his hair was shorter than it had been in more than a decade. He had taken most of it off himself with a cheap hair clipper he picked up at Walmart. Then he had gone to a salon and had it professionally done—high and tight like someone in the military. His clothes were once again the dress trousers, button downs and dress shoes he had always worn—the ones his father thought he should have brought to Florida. Once back in his old garb, he checked out his appearance in the full-length mirror on his bedroom door and wasn't sure he liked the preppy, geeky look anymore. But he thought it best to keep it for a while.

The ragged and faded jeans and the tee-shirts he had washed and tied up in a black plastic bag of the type most people used for leaves. He ran the baseball caps through a wash cycle also and put them in one of the tall white kitchen bags from under his sink. He left both bags at the backdoor of the Goodwill store on Allen Street one night around midnight. The grungy athletic shoes, also washed and dried, he set beside the bags. It was extremely unlikely that anybody would ever check the bags or any of the donated items for

207

fingerprints, but if they were to do so, they would find none. Daniel had worn latex gloves for the last time he touched any of it. Rosalynn had taught him well.

The morning after the first night back in his apartment, he had opened the envelope she had given him and discovered that it contained five thousand dollars. *You need to rest for a couple of weeks—do nothing—and this will help you,* she had said. Well, he had been busy for the first couple of days destroying evidence, but now that was done and he could relax. He wanted to call and thank her, but she had told him not to contact her. She would call him "when things blew over," and they would get together for Christmas.

Looking back at the last month of his life, it all seemed like a dream. He knew what he had done, and he believed that Rose's death had been avenged, but he didn't feel much different than he had before. In some ways, he felt a little worse. He asked himself: where was this thing people called closure? Better question: *What is* this thing people call closure? He wondered if he would ever find anything funny enough to make him laugh out loud again, if he would ever smile again in a way that made his face feel right.

For the first week, he slept a lot, often during the day in his recliner, the television on. Somehow he always managed to be awake for the news, and he began to understand his father a little better. But what he was waiting to hear was never reported. Number Four (he refused to even *think* the worked *body* or the man's name) apparently had yet to be found. Come to think of it, so far as he knew, Number One and Number Two hadn't been found yet either.

* * *

Sunrise on Tuesday made it one week, less a few hours, since anybody had heard from Eldon Landis. Sheriff Kauffman felt that the search made the day before had been thorough and should have turned up something. The fact that it hadn't meant they were lacking a key piece of information.

"Someone needs to go back and talk to that secretary of his, Janet Staubs," he said.

Deputy Buckley waited to see if Emory Shields would take the job. When the man sat with his head down and said nothing, he spoke up. "I'll do it."

Kauffman nodded. "Just ask her if there's anything else she can tell us, anything she might have forgot. If you draw a blank there, go out and talk to his wife again. Somebody knows something, and we won't find him until we know what that something is."

"I could tag along, maybe learn a few things," Debora Hicks said when Buckley headed for the door.

Kauffman waved her on without looking up, his mind already working on some other aspect of the case

They took one of the Department pickups, the one Buckley had taken out the previous day. It was a short drive to the office of Landis Realty, and that early in the morning, there was a parking space right in front of the door. Janet Staubs was sitting behind her desk when they went in, and she started to rise when she saw them, a look of hope and concern on her face.

"You found him?"

"No," Deputy Buckley said, "didn't have any luck."

Janet sunk back into her chair and put her elbows on the desk, her face in her hands.

"We'd like to ask you a few more questions, see if there's anything you can think of that you might have missed last time. Okay?"

Janet dropped her hands to the desktop and nodded. Her face was red and her eyes glassy, but there were no tears.

"Is there any place he might have gone that you haven't told us about? Anybody he might have gone off with and decided to make it... what's the word?

"An extended stay?" Debora Hicks suggested, and he nodded.

Janet gave it some thought. "I can't imagine who he would go with or where he would go and stay away this long and not tell me *something*. If he has to go out and show a property to a prospective client and I'm not here when he leaves, he usually leaves me explicit instructions. Contact so and so about whatever, take the deed to this or that property to the courthouse and get it filed, take a couple hours and find Dianne a birthday present for me. Sometimes it pisses me off. I've got my realtor's license, and I know more about running this office than he does. And Dianne's *his* daughter, not mine, so he should be the one picking out birthday gifts. I made that list I gave you guys from memory and then checked it against the files in the filing cabinet. And I only missed two or three properties. So *where* he might have gone has pretty much been covered. The *who* now, that's a whole 'nother question."

"What do you mean by that?" Buckley asked.

Janet was hesitant to answer, but after a few moments of thought, she did. "When I called his wife Marissa to tell her he hadn't showed up here at the office and asked her if she knew where he was, she seemed to think he had been spending nights with me. That never happened, not with me, but I'm guessing it happened with somebody, and I have no idea who that somebody might be. The way she snapped at me, I'm guessing his wife probably knows."

The two deputies took it all in, nodding their heads and frowning. When she fell silent, they thanked her for her time and asked her to give them, or someone in the Department, a call if she thought of anything else. They stepped outside and pulled the door shut.

"Well, that was a bust," Deborah Hicks said. "What do we do now? Go see the wife and ask if she knows who he might have been spending time with most recently?"

"I'm thinking we should give Sheriff Kauffman a call first."

They were about to get into their vehicle when the office door was yanked open and Janet shouted, "The old Cooper place!"

They stood in the open doors of the pickup and turned to look at her.

"The old Cooper place," she repeated more quietly. "It's down on 994. It's been on the market for eight years, and we haven't showed it to anybody in six. That's why I didn't think of it until now, and I just checked. The folder isn't in the filing cabinet, so he must have taken it with him. It's an old two-story farmhouse lookin' place that isn't even livable, and the owners want an arm and a leg for it. If someone called and asked to see it, Eldon would have hyperventilated just thinking about the commission he would get if he could unload it."

"Okay," Buckley said, "that sounds like a good possibility. How do we get to this place?"

"Take 26 south down through Marklesburg, then turn east on 994. The house will be on the right about a mile and a half after you pass the turnoff to Entriken. It sets back from the road a ways, and it's partially hidden by trees, but this time of year, it shouldn't be that hard to find."

Buckley nodded. "We'll check it out."

Janet went back into the office and closed the door.

"Are you gonna call the sheriff first?" Hicks asked.

"We'll call him on the way. Let him know where we're going and why."

The trip took them less than half an hour, and they spotted the house without any trouble. They left their pickup angled in toward the chain and walked up the lane, radios in their hands, keeping their eyes on the ground. There was no way to tell if any vehicles had been here recently until they got to where the Escalade and the Honda had been parked and left the dry grass matted down.

"Two vehicles. What do you think?" Hicks asked. She stopped and stood looking toward the house.

Buckley ignored her question and kept walking. When he got to where he could see past the back corner of the house, he stopped.

"Call Sheriff Kauffman and tell him we found Landis's car," he said, coming back and already heading toward the steps that led up to the front porch. "I imagine we're gonna find him inside."

While Hicks made the call, he mounted the steps

carefully. He checked the door and found it locked, then stepped to the left to peek in a window. Hicks was just picking her way up what was left of the steps when the floorboards snapped under his foot, and he dropped through up to his knee, tearing his pants and scraping his shin.

"Shit!" he exclaimed, and she hurried to help him. With a one hand on the window sill and the other on her shoulder, he was pulling himself up when he looked in the window and saw the bottoms of a pair of shoes and the legs of a pair of gray pants.

"Give Kauffman another call," he said. "Tell him he better come down here and bring the coroner. Tell him there's no need to be in a hurry."

* * *

The weather had been cool and temperatures had been dropping to near freezing and below at night, so decomposition was minimal. Landis was in almost as good a shape when they went into the house and checked for a pulse as he was on the afternoon he had last left his office—except for the two gunshot wounds to the chest, of course. Dr. Lana Cunningham, the county coroner, pronounced him dead but refused to hazard a guess about when death had occurred. Sheriff Kauffman pursed his lips, nodded and accepted her refusal but figured the man had died on the day he had left his office. He stood silently by while she and an assistant zipped the deceased up in a body bag and lifted it onto a gurney. They took it out the backdoor because it had been discovered that the steps out there were safer. For several minutes, Kauffman stood staring at the spot where the body had been and looking grim.

A forensics team arrived and, starting in the kitchen, worked for two days, going over the entire house with fine-haired brushes and black dusting powder. They found nothing, no fingerprints, nothing to test for DNA... nothing. The only indications that any person other than the deceased had been there were the second set of tire marks in the grass outside and a few indistinct smudge marks in the years' accumulation of dust on the floor.

By Friday, with no leads of any kind, Sheriff Kauffman was in a foul mood. He already had two open murder cases on the books, and he did not even want to think that this might be another one. Thanksgiving had not been a good day. He had his entire team meet him at the Cooper place late in the afternoon. They all gathered in the kitchen, careful not to disturb the marks on the floor, and brainstormed.

"So help me out here," he said, gesturing toward the spot where Landis's body had lain, his back against the wall. "Anybody have any ideas about what happened here?"

They all turned to look where he was pointing, and everybody except Debora Hicks shook their heads. She stepped forward.

"Whoever killed him followed him in here and overpowered him, very likely using a stun gun."

"And just how would you know that?" Emory Shields scoffed.

"I read the autopsy report," she told him, "and I looked at the photos. There were two burn marks on the left side of his neck like a stun gun would make."

214

"Okay, go on," Kauffman urged.

"These marks right here," she said walking carefully around them and pointing, "are most likely where he fell. And that dark spot, I believe, is blood. The report said his nose was broken."

"Okay, and then what?" Kauffman asked.

"The assailant bound him with something, maybe zip ties, something he could use quickly, and drug him to the wall by the shoulders of his jacket and set him up."

"And just how the hell could you know *that*?" Shields again.

"For one thing, his jacket was still pulled up away from his shoulders like they would be if someone pulled on them, and for another, there were wrinkles in his pants just above the knees and down near his ankles that showed something had been pulled tight around them. Also, there were ligature marks on his wrists."

Shields made a sound that suggested he thought the girl was full of it. "And why would whoever killed him do all of that?"

Hicks shrugged. "I don't know. Maybe Landis had information he wanted."

"What makes you think it was a he?"

"Landis was a good-sized man, two hundred and ten pounds an six ounces, according to the autopsy report. It would take a mighty big woman to drag him around and set him up, so I'm thinking the assailant was a man."

Shields began to feel a little respect for the girl and fell silent.

"So what do you think happened next?" William Buckley asked.

"Well, when he got whatever it was he wanted, I

think he got down on one knee—that's the spot where his knee rested right there," she said pointing, "and he took aim and fired."

"His son was killed up in Blair County just two weeks ago. One shot to the chest. Metallurgy tests show that the bullet fragments likely came from the same box of cartridges in both cases. What do you make of that?" Kauffman asked.

Hicks shook her head. "I don't know what to make of that, Sheriff. I can just read the evidence and tell you what went on here. I have little doubt that the two crimes are related, but we're gonna have to have more information and figure out a motive before we know how or why."

Kauffman smiled and nodded. He had done well in hiring this young lady. Shields? Maybe it was time for the old man to retire. "Well, I think we're done here for now," he said. "Let's lock up and go home. We'll pick it up after the funeral on Monday. You all have a nice weekend."

* * *

The funeral of Eldon Landis was held in the First Methodist Church, as his son's funeral had been, and attendance was slightly better. Most of the seats were occupied by men and women who had known the deceased and didn't like him very well but came to pay their last respects to a fellow member of their church. Janet Staubs arrived late but found a seat next to the aisle in the second pew from the back.

Members of the Sheriff's department, all in civilian clothes, were stationed at intervals along the walls on either side of the congregation. Kauffman's thinking was that whoever took Eldon Landis out might want to be in attendance as a way of giving a final finger to the man he hated enough to kill. If such a person showed up, there might be something about him—his behavior, the expression on his face—that would give him away. Kauffman himself took up a position at right front, and Debora Hicks stood across from him at left front. Buckley and Shields were stationed near the back of the sanctuary and observed the attendees as they entered.

The minister took his place behind the pulpit and asked everyone to stand. Marissa and Dianne Landis, both dry-eyed but looking appropriately grim, appeared in the doorway at the back of the church and made their way forward. They were followed by the brother-in-law pharmacist, his wife and their youngest son. The lot of them took seats in the very first pew, Marissa sitting directly in front of her husband's casket. Her face was flushed, and she didn't look well. Daughter Dianne clung to her arm protectively.

The minister said, "You may be seated," and demonstrated the direction they were to take by raising his arms, hands down, and lowering them slowly. When the members of the Sheriff's Department didn't follow his instructions, he gave them a look that suggested annoyance. He cleared his throat and began the service with the same sentence that has been used to begin such services for decades if not centuries.

"We are gathered here today to pay our last respects to…"

At this point, Sheriff Kauffman and the others tuned him out. He and Debora Hicks scanned the attendees, searching faces for any signs of guilt or glee, men's faces in particular. Buckley and Shields maintained their positions, ready to observe and possibly stop anyone who decided to leave early. Nobody showed any signs of guilt or glee, and nobody left early.

That part of the service eventually arrived where two individuals from Clarkson's Funeral Home came up the aisle, one to hold the flower arrangement that lay atop the casket, the other to open the casket and arrange the quilted cover that would keep the deceased warm for eternity. That job done, they became ushers and beginning with the last pew, urged attendees to rise and go forward for one last look at the man in the casket. Kauffman and Debora stayed at their posts as many of those in attendance stopped to give Marissa and Dianne hugs and offer condolences or to shake hands with her brother and his wife. Their son stood with his eyes fixed on the front of the church, looking like he was wishing he could be any place other than where he was.

When everyone had left except the family, Kauffman gave a signal, and his deputies followed him out onto the street.

"What do you think?" he asked. "Anything?"

All three shook their heads.

"Wasted our time," Shields groused.

"It was worth a shot," Buckley said. "What else did we have to do?"

Debora Hicks smiled solemnly and agreed.

Kauffman looked at his watch. "Well, let's all go over to Hoss's and I'll buy you all a steak on the Department expense account. We'll call it official business. Then we'll decide what to do with the rest of the day.

They had their steaks and managed to get through Monday afternoon without accomplishing much of anything significant. Funerals have a way of dampening enthusiasm and leaving a person feeling lethargic. Kauffman sent everybody home a half hour early, then sat at his desk, glaring at the Landis murder file lying in the center of the blotter on his desk.

* * *

Tuesday would be a day of revelations but no really promising leads. Sheriff Kauffman sent Deputies Buckley and Hicks out to talk to Marissa Landis first thing in the morning. They found her in light blue silk pajamas under a matching robe and with a drink in her hand. It was not yet nine o'clock. She invited them into the den and offered them drinks.

"No, thank you ma'am," Buckley answered for both of them, "we're on duty. We would like to ask you a few questions. See if you might be able to tell us something that would give us a lead we could follow in investigating your husband's murder."

She took a sip from her highball glass, said, "Shoot," and chuckled.

"Can you think of anyone who might have had a reason to want your husband dead?" Hicks asked. Question number one on the list she had written down in the little spiral notebook she took from her pocket.

"Hummm," Marissa Landis mused. "Maybe the husband of one of the women he's been bangin' these past several years. I imagine some of them were probably married, and their husbands wouldn't have taken it too well."

The two deputies looked at one another with raised eyebrows. "Would you happen to know the names of any of these women?" Hicks asked.

By then Marissa Landis had taken a seat in a wingback chair. She rested an elbow on its arm and held her highball glass against her head. "Let's see, who could it be? Maybe Linda Shontz's husband? They broke up and divorced about a year after Eldon sold them a house. But that was what... ten years ago? That would be a long time to carry a grudge, and I think both of them remarried shortly after that. Then there was Darlene Nickoloff. Her husband's a trucker and they're still married, so I don't know if he ever found out. And then there was Judy Baker, and Carol Ann Carter. Everybody always called her by both names—Carol Ann. I never understood why."

She spoke in a matter-of-fact tone, her speech slightly slurred, seemingly unmoved by her husband's infidelities. Buckley looked at Hicks, wondering what she was making of this, but his collogue was busily scribbling down names.

"Your husband must have been quite a..." Buckley started without much thought as to how he would end the sentence.

"Lecher?" Marissa Landis provided. "Whoremonger? Skirt chaser? No, those last two can't be right. Eldon would never have paid for it, and skirts were never a requirement. As long as it was female, he didn't care what it wore. But we digress. Now who was next after Carol Ann? I might be getting them a little out of order. There have been so many of them, and it started so long ago."

"Have there been any more recent ones?"

Buckley asked. "And do you know who they might have been?"

"Oh, there have been recent ones, I'm sure, but it takes the gossip line a little while for names to get to me. You might ask Janet Staubs. She has been closer to him these past few years than I have."

The front door opened and a female voice called, "Hel-low-oo!"

"In here," Marissa shouted. "In the den."

A moment later the female herself arrived and Marissa Landis said, "My daughter Dianne. These fine officers of the law are asking me who might want to kill your father."

"Pleased to meet you," Buckley said rising. His comment was ignored and cut off.

"Good grief, Mom, it's not even noon yet! Why have you started drinking this early in the day?"

"I didn't have to start early because I never stopped last night. But to answer your question: why am I drinking? I'm not sure whether it's to mourn your brother's death or to celebrate your father's. What are you doing here at this time of day? Don't you have a job to go to?"

"Yes, I have a job to go to, but I'm taking time off for awhile." She took the glass from her mother's hand and disappeared into the hallway with it. They heard a clunk as she set it on the counter, and in less than a minute, she was back.

"Do you really have to be here asking questions when she's in this kind of shape?" she asked, looking first at Buckley and then at Hicks.

"We're just trying to get a lead on your father's case," Buckley said, "just looking for someplace to start."

"Well, until she's feeling better, why don't you go look someplace else?"

And thus, the interview ended. The deputies saw themselves out with Dianne Landis's voice providing background.

"Really, Mom! You need to pull it together!"

Marissa Landis muttered something they couldn't make out, and her daughter responded with, "What? Dexter wasn't an only child, Mom! You still have me, remember? I'm your daughter!"

Then the sound of their voices was cut off by the closing door.

Buckley looked at the rust-spotted Dodge Neon parked behind their pickup and remarked, "Looks like the sun shone out of Dexter's butt, and his sister was the sunset kid."

"Maybe more like the midnight kid," Hicks said. "Just one big, happy family."

CHAPTER EIGHTEEN

From the Landis place, they swung by the office of Landis Realty. Janet Staubs was sitting behind her desk when they walked in, and she rose to greet them with a look of hope on her face.

"You have some news?" she asked. "Do you know who killed Eldon?"

"No, I'm sorry," Buckley told her. "We just came from having a chat with his wife, and she thought you might be able to help us out."

"I don't see how," she said, sitting back down. "I think I've told you all I know."

"Well, maybe there's something you don't know you know," Buckley said, a line he had picked up from television shows.

Janet looked confused.

"Something you don't realize you know," Hicks suggested.

"Like what?"

"Like someone your boss might have had an affair with and her husband found out."

Janet's face turned red and she was hesitant to answer. "I'm afraid I wasn't very honest with you, the last time you were here. I mean when you asked if I knew of anyone he might have gone off with for, what

223

did you call it, an extended stay? I just didn't want to speak ill of the dead."

"Don't think of it as speaking ill of the dead," Hicks said and offered a smile. "Think of it as an effort to help find his killer."

Marissa Landis had been right about Janet knowing more about her husband's recent conquests. When she finally started talking, she had a lot to say. In the first five minutes and after not much thought, she gave them the names of three couples, husbands' names included, the most recent clients to whom Eldon Landis had sold properties. At the end of fifteen minutes, Hicks had a list of ten more possibilities jotted down in her spiral notebook.

"I'm not saying he... that he *screwed* all of them," Janet clarified and blushed at using the word. "I'm just saying he sold them properties, and right after he closed the deal with each of them, he spent a lot of time out of the office. I hope nobody gets in trouble because of me."

"We will be discreet," Hicks promised, "and your name will never be mentioned."

They thanked her and headed back to the Department. Meagan Price, Kauffman's secretary, told them he wasn't busy and sent them on into his office

"That's it?" Sheriff Kauffman asked when they told him what they had learned. "Names of people he sold houses to, women he *might* have had affairs with? That's not much to go on."

"It's more than we had when we walked out of here earlier," Buckley said.

Kauffman stared at the wall and gave it some thought. "I guess you're right. You two got the names, so you track them down. But do it discreetly. Try not to destroy any marriages. How many names did you say the two of them gave you?"

Hicks checked her notebook. "Fourteen altogether."

"Well, talk to Meagan and get her to help you with addresses. She's pretty good with computers," Kauffman said. "I imagine it's gonna take you several days. Do what you can today, but keep at it until we find something better."

* * *

They sat with Meagan Price while she rattled keys and found them addresses and didn't get back out on the street until noon. Of the fourteen names, they had addresses for only seven, and Meagan thought that a Leslie Glaiser worked as an RN at the hospital.

"Maybe some of the women you visit with will know some of the others and help you out," Meagan suggested, and as it turned out, she was right.

Carol Ann Carter no longer lived in the home Eldon Landis had sold her, but she had been a friend of Linda Shontz's first husband, and Linda could tell them that Carol Ann had died of cancer some five years ago. She denied emphatically that she had ever had an affair with Eldon Landis or anybody else. The man to whom she was married now would have no reason to or inclination to harm anyone, and where her previous husband was now she didn't know and didn't care to know. *He* had been the one who was unfaith. She was just glad that they had had no children, nothing to keep them tied together for life.

225

Darlene Nickoloff still occupied the three-bedroom, two-story house Landis had sold to her and her husband Richard, and her husband was still a long-haul trucker. She was a shapely brunet, average in height with a heart-shaped face.

Introductions made and the reason for their visit explained, Deputy Hicks asked "Would Richard have any reason to want to do Eldon Landis harm?"

"Why, no," Darlene said, a little too quickly and her face got red.

"We don't mean to embarrass you," Buckley assured her. "Nothing that passes between the three of us will ever be made public. You must have seen on the news that Landis was murdered, and we're just trying to get a lead on who did it."

Darlene sighed. "It was a long time ago and it was stupid. Richard never found out. But even if he had, he wouldn't have killed anybody. And it couldn't have been Richard because it said on the news they found him on the fourteenth, and Richard was gone for two weeks right about then, all the way out to the west coast. And that's all I'm gonna say."

They asked her if she knew any of the names on the list and what their addresses might be. She glanced at it and her face got red again, but she shook her head and refused to say anything more. They thanked her for her time, and she closed the door practically on their heels.

Back in their vehicle, Hicks sucked in a lungful of air and blew it out through puffed cheeks. "Can you saw awkward? One who did and one who didn't, three down and eleven more to go."

"And that's if nobody gives us additional

possibilities," Buckley said. "And I'm already getting the feeling we're just chasing our tails."

"Me, too, but let's keep at it. Head for J.C. Blair Memorial. Maybe we'll catch Leslie Glasier on duty."

She was on duty, and she made no bones about what she first referred to as her dalliance with Landis. A petite blonde that brought to Buckley's mind the dingbat blonde from some television comedy, she stood behind a white counter in blue scrubs and smiled when Hicks asked about it. "It didn't last all that long. We had a fling, but it ended long ago."

"Was your husband aware of your... uh, dalliance with Landis?" Buckley asked.

"I think so, but he was having a little fling of his own, so I'm not sure."

Debora Hicks' eyes got wide and her forehead furrowed. "So he, your husband I mean, wouldn't have any reason to harm Eldon Landis?"

Leslie shook her head. "He sold us a house. He came around... hummm... three, maybe four times, and I told him that was enough. He was good, but I get bored easy."

"Thank you for your time," Buckley said, turned and headed for the elevator.

Hicks realized he was gone and almost ran to catch up. "Let's do one... maybe two more and quit for the day. This is giving me the creeps. Who's next?"

She crossed off Leslie's name in her notebook. "Rayanne Gilbert," she said. "Husband's name Jeremy. The address is a rural route number on Highway 4005 up toward Alexandria."

"How far?" Buckley asked.

"We won't know 'til we get there."

They discovered it was about three miles out of the borough limits of Huntingdon, and the house was a well-maintained two-story painted the same shade of yellow as train stations, the window and door trim in forest green. The front porch ran almost the full width of the house, and the roof a bronze sheet metal.

They had rung the doorbell and turned to admire the landscaping when the door opened.

"Rayanne Gilbert?" Buckley asked the shapely young blonde who stood behind the storm door, a frown of curiosity on an absolutely beautiful face.

She swung the door open. "No, Sandra Bowman."

Buckley stood staring at her, his lower jaw hanging.

"We were hoping to speak with Rayanne Gilbert," Hicks said. "Do you have any idea where we might find her?"

"The Gilberts haven't lived here in seven or eight years," Sandra told them. "We've been told they moved to Montana."

"You didn't know them?" Hicks asked.

"No, they were gone and the house had been sitting empty for several years before my husband and I bought it. Can I ask what this is about?"

"We're just..." Buckley started.

"Running down leads in a murder case," Hicks finished for him. "Thank you for your time." Then she took him by the arm and turned him toward the steps. Back in their vehicle, she pulled a tissue out of her coat pocket and handed it to him.

"What's this for?" he asked.

"I thought you needed something to wipe the drool off your chin."

228

"What?! I didn't…"

"No, but you were thinking about it. Let's go home and you can tell your wife about the lovely day we had."

They were almost back to town when he finally found his voice again. "Why would someone wanna move to Montana? They get snow butt deep to a tall Swede up there. The temperature drops so far it blows the bottoms out of thermometers."

"Who knows and who cares," Hicks said. "We can cross them off our list. I think we might be able to finish it in a couple of days at the rate we're going."

But Wednesday and Thursday got them no farther toward a promising lead than Monday afternoon had. They learned that another couple had moved to Georgia, close enough for a man to come back for revenge, Hicks thought, and would have to be checked out. Other than that, things went about the same. Some of the women on Hicks' list admitted reluctantly to having a relationship with Eldon Landis. Others denied it emphatically, but with a blush creeping up their cheeks, and hurried them out the door. Still others calmly said no, they had never "slept with" anybody but their husbands. All of them felt certain that their husbands would never harm anyone.

The last woman they interviewed on Wednesday afternoon used the "slept with" phrase, and once on the street, Buckley chuckled.

"She never 'slept with' anybody other than her husband," he said, using finger quotes. "I was tempted to tell her we weren't talking about sleeping."

Hicks laughed. "Well, don't you 'sleep with' your wife?" she asked and copied his finger movements.

229

"Yeah," he grinned, "It's usually 'after.' Know what I mean?"

Hicks blushed and told he was bad. Then the two of them sobered up.

"So now we go back and tell Kauffman we used up two and a half days, and we've learned nothing. We're no closer to finding out who killed Landis than we were the day we found him," Hicks said.

"That's the way it goes sometimes," Buckley said, then started the pickup and repeated, "That's the way it goes."

* * *

Charles Bond, Chief of Police in Mount Union, poked his head in the door and asked, "Anybody got time for a visitor?"

Meagan Price looked up and let out a little squeal. "Someone here always has time for a visit from you," she said, pushing her chair back and rounding her desk to give him a hug. "We haven't seen you in awhile. Been busy?"

"Not so much, but I had papers to bring up to the courthouse today. Thought I'd stop by and see how things are going."

"He's in there talking with Billy Buckley and that new girl, Debora Hicks. They've been in there awhile, so they should be out soon."

She had hardly finished her sentence when the door to Kauffman's office opened and the two of them walked out looking none too happy. Buckley's face brightened a bit at the sight of Bond.

"Hey, Chief, nice to see you! Everything okay

down there in Mount Union, or do we need to come down and give you a hand." He offered his hand for a shake and Bond took it.

"This your new partner?" he asked.

"Yeah, meet Debora Hicks," Buckley said. "We've been out pounding the pavement, and we came up with nothing but tired feet.

Hicks smiled and shook Bond's hand, and she and Buckley left.

"You can go in now, but I don't think you're gonna find him in a very good mood," Meagan said. "I'll let him tell you why."

Kauffman was sitting behind his desk glaring at the same case folder that had been keeping his attention for days. He looked up when Bond walked in, but the scowl on his face did not quite morph into a smile.

"Have a seat," he said, nodding at the visitors' chairs that sat against the wall opposite his desk.

Bond sat down. "What's happening?"

Kauffman raised his eyes to look at the wall and blinked several times before he spoke. "You remember the Johnson and Collins cases from two years ago, the ones we never closed? Well, it looks like we've got another one."

Bond frowned. "Maybe you're trying to rush things. Contrary to what they say on detective shows, few cases are solved in the first forty-eight hours."

"We're way past forty-eight hours with this one. It's been eight days since we found Eldon Landis's body. So that's what, a hundred and ninety hours, give or take? And we've got nothing."

"Exactly how much nothing?" Bond asked.

231

"You remember the nothing we had with the two cases I mentioned a minute ago? Well, we've got more nothing with this one than we had with those."

"Do you want to bring Gray in again?" Gray Ballard had been a homicide detective in Harrisburg until he was forced into retirement when his partner shot him in the knee. Gray had an uncanny ability to see what others missed, and had been asked to help out with the cases Kauffman had just mentioned. His input had helped them with some aspects of the two cases, but both of them had turned cold and were still unsolved.

"There wouldn't be any point," Kauffman said. "We already know all there is to know about what we know. We just don't know all that much."

"Maybe fresh eyes would see something," Bond suggested.

"Fresh eyes lookin' at nothing see the same thing tired eyes see. If and when we find *some*thing we can't figure out, I'll be glad to bring Gray in."

"Mind if I take a look?" Bond asked.

Kauffman picked up the case file and tossed it to him. He sat reading for all of three or four minutes and tossed it back on the desk.

"I see what you mean," he said. "No fingerprints left at the scene. No prints of any kind. In a vacant house out in the country, so no witnesses. His son was killed up in Altoona about a week before you found him, wasn't he? Seems to me like the two cases have to be connected."

"I won't argue with you there. I've been sharing information with the sheriff up there, and the only connection we've made so far is that, according to a metallurgy test, the ammo used came from the same box. If there's any other connection, I don't have the foggiest idea what it is. They do have one piece of evidence, though, a plastic card case, like some women carry their credit cards and driver's license in, and sometimes their change. It had a great surface for fingerprints, and they found two sets. Neither of them was in the system. The young woman who found the body had been spending some nights with the victim, I understand, but she insisted the case wasn't hers."

"Do you think the two of them might have been professional hits? That maybe they were mixed up in some kind of drug deal and it went sideways on them?"

Kauffman shook his head. "There's no evidence that the two of them were working together on anything. The son Dexter was a pharmacist at a Walgreens up there in Altoona. Eldon Landis was selling real estate from his office here in Huntingdon and getting as much on the side as he could, if you know what I mean. We thought he might have been killed by a jealous husband, but two of my deputies looked into that and couldn't find anything.

"As for professional hits, I would think a professional would have tracked each of them down and put a bullet in the back of their heads, and they would never have seen it coming. This seems more personal, like whoever did it wanted them to know why they were getting it and wanted them to see it coming."

"Did his wife know what he was doing?" Bond asked.

Kauffman nodded. "She's the one that put us onto

the possibility of a jealous husband. Seems like she knew about his extracurricular activities for years and just chose to ignore it."

The two of them fell silent for several minutes, each thinking his own thoughts, then Kauffman asked, "What's going on down in your area of the world?"

"Oh, the usual, a couple of homes burglarized while the residents were gone, shots fired down on The Flat. One person called it in; nobody else heard or saw anything. We made a couple of arrests for possession, small-time dealers. That's why I'm up here filing paperwork. I'd like to catch the big guy or guys that are bring the stuff in, but I've got what you've got—nothing."

Kauffman's eyes went back to the folder lying on his desk. Bond sat frowning at the floor for a minute or two, then he roused.

"Well, I'll leave you with it then. Let me know if I can help with anything, or if Gray can."

Kauffman raised a hand in goodbye, and Bond stood and left.

CHAPTER NINETEEN

November turned into December, and most of the citizens of Huntingdon County, like everybody else across the nation, scurried around buying gifts in anticipation of Christmas. On the fifteenth day of the month, Rosalynn June Holder did some shopping of her own. At around four-thirty in the afternoon, the sky was overcast and the street lights had already come on when she entered Hillman's Jewelry on Washington Street. The weather was seasonably cold, and a lot of folks were hoping for a white Christmas, so she was wearing boots and a burgundy parka with a fur-lined hood. The bell above his door jingled, Delbert Hillman looked up from were he stood behind a display case of diamond rings, recognized her and spoke.

"Well, hello, Rosalynn. It's nice to see you. How have you been?"

She walked toward him without saying a word, pulled what looked like a pillowcase out from under her parka and a hammerless thirty-eight pistol out of a pocket. She threw the pillowcase at him and he caught it to keep from getting hit in the face. He frowned at it and then looked up at her.

"Fill it up," she said, and aimed the pistol at his chest."

"Now, Rosalynn," he said, "what are you doing?"

She raised the pistol and brought the butt of it down on the top of the display case. Glass shards flew everywhere, and she aimed her weapon at his face.

"Do what I tell you and save yourself the cost of another display case," she said. "Fill it up."

"Okay," he said, more angry than scared, and began picking up the rings that were on display and now easily accessible. Careful to shake out any glass particles, he closed the little velvet boxes and dropped them into the bag she had provided. When the case was empty, she told him to get the key and open the one next to it.

"Now, Ms Holder, this isn't like you. What's going on?" he asked.

Rosalynn raised her arm over another display case threateningly and gave him the meanest look she could muster.

"Okay! Okay!" Delbert said and dug a key ring out of his pocket.

The contents of the second display case went into the bag, and she held out her hand for it. He gave it to her and then backed up against the wall, his arms spread wide in surrender. Rosalynn kept her eyes on him and backed away slowly. At the door, she shoved the pistol into her pocket, opened the door and stepped out and walked calmly away.

Delbert stood where he was in a kind of paralyzed state. Did what had just happened really happen? Coming out of his trance, he rushed to the window and looked in the direction Rosalynn had gone. She was nowhere in sight. He scratched his head and sighed and went to his phone.

A squad car pulled to the curb in front of the store minutes later, two uniformed officer got out and entered.

"You were robbed?" one of them asked.

"That's why I called," Delbert said. "She came in here waving a gun around and gave me a pillowcase and told me to fill it."

"Can you describe this individual?" the second officer asked, pulling a notebook from a coat pocket.

"I can do better than that," Delbert told him. "I can tell you who it was."

Both of them looked at him like he had sprouted horns.

"You can? Who was it?" the first officer asked.

"Her name is Rosalynn Holder."

"The school teacher?! My son was in her class a couple of years ago!"

The second officer took a pen from his pocket. "Tell us in detail what happened."

By the time Delbert had gone through his story and the man had the details written down, it was well past closing time. He locked the door behind them and watched in a daze as the squad car pulled away.

* * *

They got Rosalynn's address from the man who had been her boss, the principal of the school where she had taught. When they arrived at her house, lights were on in the living room and kitchen, but no one responded to their knock.

"It's the police!" one of them shouted. "Open up!"

He was rearing back to kick the door in when his partner tried the knob and the door swung silently open. Both of them drew their weapons, crouched and slithered inside like two television cops expecting a hail of lead. Rosalynn Holder was sitting in her recliner, the foot rest up, still in her parka and boots, waiting for them. When they ordered her to stand up, she struggled to do so, and one of them had to help her out of the chair. He handcuffed her, and she was led silently to the squad car and locked into the back seat.

Back in the house, they discovered the pillowcase Delbert Hillman had filled with jewelry from his display cases. It was lying on the kitchen table. The jewelry it contained would eventually be assessed and discovered to be worth tens of thousands of dollars. Rosalynn would be charged with grand larceny. Lying beside the bag of jewelry was a hammerless thirty-eight pistol, pink and chrome with a black rubber grip. When it was examined later, they would discover that it needed to be cleaned and that there were five empty cartridges in the cylinder. Sitting beside the pillowcase and pistol was a box of frangible ammo with five cartridges missing. Metallurgy tests would eventually prove that the bullets that killed Dexter and Eldon Landis came from that box.

The case seemed like a slam dunk. They had found and apprehended their thief, and in due time, she was taken back to the station, fingerprinted and shown to a cell. Throughout the entire process, Rosalynn never said a word.

She had timed her arrest and incarceration perfectly, so late in the day and in the week, after quitting time for weekday nine-to-fivers, that getting a lawyer to come to the station was unlikely. And the probability of getting one there was made even less likely by the fact that the individual who need one refused to say which law firm she used. In fact, Rosalynn refused to say anything and declined to make the one phone call that was guaranteed to her by law. Following a couple of hours of questioning, which got her interrogators nothing except frustration, they led her back to her cell.

They took her breakfast on Saturday morning and slid it through the space in the cell door meant for that purpose. She was lying on her back on the cot and covered to the armpits with the single blanket provided, staring at the ceiling.

"Eat up!" the officer said and left.

When he came back for the tray an hour later, the food had not been touched. Lunch and supper were replays of the morning. Rosalynn ate nothing all day and, so far as anyone could tell, never left the cot.

"You think she needs medical attention?" one of the officers asked.

"She's just being stubborn," his superior said. "She'll eat when she gets hungry,"

On Sunday morning, a different officer brought her breakfast, a young man who had been one of her students. Rosalynn was standing at the bars.

"Mrs. Holder? Are you okay?" he asked.

For answer, she held out her left hand, palm up, and with her right hand, appeared to be writing on it with and invisible pen. The officer watched her for several minutes before the light dawned.

"You want to write something?"

Rosalynn nodded.

"I'll be right back," he said and left the cell area.

In less than a minute, he was back with a pen and a notepad. He handed them to her through the bars and watched as she wrote a couple of lines and handed both items back. Then she turned and went back to the cot. The young man watched as she lay down and covered herself again. Then he looked down at the notepad and saw that she had written a man's name: Murray L. McCartney. Below the name was a local phone number.

* * *

In his apartment in State College on Wednesday morning, Daniel was in a quandary. Given what he had done (*There's no need for either of us to say it out loud*), he asked himself, would it be ethical for him to ever practice law? He had spent most of the last ten years preparing himself toward that end, and as he had told his father, he had done so because he wanted to help others, especially people like Rose Lynn Holder who didn't have the ability to help themselves. Before he had gotten the call from Rosalynn, he had applied to several law firms, and in the past couple of weeks, he had gotten calls from some of them asking him to come in for an interview. He had put them all off because he wasn't sure he felt worthy. It would be years before the irony of even asking himself the question finally dawned on him, and he realized that ethics went out the window when he went to San Antonio and took the first step toward evening out the numbers for Rosalynn.

But then, if he didn't accept a position and practice law, how would he earn a living? Rent and bills had to be paid. He had to eat. Go back to the job he had when he first enrolled in college—flipping burgers? To say that thought was not appealing would be the understatement of the century. But that and law were the only two skills he had.

He had learned to live frugally in college and law school, and much of the five thousand Rosalynn had given him the last time he saw her was still in his account. He was trying to figure out how long he could make it last when his phone rang yet again. Another prospective employer, he thought, and was about to let the thing ring until whoever it was gave up when he changed his mind and answered it.

"Hello?"

"Daniel Miller?" a male voice asked.

"Yes, this is Daniel Miller."

"Daniel L. Miller?" the man asked. "And your mother's maiden name?"

"Lamont, just like my middle name. Look, if this is about a job offer, I need to do some thinking before I come in for an interview. I'm not sure…"

"This is not about a job offer, Mr. Miller," the man interrupted. "This is about the last will and testament of Rosalynn June Holder."

"What?! Who is this? Who am I speaking to?"

"Murray J. McCartney. I am... was Mrs. Holder's attorney."

"Was?! You mean she's dead?!"

"I'm sorry I have to be the one to inform you, and over the phone yet, but yes. Mrs. Holder has passed, and she left explicit instructions, not the first of which was to call you. Could you possibly come to my office this afternoon?"

Daniel was struck speechless for several moments.

"Mister Miller? Are you there?"

"Yes. Yes, I'm here."

"Would it be possible for you to come to my office this afternoon? There are some things we need to discuss, you and I. If your schedule doesn't allow it, we could put it off until another day?"

"No," Daniel said when he found his voice again. "I have nothing pressing. Just tell me where your office is and I'll be there."

McCartney gave him an address in Huntingdon, thirty-some miles away. Daniel had made the trip hundreds of times going down to visit Rosalynn, and he knew the shortest and fastest route. He looked at the clock on his microwave and saw that it was a little after eleven.

"I can be there by one, no problem."

"Excellent," McCartney said. "I usually have a sandwich for lunch right here in my office, so if you get here a little early, just come on in."

Daniel hung up without saying anything more. He went looking for the keys to his Impala, realized that they were in the pocket of the kakis he had worn the day before and that he was still in his pajamas and tee-shirt. Put on fresh pants and dress shirt or wear the ones his keys and wallet and change were in? He couldn't seem to get his mind to work. Rosalynn dead? How? Why?

Yesterday's clothes were good enough, he decided. Dressed and headed for Huntingdon, he drove in a daze. Why hadn't she said something? Was her health that bad? Did she know how long she had, and was that why she wanted things "dealt with"?

The comments she made about television commercials that advertised drugs came back to mind. *Any reasonably intelligent person would realize they might as well forego treatment and let their ailment run its course. Use whatever time they have left to get their affairs in order.* And when she wanted to put off taking care of Number Four. *It would maybe give the Landis family time to get past their grief. I think there's time for that.* And when he asked her about wearing pajamas to the breakfast table, she had said that life was too short to worry about inconsequentialities. He thought about how she had struggled to raise the footrest on her recliner and how she had left it up. Why hadn't he picked up on any of that? He asked himself these and a dozen more questions, castigated himself for being so unperceptive.

He passed the Huntingdon city limit sign and realized he had arrived at his destination and could not remember seeing the landmarks he usually used to mark his progress. The narrow streets of Huntingdon were crowded, so he was forced to pay attention to his driving, and he found the office of Murray J. McCartney with little trouble. It was in and old storefront building, between Washington and Mifflin Streets. Large display windows on either side of the inset door were closed off with Venetian blinds, their slats in bad need of cleaning. The exterior woodwork was rough and had been painted a myriad of times. Currently, it was a dark green. The only thing that indicated it was an office of any kind was a small sign that read Attorney at Law—white with black lettering—that was hung in such a way that anyone passing on the street could see it.

There were no parking spaces in front of the

place, so Daniel took his Impala, to the lot on Penn, and left it there. He walked back, the hood of his parka up and head bowed against the December wind. The building looked a little seedy, he thought, and was surprised to find gold gilt lettering on the window of the door that announced: Murray J. McCartney Attorney at Law. When he stepped inside, it was Murray J. himself that rose from behind a desk in what Daniel thought would have been a room occupied by a secretary or receptionist.

"Murray McCartney," he said, rounding the desk and offering a hand. How can I help you, sir?"

He was a man in his mid-forties, Daniel guessed. His face was clean-shaven and free of wrinkles, but much of his full head of hair had already turned white. His suit looked like it had come from Goodwill but appeared to have been freshly pressed. His smile seemed genuine and his handshake was firm.

"Daniel Miller. You called me earlier."

"You came from State College? My, but you made good time. Please, have a seat," he said and indicated one of the scarred wooden armchairs that faced his desk.

Daniel sat down and pushed his hood back.

"I'm sure you have a lot of questions," Murray said, "but before you ask them, let me explain how I came to know Rosalynn Holder and what she retained me to do. Mrs. Holder came to me sometime around the last of November. I don't remember the exact date, but I could find it if you would like me to."

He had already begun pawing through the papers on his desk when Daniel told him it wasn't necessary.

"Okay, so sometime around the last of November,

244

she came in with a large envelope. She told me that she didn't have much time left and asked me to hold it until after her death, at which time I was to contact you."

"What caused her death, and where is her body now?" Daniel interrupted.

Murray held up a finger. "As per her instructions, when I was notified of her death and before I called you, I was to have her body cremated, her ashes put in an urn and buried on the grave of her daughter Rose Lynn Holder. That has been done. As to her cause of death, she was suffering from pancreatic cancer. It was already stage four when she was diagnosed she told me, and she refused treatment. It would have been a waste of time and money she said, and she had put what little time she had left to good use. I asked her doing what, and she told me rather quickly that I did not need to know."

If Daniel had not been in such a stunned state, he might have smiled. He had certainly experienced that side of Rosalynn's controlling personality. Murray stopped speaking, and he let the silence build. Vehicles passed on the street outside. A woman yelled at someone not to cross the street until she got there.

"She didn't want me to see her again?" Daniel asked. "Why?"

"She didn't share that with me."

"Well, where was she when the end came? Can you tell me that? Did she suffer? Was she in the hospital?"

Murray's expression was grim. "I don't think she suffered, no. As to where she was, I had to request the mortuary to pick her up at the city jail."

"The city jail!" Daniel exploded. "What the hell was she doing in the city jail?"

"I'm told she robbed Delbert Hillman's jewelry store, and the charge was armed robbery."

Daniel looked at the man like he had lost his mind. Rosalynn Holder committing armed robbery? The very idea was absurd. What could she hope to gain from...? His mind stopped the question mid-sentence. Fingerprints. Hers had to be on the lipstick, the compact and the credit card case he had left at the scenes. She wanted to make sure they were in the system—or would get there eventually. What was it she had said? She *would see that there was enough misdirection.* Her fingerprints on items found at crime scenes where she had never been. It would add an element of confusion to the investigations and draw suspicion away from him. He sat staring at the wall beyond Murray McCartney's shoulder, nodding his head.

"Do you know what she might have been up to?" the man asked.

Daniel pulled his thoughts back to the present, looked him in the face and shook his head. "I have suspicions but like you, I don't really know."

"Do you have any other questions?"

"Not at the moment," Daniel said. "Maybe when I've seen what's in the envelope she left for me."

McCartney nodded, got up and went to a filing cabinet, OD green Army surplus. From the top drawer, he took a nine by twelve yellow envelope and held it to his chest.

"Her final instruction to me was to have you read the contents of this envelope before you left my office.

246

Do you mind? I'll just sit at my desk and have the sandwich I brought for my lunch."

Daniel nodded and held out his hand. McCartney handed over the envelope and took his seat.

"Was it sealed when she brought it to you?" Daniel asked.

Murray stopped with his sandwich halfway to his mouth. "No, she had me make out a will for her, and I called a friend to come in and notarize it. She put the will in it and then sealed it in my presence."

Daniel undid the metal clasp and ran a finger under the flap. He pulled out a thin stack of papers and laid them atop the envelope on his lap. The top sheet was the will McCartney had just mentioned. It was a surprise and surprisingly brief: All my worldly property, goods and possessions I hereby bequeath to Daniel Lamont Miller.

"She left me everything?!" he asked.

"Yes, she did," McCartney said. "She said you were her last remaining friend in the world—those were her exact words, 'last remaining friend'—and that at one time she had hopes that you would be the father of her grandchildren someday. So whatever she had, it's all yours now."

The next surprise was titles to not one but two Honda Accords, both two thousand-ten models. What was she doing with two vehicles? He had only ever seen and driven one, so where was the second one? A possible answer came from the tag on a key that had gotten stuck between the papers. It was to a storage unit. He put it aside and would think about why she had two of them later.

He shuffled the titles to the bottom of the pile and

found himself looking at a letter that Rosalynn had handwritten. His hands shook as he picked it up and read:

To my dearest Daniel,

It goes without saying that when you read this, I will be gone, but there I've said it anyway. I could never thank you enough for what you did for Rose and for me. Please believe me when I tell you that because of what you did, justice has been served. Don't ever doubt that your actions were right and necessary and that the world is a better place because you took them.

If things had gone differently, we would have been family, you and Rose and I. Fate was cruel to us, but we made the best of it, and you still survive. Don't waste your years lamenting what might have been. Find yourself another Rose, raise a family and be happy.

You will find in this envelope keys and the means to get you started. Keep of it what you will and sell or donate to charity whatever doesn't suit you. I think you will find it sufficient to provide for your needs and to launch the next chapter of your life.

One item you will find is the key to a safety deposit box at Community State Bank. In it, you will find the deed to the house and other papers you might need.

There are also a checking account and a

savings account in my name there. I urge you to retain the services of Murray McCartney in dealing with the legal problems that will inevitably crop up. I believe he is an honest man.

Do not keep this letter. When you finish reading it, take it into the restroom and burn it with the lighter provided. What I have written in the first several paragraphs could be incriminating.

Use the birth certificate and other papers included if you want to or feel you need to. You will always be Daniel Lamont Miller to me. Always remember me and our darling Rose.

Love forever,
Rosalynn June Holder

Daniel bowed his head and took a moment to get his emotions under control. Where would he ever find another Rose? Where would he ever find another Rosalynn?

The birth certificate she referred to in the letter turned out to be in the name of William D. Perkins. He looked it over carefully and saw that it was in every way like his legitimate birth certificate, including the date and the place where he was born. The only change was that now his parents' last name was Perkins, also.

The last item in the pile was a sheet of crisp, white stationary with the letterhead of a bank in the Cayman Islands. He scanned it casually until he came to a number at the bottom that represented the balance of an account that had been taken out in his name. The number of digits it contained made his eyes pop.

"Whoa!" he exclaimed aloud. "Where did she get this kind of money?"

"She won the lottery," Murray McCartney said calmly.

Daniel looked up at the man

"And you're just now telling me?" Shock made his expression and his tone angry.

"As per her instructions," Murray answered. "She said you were to open the envelope and examine its contents in my presence, but I wasn't to say anything until you had done so or unless you asked a question. And the one you just now asked is one she expected."

Daniel turned his attention back to the paper. He counted the digits in the number just to be certain he wasn't misreading it. There were eight of them to the left of the decimal point. When the shock and numbness wore off, he realized that the question of how he would earn a living if he didn't practice law had been answered. He was financially free to do whatever he wanted. Whether to practice law or not to practice law was no longer a pressing question.

He pulled the envelope out from under the stack and poured the remaining contents into the palm of his hand. Only three items fell out: the flat silver key for a safety deposit box, a ring with two keys to the house he had just inherited and a blue Bic cigarette lighter. He smiled to himself when he saw the lighter. Blue had been Rose's favorite color. There was nothing random about even the smallest details of Rosalynn's plans.

"Can I use your restroom?" he asked.

Murray nodded and pointed to the door in the back wall. "Right through there and to your left."

He never made it to the restroom. Once through the door, he discovered that Murray's office space was the only modern improvement in the place. The back room had a twelve foot ceiling that was covered in ancient stamped tin with layers of white paint flaking from in, and it was not heated. Stacks of boxes and items of every description were piled everywhere. He laid the envelope and papers on one of the stacks, stood in the space between them and the bathroom door and held the flame from the lighter to the corner of Rosalynn's letter. It blackened and curled and part of it fell away. When there was only the corner he held remaining, he laid it on the floor and watched as the last of it turned into gray ash. He tapped it with the toe of his shoe, leaned down and blew on it, and it scattered and became a part of the ancient dust that covered the floor's filthy black and white tile.

When he got back to the chair where he had been sitting, McCartney looked up and smiled as if he knew what had just happened. "So, it's done."

Daniel nodded and sat there silently for more than a minute. Then he said, "She said that I should retain your services, let you deal with any legal problems I run into. Would you be willing to do that?"

"I most certainly would," McCartney smiled.

They haggled a bit until both of them agreed on a yearly fee. Then McCartney gave him advice on how to deal with the Grand Cayman account and how to go about getting access to the safety deposit box and the accounts in the bank right there in town.

"Whatever you need me to do," he said, "just give me a call."

Out on the street after a firm handshake, Daniel inhaled deeply. Did the world seem a little brighter, a little warmer after his visit with Murray J. McCartney? Maybe it was because the sun had come out and the wind had died down. Or maybe it was because he was free to go wherever he wanted, to do whatever he pleased. The only thing that threatened to cast a pall over his spirit was the knowledge that Rose and Rosalynn were gone.

CHAPTER TWENTY

"Unka Cha-wee! Unka Cha-wee!" Three-year-old Clara Ann Ballard came running and threw herself at Charles Bond. He picked her up and tossed her into the air and then settled her on his arm.

"Look at you!" he said and poked her gently in the ribs. "You are twice as big as you were the last time I was here, and that was only last month!"

The little girl giggled and squirmed away from his finger.

Daddy Gray heard the comment where he was sitting in the living room and was smiling like the proud father he was when Bond carried his daughter through the archway. A six-foot, artificial Christmas tree stood at the front window, lights twinkling and multicolored ornaments gleaming. Flames leapt in the fireplace, and the room was toasty.

"She's growing like a weed," Gray said, standing and relieving Bond of his burden so the man could take off his heavy winter coat.

"Not a weed," Bond said, "more like a flower."

"Did you tell Uncle Charlie Merry Christmas?"

Clara Ann ducked her head, uncomfortable with the new words. "Ma-wee Cwis-mas."

Gray set his daughter back on her feet. "Now why

don't you run into the kitchen and ask your mother how long it will be until dinner is ready while I hang up Uncle Charlie's coat?"

Clara Ann took her father at his word and took off running. Gray was just resuming his seat on the sofa when she reappeared in the archway to the dining room. She held up one little hand, fingers spread and said, "fi'e minutes" and was gone before he could thank her.

Bond had taken a seat in the recliner that was angled in the corner of the room and was holding out his hands toward the fireplace.

"So, what have you been up to?" Gray asked.

Bond smiled. "The same ole same old. Things have been pretty quiet, law enforcement-wise. I guess maybe people have been two busy getting ready for the holidays to think about breaking the law. 'Tis the season to be jolly and all of that."

"It comes in waves sometimes, doesn't it? When I was on the force in Harrisburg, we would have a lull in homicides, and then there would be an up-tick. We would have more cases on our hands than we had detectives to handle."

Before either of them could say anything more, Anna called from the kitchen. "Gray, if you would come in her and carry the turkey to the table, everything would be ready."

Everything on the table, the four of them took their usual seats—Gray at the head of the table, Anna to his left and Clara Ann in a youth chair to his right, Bond at the end opposite Gray. After a brief blessing, Gray carved the turkey and helped Clara Ann's plate. Then plates and bowls were passed from hand to hand and portions taken.

"Did I hear you say things have been quiet?" Anna asked when everybody had settled down to eat.

"Yes, you did," Bond answered. "But I don't imagine it will last."

"I was surprised to see Richard Hogan's obituary in the paper last week," she said. "I didn't think he was that old."

Hogan, known none too affectionately as "Bulk Hogan," had been the Chief of Police when Gray first moved back to Mount Union. He had arrested Gray for a murder that Gray had eventually helped to solve.

"He wasn't that old," Bond said, "but he was that overweight, and he had a thing about doctors. In the years I worked under him, I never knew him to go to one."

"And that red face of his was likely a symptom of high blood pressure," Gray suggested, remembering the man's temper. "The paper didn't say, but I imagine it was a heart attack."

Clara Ann concentrated on her food and ignored the adult conversation.

"Do you have any idea how the Landis case is progressing?" Gray asked.

Bond nodded. "I was up there a week ago and stopped in to see Sheriff Kauffman. He says they've still got nothing. It looks like whoever did it was very careful and made no mistakes."

"Another one for the cold case file?" Gray suggested.

"It looks that way."

"And his son was killed up in Altoona. What do you hear about that?" Anna asked.

"Same thing. Similar situation and more than likely

the same assailant, but other than that, nothing to connect the two yet, as far as I know. In both cases, the killer left nothing—no prints of any kind, no DNA."

"Well, the best detectives in the world don't close them all," Gray commented.

Bond frowned and nodded in agreement.

* * *

"So, now that we've all got this Christmas stuff out of the way and had time to think about it, have any of you come up with an idea on how to proceed with the Landis case?" Sheriff Kauffman asked.

Meagan Price had gathered Deputies Shields, Buckley and Hicks in the conference room at the boss's request. Now she waited with her notepad and pen to take notes of the meeting.

"I was thinking maybe, since he had no respect for the marriages of his clients," Buckley said, "maybe he didn't have any respect for other realtors either. Way down there in the boonies at that hunting cabin, I asked myself why he would take on something that far away. I mean, it was like in the middle of nowhere. And it occurred to me that Landis Realty probably wasn't the only company handling it. Maybe whoever owns it has it listed with other companies, too. Maybe Landis was, like, in competition with other realtors to sell a piece of property, and somehow he screwed somebody out of a nice commission."

Kauffman nodded. "Sounds like a good possibility. Good job, Buckley. You look into it. Let me know if you need help. Anybody else?

Debora Hicks raised her hand. "I was thinking

maybe his wife's indifference to his cheating was a put on, a cover up. She might be behind the whole thing. Maybe she paid someone to do it. If we could get a look at her finances, her bank records, we could at least rule her out."

"You'll need a warrant for that. See if you can get one and have someone in the accounting department help you with it," Kauffman told her. "Anything else?"

Emory Shields sat with his head down and ignored the question.

"Okay," the Sheriff said, "go to it. Emory, let's go into my office."

Buckley's first stop after their meeting was Landis Realty. Janet Staubs was more than happy to cooperate, and together, they were able come up with a list of properties that were not offered exclusively by Landis Realty. Buckley took the list back to the office with the intention of calling each of the realtors on the phone and asking if they had had any dealings with Eldon Landis. Kauffman caught up to him just as he was about to make the first call.

"What have you got so far?" he asked.

Buckley showed him the list. "I thought I'd call them and…"

"No, not over the phone," Kauffman interrupted. "Do it in person, and watch their expressions when they answer your questions."

"What?!" Buckley exclaimed. "Some of them are as far away as Bedford and McConnellsburg!"

"Then I'd say you better get started."

Hicks walked up just as Buckley was leaving. "I haven't been able to get a judge to sign off on a warrant for Marissa Landis's accounts."

"Let me make some calls," Kauffman said and headed back to his office.

Judge Blakemore turned him down flat. Marissa Landis had contributed heavily to one of his favorite charities and was not the kind of woman who would hire someone to kill her husband. Yes, he knew her husband had been cheating on her for years, and yes, he knew that she knew, but that was no indication of guilt. His final statement was: "Take your investigation in some other direction."

Hicks' investigation was over before it started.

The following day, she joined Buckley and they visited the remaining names on the list he and Staubs had compiled. Few of those they interviewed had known Eldon Landis personally. Some of them knew him by reputation and thought him to be a good businessman but maybe lacking in integrity otherwise. None of them admitted to ever having worked with him or having lost a commission because of anything he might have said or done.

When they were finished with the list, Buckley's suggestion had netted them the same results as Hicks'—nothing. The only things they had managed to do were to eliminate some people who had never really been suspects and to put some miles on a Department vehicle.

"So, we're back to square one," Kauffman said.

At square one was where the investigation would stay until after the New Year, and then a lead would come from a source that no one had expected.

* * *

Ella Mae Gibbons had a voice that sounded like someone running a coarse file over the edge of a piece of rusty tin—way beyond fingernails on a chalk board—and once she set her mind to something, a brick of C4 couldn't change it. Anybody who ever made the mistake of calling her Elly May usually only did it once. Being compared to that blonde-haired bimbo from *The Beverly Hillbillies* would put her on a fifteen-minute tirade that would leave their ears ringing for a week. Classmates on the playground in grade school had teased her by singing "Elly May Clam-pett! Elly May Clam-pett!" until she learned to run at them screaming and make them take off, holding their ears. And the passage of years had not made her any fonder of the name. Just ask her husband Walter. He had learned his lesson the first week of their marriage, and usually when he spoke to her by name, he used just Ella. Still, given her determination to get done whatever it was she had decided needed done at any given time, his ears had been ringing for most of their married life.

The house on Route 11 just north of the town of Greencastle, PA where Ryder Robinson had lived was her parents' "old home place," and one of the things that had been making Walter's ears ring since November of the previous year was his inability to find a new tenet. When he went to collect the rent back then, he found the house empty and no pickup in sight. Not knowing anything about his young renter, except that maybe he worked at Walmart, he didn't know of anyone he might call about the young man's absence. No problem that he could see. The place was fairly clean. All he had to do was find someone to occupy it,

259

and now he could advertise the place as furnished. As it turned out, nobody seemed to want to rent an old house that far out from town. Everybody these days wants to live not more than five minutes from everything. Ella Mae seemed to think he could pull a new tenet out of thin air.

"Any man worth his salt would a found somebody to rent it by now," she harped daily. "A house settin' empty like that always ends up just fallin' down. You need to get somebody in there so's the place don't get taken over by squatters and rurint."

Walter knew that, even with a family of twelve living there, *he* would be the one who did the work to keep the place from fallin' down. In fact, if he had his way, Ella Mae wouldn't have to worry about the place *fallin'* down; he would have the damn thing *bulldozed!* How, he wondered, could the fact that her "mom and dad lived there and raised their family there" make up for the fact that the plumbing was shot, the well went dry in a long, dry summer, and if they didn't throw money away having the roof tarred soon, tin blown loose by high winds was going to let rain blow in and ruin the plaster walls? He had built her a new house right here in Greencastle, hadn't he? You would think a woman that had the luxury and convenience of central heat and air would appreciate what he had provided for her and let go of things that were past fixin'. But you would be wrong where Ella Mae was concerned. *Ashes to ashes and dust to dust and all that applies to more than the human body*, Walter thought. *Let the old place fall!* Still, he did his best to satisfy her, if for no other reason than for the sake of his eardrums. His best just wasn't good enough.

"I put ads in the papers in Greencastle and Chambersburg and Shippensburg and even down in Hagerstown. We ain't heard nothin'. What do you want me to do?"

"Well, you haven't been up there to look at things since before Christmas. Somebody might a hauled the whole place off by now. What I want you to do, and I want it done today, is I want you to go up there and check on things. And while you're up there, I want you to get my mother's old coffee table out a the barn out back a the house, and I want you to bring it in here and refinish it for me in that shop out back you put so much money into and you never set foot in. Why don't you make it a New Years resolution to spend less time on your dead butt and more time doin' something useful for a change?"

"There's no coffee table in that barn anymore, Ella Mae. You let one of the girls take it when they got married and moved out. It's somewhere down there in Tennessee or South Carolina, and that's if they haven't tossed it for something store-bought by now." *Where I wish I was*, he thought but kept it to himself.

"I did no such thing! I would never give away something that means so much to me. I used to do my homework on that table when I was a little girl in grade school. It's up there in that barn, and I want it brought in and refinished."

The longer she talked, the higher pitched and louder her voice got. Darn woman, Walter thought, how come never once in all the years they'd been married, had she ever tried to use what folks call the silent treatment to get her way? He slipped on his winter coat and the red and black plaid cap he wore

261

when he went deer hunting and slipped past her where she was standing with her back turned at the kitchen sink. He opened the door to the garage, stepped out, and closed it as quietly as possible. Ella Mae was still ranting.

"My grandfather Carter made that table for my grandmother with his own two hands. Grandma passed it on to my mother, and she passed it on to me, and I'll pass it on to one of the girls, but neither one of them is gettin' it 'til I'm dead and gone."

Walter got into his pickup and eased the door shut. It caught but wasn't closed all the way. When he turned the key in the ignition, the engine came to life, humming quietly, and he backed out of the garage, congratulating himself for leaving the overhead door up earlier. And still he could hear her talking.

"Grandpa cut down that tree himself and dragged it to the sawmill with a team of mules. I would never even think about…"

The sound of her voice faded slowly as he drove out of range. Walter shook his head and smiled, enjoying the quiet and wondering to himself how long she would talk before she figured out he was gone. He opened the truck door and slammed it shut.

The drive up Route 11 was pleasant. The road was dry and the sunshine was bright and warm. It was a beautiful morning for January. Once the pickup warmed up, he didn't mind being out at all. It was the *reason* he was out that bothered him.

"A fool's errand," he muttered to himself, "Checkin' on a house that ain't worth checkin' on and pickin' up a coffee table that ain't there and wouldn't be worth the time and effort it would take to finish it if it was. Wonder how long it takes to refinish a table that ain't there?"

He had to admit that Ella Mae was right about some things, though. A house that was left sitting empty would eventually become a target for kids out and about and up to no good. The windows would go first, the victims of rocks hurled just so someone could enjoy the sound of breaking glass. Then someone would kick in a door and the walls would get covered with graffiti, and there was no telling what other damage might get done. Maybe he should try harder to find a new tenet.

He turned left off Route 11 onto Frank Road and then right into the lane. The house was still standing, and the windows still had all their glass. Walter experienced a mild feeling of disappointment. If it ever fell into obvious disrepair, maybe Ella Mae would agree to have it demolished. He looked the place over as he slowly drove by it, heading for the barn out back, the building where the coffee table wasn't that he had come to get. His brow furrowed when he saw the three buzzards sitting on the peak of the roof.

"What the devil?" he said aloud.

He stopped his pickup some ten feet in front of the building's double doors, opened the truck's door and stepped out. Two of the buzzards took flight. He slammed the pickup door, and the third one joined the first two. Walter stood watching as they began to slowly circle overhead. Then he tossed aside the two-by that propped the doors shut and swung one of them open. Because of the cold weather, the odor wasn't real strong, but his nose told him immediately that something had died in there somewhere. And adding

263

to the shock and the mystery of it all was the front end of Ryder Robinson's red Dodge Ram pickup.

Walter swung the other door open to let more light in and then stepped inside. His foot slipped in something, and looking down, he saw a swath of opossum scat that practically encircled the vehicle. Careful not to step in any more of it, he made his way along the side of the truck and peeked over into its bed.

"Damn!" he said and jumped back. Seconds later, he was out in the sunshine several yards behind his own pickup, bent over with his hands on his knees and sucking in the fresh cold winter air—with no memory of leaving the barn. When the bile that threatened to climb up his throat had subsided, he straightened up and headed back to the pickup to get his phone. With shaking hands, he dialed the number for his landline back in Greencastle. It rang five times, and then the answering machine picked up. Ella Mae was punishing him for slipping away without telling her he was going. *There's times*, he thought, *when Caller ID ain't a good thing.* Impatiently, he waited for the beep and then spoke.

"Pick up, Ella Mae! There's a dead body in the barn! Pick up!"

His tone got her attention and she did what he asked.

"What did you say, Walter?"

"There's a dead body in the barn," he repeated more calmly now that he was sharing the information with another human being, "call 911."

"Did you find the coffee table?" Ella Mae asked.

"No, I didn't find the coffee table!"

"Then call 911 yourself," she said. There was a loud *clack!* And she was gone.

Walter made the call, wondering why he thought he had to call Ella Mae in the first place. The shock of finding a dead body, he supposed. He reported what he had found and was told to remain where he was until someone got there. The first someones to arrive were the county sheriff and a deputy. They were followed shortly by two state policemen in separate patrol cars. Two news vans equipped for remote broadcast showed up in a surprisingly short time and were denied access to the lane. They set up on Frank Road, and their cameramen filmed the activity around the barn with zoom lenses. Last to arrive was the coroner. By late afternoon, the body had been officially pronounced dead by the coroner and hauled away in his van. A tow truck had showed up, causing a scramble as everybody got their vehicles out of the way so it could hook onto the Dodge Ram and haul it away as evidence.

When everybody else was gone, Walter stood beside the house and looked back at the yellow crime scene tap stretched around the barn. What a mess! Now he couldn't go in and look for the table that wasn't in there, and he could hear Ella Mae already:

"Well, it's in there! I *know* it's in there! If you had just thought to look for it before you called 911, you could a found it and had it loaded on your pickup before anyone knew it was even in there!"

He dropped his chin to his chest and shook his head. "Get ready, ears, you're gonna catch it," he said, and headed for his pickup.

CHAPTER TWENTY-ONE

The discovery of the body made the evening news in southern Pennsylvania and northern Maryland. Although there wasn't much doubt in the authorities' minds that the deceased was Ryder Robinson, his name was withheld, pending positive identification and notification of next of kin. Eventually, the story reached Huntingdon County and was reported in *The Daily News,* an issue of which was delivered to the office of the Huntingdon County Sheriff's Department each weekday afternoon. Meagan Price worked hard to keep her filing done and her desk clean and was almost always the first one to read it, beginning with front page headlines and then skipping straight to the obituaries. Ryder's name seemed to leap off the page at her, but for several long minutes, she couldn't figure out why.

"Ryder Robinson," she said aloud to herself, "Ryder Robinson. Why does that name sound familiar?"

She had already turned to the comic page when it hit her.

"Ryder Robinson and Dexter Landis!" she said more loudly. "And there was another one that had one of those names people use for a boy or a girl!"

266

She turned back to the obituaries and left the paper spread out on her desk. This was something Sheriff Kauffman had to hear about and the sooner the better. And it needed to be done face to face. She went through his office door without knocking and took a seat in a visitor's chair without being invited to do so. Kauffman looked up, his eyebrows raised in surprise.

"What is it Meagan?"

"I think I might know why Eldon Landis and his son were killed," she blurted.

"What?!"

"I think I might know…"

"I heard you," the sheriff said, frowning. "What makes you think so?"

"Do you remember reading in the paper about three boys being tried for assaulting a retarded girl about ten years ago and being found innocent?"

Kauffman had to think a minute but finally nodded and said, "Yes, I think I have a vague recollection of something like that. What about it?"

"One of those boys was Dexter Landis, and another one was Ryder Robinson. I just read his obituary in *The News.* He must have been the one they've been talking about on the television, the one they found shot to death down below Chambersburg. And there was a third one that had a name like a girl. The three of them picked up a teacher's daughter and took her out in the country and assaulted her. What was her name?" Meagan bowed her head and rubbed her temples with a thumb and two fingers. "Some kind of flower... Rose! Her name was Rose! Rose what? Rose Howard... Rose Holden... Rose *Holder!* Her name was Rose Holder, and her mother was an English teacher!"

267

"That was before I took office," Kauffman said. "What else do you remember?"

Meagan shook her head and looked disappointed in herself. "That's all for right now. But the whole case is in one of our filing cabinets. I'll just have to hunt it down."

"Okay," Kauffman said, "do that. You just might have come up with the best lead we've had yet."

"I'm on it," she said, and in one swift and graceful move for such a large woman, she rose and went out the door.

Twenty minutes later, she walked back in and laid a folder on his desk. "Sorry it took me so long," she said, "but I thought it would be in the Closed file, and it was in the Cold Case file. I remember Sheriff Wakefield wasn't too happy about the way things were left when the investigation ended."

"Why was that?" Kauffman asked and then said, "Have a seat."

"Well, at the time, everybody I talked to thought the boys had done it, and they weren't found innocent. The trial ended in a hung jury. The girl's mother was pushing the DA for a retrial, and then the girl died, committed suicide supposedly, and even though the mother—what was her name?—Rosellan? No, Rosalynn Holder, even though she kept pushing, for another trial, it never happened. Sheriff Wakefield was never satisfied with the way those boys got off, mostly because they were the stars of the football team and everybody was hoping they would win State that year."

"Well, shit!" Kauffman said. "Pardon my French." He had flipped the folder open and was scanning through the papers.

268

"What brought that reaction?" Meagan asked.

"Ronald A. Parsons."

"Oh, yes, he was the one that represented the boys. Some people say that's what got him the backing to get elected District Attorney."

"Okay, here's a list of their names: Dexter Landis, Ryder Robinson and Jordan Harris. Can't do anything for the first two, but we better get a hold of the Harris family and have them give their son a heads up. He might be next. Have Buckley and Hicks come in here," he said, "and, Meagan, good job. I think you just gave us the lead we've been needing."

She left with a nod and a smile.

Buckley came through the door in less than five minutes. "You got something for me to do, Sheriff?"

"Where's Hicks?"

"She's just finishing up a report. She'll be here in a minute."

"I want the two of you to go have a visit with the parents of a Jordan Harris. He was involved with Dexter Landis and Ryder Robinson in an assault on a young girl when the three of them were in high school. Meagan just found Robinson's obit in the paper. He's the man that was found shot to death down below Chambersburg recently. If what they were accused of in high school has something to do with why Landis and Robinson were killed, Harris might be next on the killer's list."

"How would Mister Landis fit in?" Buckley asked.

"I don't know the answer to that right now," Kauffman said, handing him a scrap of paper he had just scribbled on. "We'll figure that out later. Here's

269

the address where they lived back then. Hope they haven't moved. Get Hicks and go."

Buckley filled Hicks in on the way.

"Three of them assaulted a retarded girl?" she asked.

"That's what Sheriff Kauffman said."

"And two of them are already dead?"

"Yes."

"So why are we going to the Harris place?"

"To tell his parents so they can tell their son to be careful. He might be next."

Hicks turned her head to stare through the windshield and said nothing more.

"What?" Buckley asked when he sensed she was angry about something.

Debora Hicks shook her head and tried to put him off with a wave of her hand.

"No, come on. If something is bothering you, share it."

"Okay, but it's not very professional," she said, and after a pause, "I was just thinking if the three of them assaulted a girl, maybe he *should* be next."

Buckley was quiet for several minutes. "No, that's *not* very professional, especially for the profession we're in," he said. "But I tend to agree."

They found the Harris place with no trouble. It was a two-story in need of a coat of paint and other maintenance, but it was habitable. A heavyset man with graying red hair cut in a burr, and a beer gut that strained the buttons on his red and black flannel shirt responded to their knock. He frowned at them but didn't speak.

"Mister Harris?" Buckley asked.

"Yeah, I'm Joe Harris."

"The father of Jordan Harris?"

The man's face got red and he closed the door in their faces.

"Sir, we need to talk! It's important! Your son might be in danger!"

The door was jerked open. "What the hell kind of joke do you two think yer pullin'?"

"It's no joke, sir," Hicks said, angry at the man's anger. "Your son was involved in an incident with Dexter Landis and Ryder Robinson when he was in high school. Both of those men have been murdered, and your son might be next."

Joe Harris looked at them like they had lost their minds. "My son was murdered in October last hear. He's been cremated and buried. He ain't in no danger of bein' next."

The door started to close, and Buckley got his foot in it. Harris jerked it open and glared at him.

"We need to know when and where and how it happened," he said.

"It happened in San Antonio, Texas, October of last year. Somebody shot him in the chest and stuffed him under a house. Now, if you like two feet to walk around on, you better git that one outa my door, or yer gonna be hoppin' around on one leg."

They took what little information they had gotten back to Sheriff Kauffman.

"Last year in San Antonio?" he asked. "How come we never heard anything about it?"

"I got the feeling he wasn't too proud of his son," Hicks said, "maybe because of that incident in high school."

Kauffman gave the idea some thought and then nodded. "Well, it's late, so you two can call it a day. We'll get in contact with the authorities down there in Texas and find out what they know and have them send us whatever evidence they can. They're all tied together, these four deaths. We just have to figure out how and who's responsible."

* * *

The following day began with a flurry of activity. Emory Shields was given the task of finding and questioning Rosalynn Holder. She was, Sheriff Kauffman thought, the one most likely to have held a grudge against the boys who had allegedly assaulted her daughter.

"Where would a school teacher get the means to carry out four murders?" Shields asked, his tone suggesting strongly that he would rather just sit at his desk until he could retire.

"I have no idea," Kauffman said. "Maybe that's one of the questions you should ask her when you find her." He turned to Buckley and Hicks. "Go back and talk to Harris's father again. See if he can give us any more details about his son's death. The more we know, the better our chances of solving these cases."

Meagan Price was given the task of calling the Altoona and San Antonio police departments and asking them about sharing evidence collected from the crime scenes in their jurisdictions. Representatives of both departments said they would be glad to do so and asked that they be kept in the loop and be informed of any progress.

Deputy Emory Shields was back in less than an hour. He stalked past Meagan Price with a folder in his hand without giving her so much as a glance, pushed through the door of Kauffman's office and sat down in a visitor's chair. Kauffman looked up at him and raised his eyebrows.

"Are you gonna set there glaring or are you gonna tell me how your interview with Rosalynn Holder went?"

"There wasn't no interview," Shields said. "She's dead."

"Dead?!" Kauffman made no effort to hide his surprise.

"Dead, cremated and buried, according to her neighbor. Her house was locked up tight and looked deserted. I got no answer when I rung the bell, so I went next door, and the lady there said Holder robbed a jewelry store back in November or December, the woman couldn't remember which. She got taken to jail and never came back home."

Sheriff Kauffman just looked at the man in shock. "Robbed a jewelry store! You're kidding?"

"I stopped off at the Police Department and got copies of everything they had. It's all in here." He tossed the folder on Kauffman's desk. Then he sat in a glum silence while Kauffman shuffled through the sheets of paper it contained.

"She robs Hillman's Jewelry, goes home and lays the jewelry and the gun on her kitchen table and sits down and waits for the cops to show up?" he asked. "That doesn't make any kind of sense at all! What do you make of it?"

Shields shrugged. "I have no idea."

"She pulls her stunt late on a Friday and refuses to say a word when they pick her up, and she doesn't call an attorney? She's found dead in her cell late Sunday morning, and it doesn't even make the news? How is that possible?"

"I have no idea," Shields repeated. "Maybe you should talk to her attorney. His name's in there somewhere."

Kauffman sat frowning at the man until Shields became uncomfortable and decided he had better say something.

"I've been remembering some things about that case. The daughter was eighteen or nineteen, but they said she had the mind of a five-year-old because of an operation she had on her brain. They picked her up off the street one night and took her out in the country somewhere, kept her out there for an hour or more and then dumped her out in front of her house. The case seemed cut and dried, and everybody was surprised at the way the trial went."

Kauffman's frown disappeared and he nodded.

"So what do you want me to do next?" Shields asked.

"Just stay lose for now. I'll let you know when I figure it out myself."

* * *

Buckley and Hicks experienced a moment of *deja vu* when they rang the bell at Joe Harris's house for the second time. The man opened the door, saw who it was and slammed it in their faces. Buckley pounded on the door with a fist.

274

"Open up," he said loudly. "We need to talk to you."

There was no response.

"What now?" Hicks asked. "Put him in cuffs and take him to the office?"

Buckley shook his head and headed back to their vehicle. "He isn't a suspect, and he hasn't committed a crime. I guess we call Kauffman and ask him what he wants us to do."

Hicks pulled out her cell phone and was dialing a number when the door to the Harris residence opened and a young woman with dyed black hair, obviously a professional job, came out.

"What do you want?" she asked.

"We need to ask Mister Harris about his son Jordan's death," Hicks said.

"I'm Jordan's sister Joanne. What do you need to know?"

"Four people have died, have been murdered," Buckley told her. "We think your brother might have been the first and that the murders are connected to an assault he was indicted for in high school. We need to know the details of his death—whatever you can tell us."

"You mean the thing with Rose Holder."

"You know about that?" Hicks asked.

"Everybody that lived in the area at the time knew about it. I'm four years younger than Jordan, and I was fourteen back then. So, yes, I know more about it than I want to."

"Do you think they were guilty, your brother and his friends?" Buckley asked.

"I don't think," Joanne said, "I *know!* Jordan and

275

I were close, up until then. He came home bragging about it, thought it was funny the way that girl got into it once they got her started. He laughed and said it was like she wouldn't ever get enough. Dexter Landis was the one that came up with the idea, he said, but they all had her, and then they took her home. Dad didn't hear about it until the cops came and got Jordan, and after that, it was like he didn't have a son anymore. They never got along all that well anyway. Once he got to hanging around with Landis and Robinson, Mom couldn't do anything with him. Dad was off on construction jobs, and she would rat on him when he got home on weekends. Dad would whip him with a belt, but it only made things worse. When the trial was over, he wasn't welcome here anymore. Dad let him stay until he graduated, and that's when he went to the Air Force."

Buckley pursed his lips and nodded his head.

"Do you have any idea about when he died?" Hicks asked.

"I think the last time anybody saw him alive was, like, the third week in October last year. They didn't find him for a while, and I understand he was pretty messed up when they did. He had to be identified with DNA. I think they keep a sample of everyone that goes into the service. They wanted one of the family to go down there to take charge of his remains and arrange to have them shipped back, but none of us had the money to go. Dad hadn't had work in a couple of months and was drawing unemployment. Even with tips, Mom's waitress job didn't bring in enough for that kind of an expense, and me and Jeff just get by on what I make at the beauty shop and what he makes at

276

Walmart. Dad told them to cremate him and send us the ashes. I think they might have come FedEx, but I don't know. Dad had him in the ground before I ever even saw the box.

"Anyway, Dad's upset that the whole thing is getting brought up again, so you won't get anything out of him. None of us ever seen him after he went to the service, and all any of us knows is that he was shot and stuffed under the house he was living in. If you want more details than that, you'll have to talk to the people down there in Texas." She looked at her wristwatch. "And I'm gonna be late for work."

They thanked her for her time and watched as she got into a ten-year-old Ford Ranger and left.

"So what we got is a lot of nothing," Buckley said.

"Right," Hicks agreed. "Let's go share it with Kauffman."

Fifteen minutes later, they were back at the Department.

"Go on in," Meagan Price said. "He's been waiting for you."

"How did it go with Mister Harris this time?" Kauffman asked.

"Just about the same way it did before," Hicks said, "but we lucked out this time. His daughter was visiting, and she was more cooperative."

Together, they filled him in on what Joanne Harris had told them. When they were finished, Kauffman sat frowning at the wall and said nothing for several minutes.

"Her brother bragged about it and laughed about it?" he finally asked.

277

Buckley and Hicks both nodded. When he said nothing more, Buckley asked, "What do you want us to do next?"

"Run up to Altoona and see if they got the copies we requested ready yet. I don't imagine we'll get anything from San Antonio until the end of the week."

The two deputies left him sitting at his desk and staring at the wall and looking angry.

* * *

By noon on Friday, they had collected all the evidence they were going to get from the other investigations. Sheriff Kauffman had it all laid out in the conference room and spent a lot of time walking from one end of the table to the other and looking it over again and again. Emory Shields, William Buckley, Debora Hicks and Meagan Price sat silently and watched.

"Okay," Kauffman said without turning around, "a lipstick in San Antonio, a compact in Chambersburg and a credit card case in Altoona—all items that didn't fit, that shouldn't have been there. Why didn't we find something like that down at the Cooper place? Was it there and we missed it?"

"I suppose that could be," Emory Shields said, "but suppose there was. What would it add to what we've already got? Tests already show that the bullets that killed all four of them came from the same box of ammunition, and the police recovered that box and the gun that was likely used from the kitchen table in Rosalynn Holder's place. Seems to me like we've got enough to prove she's the one that done the killin'.

The prints on those items you just mentioned are a match to the ones they took when they arrested her for robbin' Hillman's. Looks to me like case closed."

"Buckley and Hicks canvassed her neighborhood yesterday, and her neighbors all said there wasn't a time when she wasn't here in town," Kauffman said. "How do you explain that? And given the state of her health, how could she possibly have driven all the way to San Antonio and back anyway? What's more, according to the autopsy report, Ryder Robinson weighed somewhere between two-fifty and three hundred pounds. How could she have possibly gotten his dead weight into that pickup where they found him?"

Shields answered with a shrug.

"We need more information," Buckley put in. "Maybe her financial records would tell us something. Like, maybe she hired someone to do the job for her."

"I already have a subpoena," Kauffman said. "I want someone to go to the bank this afternoon and get copies of everything her name's on."

"Me and Hicks can do that," Buckley volunteered.

"Something I've been wondering about," Meagan Price spoke up. "Rosalynn Holder robbed a jewelry store, died in the city jail, got cremated and buried, and I never read a single word about it in the paper. None of it was ever printed in *The Daily News*. And she had no family left, so who arranged for her cremation and burial?"

"Good question," Kauffman said nodding. "That very thought came to me when Emory first told me she was dead. So, Emory, that's your job. Go talk to her

279

lawyer..." he flipped through one of the files until he found the man's name and address, scribbled them on a scrap of paper and handed it to his Chief Deputy... "Murray McCartney. Find out if he's the one that arranged for the body to be picked up, cremated and buried. She must have left instructions with somebody. If it wasn't him, find out if he knows who it was. Maybe that will give us some idea of what direction to take next. Me, I'm gonna make a run down to the Cooper place and take another look around, make sure we didn't miss anything."

CHAPTER TWENTY-TWO

By the end of January, Daniel had closed up his apartment in State College, donating most of the furniture to Goodwill and moving what few items he wanted to keep down to the house in Huntingdon that Rosalynn had left to him in her will. The old red Impala he traded in for a late model Camaro, a silver one with two wide black stripes on the hood and trunk lid. The two gray Hondas he had put into the hands of Murray McCartney to be sold, told the attorney to price them to go, and they had. The proceeds, less McCartney's commission, went straight to the bank in the Caymans. On the last Sunday of the month, he loaded the last of his clothes into the backseat of his new vehicle, dropped his apartment keys in a box next to the office door and headed for his new home.

He had just pulled into the driveway of the house in Huntingdon, gotten out of the car and had his arms loaded with clothing when an elderly couple in a Buick sedan pulled into the driveway of the house next door. The gray-haired woman in the passenger seat locked eyes with him and frowned.

"Who are you and what are you doing?" she demanded when her husband had opened the door for her and helped her out.

The two of them looked like they were dressed for church. The man's tan suit pants were still sharply creased and his cordovan wingtips brightly polished below his long camel overcoat. The woman was wearing a blue flowered dress under a navy jacket that looked too light for the chill that was in the air.

Daniel smiled. "I'm Daniel Miller and I'm moving in here."

"That was Rosalynn Holder's place. Did you buy it from her before she died?" the woman asked, her tone suspicious and demanding.

"No, she left it to me in her will."

Her frown did not diminish. "Why would she do that?"

"Because I lived next door to her and her daughter when I was young—in the house you and your husband are currently occupying, in fact. I was her daughter's best friend, and Rosalynn was like a mother to me."

"She never mentioned you to me," the woman said, and her tone was filled with doubt.

"She never mentioned much of anything to you, Mother," her husband said and approached Daniel with his hand out. "We're the Donoffs. I'm Gerald and this is my wife Louise. Welcome back to the neighborhood." Then he turned to his wife, "Come, Mother. Let's go in and have some lunch. Let this young man get his things unloaded. It's cold out here, and we don't want you to get a chill."

She allowed her husband to take her arm and turn her, but she kept looking back over her shoulder and frowning. Daniel smiled as best he could and gave her a finger wave.

He hung his clothes in the closet of the guestroom he had used the last time he had visited Rosalynn. Taking over the master bedroom so soon after her death seemed disrespectful somehow. His underwear and socks were already in one of the drawers in the dresser from an earlier visit.

He made himself a pot of coffee, smiling at the fact that Rosalynn had stocked the house before her little adventure into a life of crime. There was no doubt in his mind that she had done so in anticipation of his moving in. He poured himself a cup, took it to the living room and sat down in his usual spot on the sofa. Staring at her recliner brought a lump to his throat, so he got up and went into her office and sat down in front of her computer. Had she erased the history as she said she would, or did she leave it as part of the "misdirection" she had mentioned? He had his fingers on the keyboard and was about to type in what he thought might be the password when the doorbell rang.

When he opened the door, a uniformed policeman was standing on his porch. *I guess Louise won that argument* went through his mind, and he pushed the storm door open.

"Can I help you, officer?" he asked.

"We got a call that someone was breaking into the house at this address," the man said. "Let me see some identification."

Daniel pulled his wallet out of his hip pocket, took out his driver's license and handed it over. The officer looked at the photograph on it and then up at Daniel's face.

"This was Rosalynn Holder's place," he said. "How did you get in here?"

Daniel pulled his key ring out of his pocket and selected the right key. "I used this. Rosalynn left the place to me in her will."

The officer took the key from his hand and inserted it into the lock on the door. It went in with no problem. He turned it back and forth a couple of times, then withdrew it and handed the key ring back to Daniel.

"Mind if I get a shot of you?" he asked and pulled a cell phone from a pocket.

Daniel stood still and looked at the little lens in the corner of the phone, surprised at how little concern he felt. He had no record, and except for a convenience store clerk and one customer in Texas and maybe a few people in the Walmart in Chambersburg, nobody had seen him in the area of any of his... he refused to even think the word crimes... in the areas he had visited. Besides, with his short haircut and the absence of the beard, he looked nothing now like he had back then. What could it possibly hurt to let them have a photograph?

"Thank you," the officer said, returning the phone to his pocket. "We'll be in touch." He was already halfway back to the squad car parked at the curb when he stopped and turned around. "Which lawyer did Mrs. Holder use when she made her will?"

"Murray McCartney," Daniel told him and then watched until the squad car pulled away and disappeared down the street. "Welcome back to the neighborhood," he muttered to himself and then closed the door.

* * *

"This investigation is like a dog chasing its tail," Sheriff Kauffman said. "Just when we think we have something, it turns out to be nothing."

The financial records Deputies Buckley and Hicks were sent to retrieve looked promising at first. Over a period of nearly a year, Rosalynn Holder had made weekly, sometimes bi-weekly, deposits of anywhere from five to eight thousand dollars in an account at Community State Bank until there was a total of just under a hundred thousand. Then she had begun to make similar withdrawals until she had taken out eighty thousand of it. Very likely payment for four hits, Kauffman suspected, but that particular trail ended right there. Nobody knew where the money came from or where it had gone.

Deputy Shields came back from his visit with Murray McCartney looking more glum than usual. "The man admitted he was the one they called when Holder died in jail, and he was the one that had her cremated and buried. I asked him why him, and he told me he didn't really know. She walked into his office a couple of weeks before she died and gave him a retainer, and that's what she wanted. He kept sayin' 'as per her instructions' every time I asked him why things were done the way they were. Like, I asked how come there was no mention of her death in the paper, and he said he took care of that 'as per her instructions.'

"I asked him if he knew anything about the murders of Jordan Harris, Ryder Robinson, Dexter Landis and Eldon Landis, and he said only what he read in the papers and saw on the news. I asked if he thought Rosalynn Holder was involved, and he told me

285

he had no idea whether she was or not, but even if he did, it would be covered by attorney-client privilege. I could go back and ask if he knew where the eighty thousand came from or where it went, but I'm sure I'd get the same answer."

Kauffman sat behind his desk with his head down.

"What did you find down at the old Cooper place?" Shields asked.

"Nothing," Kauffman said. "In fact, less than when we were down there before. Someone broke the seal and went in and cleaned the place up. The marks in the dust on the floor are gone because the dust is gone. Somebody went in there and mopped the floor and, I think, maybe painted that wall where Landis was sitting when he was shot. I looked everywhere, inside the house and out around it. Whoever it was took down the saplings behind the house where we found Landis's Escalade and the whole area has been mowed. There wasn't anything down there that doesn't belong there."

"Well, it was a long shot like everything else," Shields said.

Buckley and Hicks both nodded their heads and said nothing. They had all given it their best shot, and there was nothing much left to say.

* * *

February was its usual miserable self. The first two weeks brought no snow, but most days were overcast, cold and wet and nasty. Police Chief Charles Bond and Gray sat in the living room of the Ballard

286

residence in Mount Union, enjoying the warmth from logs blazing in the fireplace and saying little while they waited for Anna to join them. They heard her soft footsteps on the stairs, and she came through the archway smiling, took a seat beside her husband and reached for his hand.

"Okay, she's down for the night," she said. "Tell us what you know."

"Well, there's not a whole lot to tell," Bond said. "Sheriff Kauffman says every lead they come up with takes them only so far and then dead ends. Most recently, they had a tech go into Rosalynn Holder's computer. Their suspicion or hope, or whatever you want to call it, was that there would be something in its history that would tell them she had been on the dark web, looking for a hit man. Or that she had used it to locate the four men that were murdered. The hard drive was blank."

"Blank?!" Gray exclaimed.

Bond nodded. "The thing had never been programmed."

"And they think the Holder woman installed it and destroyed the old one?"

Again, Bond nodded. "She took some courses on computers at the vo-tech in Mill Creek, so odds are she knew how to do it. It was either her or the young man she left the place to, a Daniel Miller. He and his family used to live next door. Her parents were gone and her daughter, so she had no blood kin to leave it to. Kauffman says that, given other circumstances, the guy would probably have been her son-in-law."

"But there's nothing to suggest he was involved in any of it?" Anna asked.

Bond shook his head. "Miller has no criminal record, and has a clean-cut, preppy look about him, Kauffman says. He just graduated from law school and passed the bar exam last year. Nothing about him seems suspicious. They got a photograph of him and one of Rosalynn Holder and sent them to San Antonio, Chambersburg and Altoona. Authorities showed them around, and nobody anywhere remembered seeing Miller. A man that works at a CVS Pharmacy on Plank Road up in Altoona thought Rosalynn Holder might have been in his store once not long ago, but he wasn't sure and couldn't pinpoint the date. And a woman up there at the Chamber of Commerce thought she had seen her but wasn't sure, either. Both of those locations are clear across the city from the neighborhood where Dexter Landis lived and was killed.

"The odd thing about it is that in three of the cases whoever did the killing left items that had Rosalynn Holder's fingerprints on them—a tube of lipstick, a compact and a small plastic case that a woman might use for her credit cards . You know about her robbing the jewelry store." Bond paused until Gray and Anna nodded. "Well, the gun she used was the one used in all four murders. Five empty cartridges were left in it, and her fingerprints were on all of them, too. Kauffman thinks the reason she pulled the robbery was so her prints would be on file."

"And this Daniel Miller and the Holder woman are the only suspects they have?" Anna asked.

"Well, I suppose technically, Miller would have been more like a person of interest and Holder a suspect. But, yes, given that the motive seems to have been revenge against the boys who assaulted her daughter and his... I'll call her his girlfriend... Rosalynn Holder and Daniel Miller are the only two who fit the bill. No one else seems to have a reason for wanting any one of the four victims dead. There are no other suspects."

"And the Landis boy's father?" Gray asked. "How does he fit in?"

"It's mere speculation," Bond began, "but Kauffman is of the opinion that he was the one who fed the daughter the capsules that killed her. She had the mind of a five-year-old and wouldn't have known what to take even if she wanted to kill herself."

"And this Daniel," Anna asked. "Where is he now?"

"The last Kauffman knew, he was heading down to Florida to visit his father and step-mother. Goodness knows where he might be now."

* * *

Six months after Rosalynn Holder's death, Murray McCartney—as per her instructions—paid a visit to Donna McCreary, the mother of the little girl Dexter Landis had sired. The woman had just gotten home from picking her daughter up a daycare and was in the process of unlocking her front door and was surprised when a strange man walked up and addressed her by name.

"Who are you and what do you want?" she asked, turning around, her tone somewhat hostile. The little girl in her arms hid her face against her mother's neck.

"I believe it might be best if we keep you in the

289

dark where my name is concerned, but be assured, I mean you no harm," he said, at the same time pulling a folder out of his suit coat. "I have been entrusted with the task of bringing you this information which concerns a trust fund that has been set up for your daughter."

"A trust fund? Set up by who?"

"Suffice it to say by a client of mine who wishes to remain anonymous but who is aware of your daughter's... um, parentage... and who would like to help with her needs and contribute to her education."

Murray held out the folder, and she took it, her brow drawn in suspicion.

"You will have question, I'm sure, so I would urge you to contact your lawyer and have him or her discuss the terms of the trust fund with you. I'm sure the amount my client has included allows for his or her fee," Murray said, and then turning to go, he smiled at the little girl. "Have a good life, sweetheart."

Donna watched him go until he disappeared around the corner. Then she pushed the door open, stepped inside and set her daughter on her feet. With trembling hands, she undid the string on the flap on the folder and withdrew a sheaf of papers. Brow still drawn, she began to scan them. They were covered with legal jargon, and she didn't understand much of it. But the number at the bottom of the final page, that she understood. Reading it for the first time, her breath caught in her throat, and tears began to stream down her face. They would have to see a lawyer, no doubt, but if this was legit, her daughter's future was secure.

* * *

After two months, Daniel Miller was getting used to the narrow streets of Paris and the French language, not that he understood or could speak more than a few simple phrases. But he was getting used to the sound of it everywhere he went. It would be nice to live in a country that spoke English, he thought, but he had found London, England intolerable.

The food was something else again. Not that it was bad. But what do you eat when you don't want to eat anything you can't pronounce, and you can't pronounce anything on the menu? He had gotten into the habit of dining only in places where someone spoke English and could explain to him what he was about to ingest. On days when he didn't want to deal with it, he went to McDonalds and had a burger and fries. A taste of something from home? The house he had inherited from Rosalynn was waiting for him to return, but he wasn't quite sure where "home" was anymore. There were times when he had half a mind to get in touch with Murray McCartney and tell him to sell the place, not that he needed the money or that he would ever need the money. Given the habit of frugality he had developed in college and law school, Rosalynn had left him more than he would ever likely spend.

Apparently he was beginning to look like a native, maybe because his hair was longer again. Not as long as it had been when the numbers were evened out but brushing his collar again. Just yesterday, he had been stopped on the street and asked directions to the Eiffel Tower, a structure that he no longer found fascinating. The man and woman had stammered at him in what he supposed was Americanized French

291

until he told them English would be better. Their faces seemed to relax into an expression of both embarrassment and relief, and they invited him to join them for dinner. He had declined and sent them on their way, the Eiffel Tower their destination.

Most days he left his hotel room sometime around ten A.M. and made his way to one of the more than twenty Starbucks scattered around Paris. He always ordered a Grande— just coffee, no cream or sweetener of any kind—and if the weather was nice, he took it outside to one of the tables on the sidewalk, sipped it quietly and watched the people until noon. Most of them ignored him, but more recently, some of them would smile and say something to him in their native tongue. He would smile and nod, sometime raise his cup in a silent salute.

Daniel had just set his cup down and was staring at it, thinking about the strong black coffee Rosalynn had made for him back in the States when a young woman walked by. He looked up just in time to catch a glimpse of her face in three-quarter profile, her short dark hair tucked behind her ear. She reminded him so much of the post-surgery Rose that his breath caught in his throat. Before he thought to react, she disappeared around the corner of the building. He left his coffee sitting on the table and made it to the corner in time to see her going through the door of the restaurant.

He followed, stood just inside the door and watched while she ordered a latte. She looked and dressed like a native Parisian and spoke French. When she turned with her purchase and headed for the door, he stepped in front of her.

"*Pardon moi, s'il vous plait, mademoiselle,*" he stammered, "*je...* I..."

"Maybe English would be better," she suggested and gave him a smile that made her dark brown eyes almost disappear. Her upper lip folded up almost against her nose and revealed small, even, white teeth.

"Yes, English would be much better," Daniel said. "I'm afraid I've already used up almost my entire vocabulary in French."

"So, what can I do for you?" she asked when he just stood there and stared at her.

"Oh! You walked by me on the sidewalk, and you reminded me of a very good friend of mine, and I... I had to speak with you. Do you mind? I left my coffee on the table outside."

"Not at all," she said. "Lead the way."

She followed him outside and around the corner, Daniel looking back over his shoulder to make sure she was still coming. The table was still vacant, and his cup was still sitting where he had left it. He pulled out a chair for her and then returned to the one he had been occupying when she passed.

"What did you want to talk about?" she asked, and Daniel came out of his trance.

"I'm Daniel Miller," he said and offered his hand across the table. She placed hers in it and they shook. "And you are...?"

"Rosemarie Broussard."

Daniel's jaw dropped for several seconds. "Rose Marie Broussard," he said, nodding with each name.

"No, Rosemarie Broussard." She nodded only twice.

"You're an American?"

293

"Yes, I'm from southern Louisiana, a little town just out side New Orleans," Rosemarie said.

"But you speak French very well. Even your English has a bit of a French accent." Daniel was confused.

Rosemarie gave him another one of those smiles that did things to his heart. "I speak Cajun French. It is not considered, how do you say? Not considered very classy here, but I can get by. And I suppose my English is a bit off because I have been here so long, much longer than I wanted to be."

"So why don't you just go home?" Daniel asked.

"I came over with a boyfriend. His family has the money," she said and rubbed her thumb and fingers together. "He found someone else and left me behind. I try to save enough for an airline ticket, but I have no skills, so I work as a waitress, and I have to pay rent and eat. It is hard to save."

Daniel nodded in sympathy for her plight and words from Rosalynn's last letter came to mind: *Find yourself another Rose*. Was this Fate intervening?

"Maybe I could help you with that," he said.

"And what would I have to do to pay you back," Rosemarie asked.

"You would have to let me go with you."

"You do not like it here?"

"I didn't until I saw you pass by on the street, and I don't think I would like it if you went back to Louisiana and left me here."

Rosemarie raised her chin, turned her head aside and looked at him out of the corner of her eye. "Are you thinking it was love at first sight?"

"Maybe not love," Daniel said, "but definitely

something similar. I would like the chance to get to know you better."

"You are not joking? You are being serious?"

"I have never been more serious in my life. We fly back together and spend some time together and see what happens. If things don't work out the way I'm hoping they will, we go our separate ways. What have you got to lose?"

"I guess I have nothing to lose. Should we go pack our suitcases then?"

"We should go pack our suitcases," Daniel agreed, and there was a smile on his face that felt right for the first time in a decade.

ABOUT THE AUTHOR

Charles C. Brown was born in Pennsylvania where he lived the first seventeen years of his life. After high school, he enlisted in the U.S. Army and spent the bulk of his enlistment in Germany. Following a year as a laborer at Letterkenny Army Supply Depot in Chambersburg, PA, he moved to Oklahoma where he attended college in Durant, receiving a bachelors degree in education in December of 1970. Retired from teaching after thirty-six years, he now lives in Davis, Oklahoma, with his wife of more than fifty years and a very spoiled cat. Brown is the author of eight previous novels: *Say I Do and Die, Dead Man Waiting, Cold in the Ground, Suffer the Consequences, Up From the Grave, Best Served Cold, Catch and Release,* and *Justice Comes Late.*

Made in the USA
San Bernardino, CA
08 August 2018